I0738948

BULLDOG AND RATS

A FANTÔMAS DETECTIVE NOVEL

BY MARCEL ALLAIN

Translated by A. R. Allinson

Bibliographical Note

This Antipodes edition, first published in 2017, is a republication of the work first published by Stanley Paul & Co, London, in 1928. The original translation has been altered to reflect modern spelling and usage.

ISBN 978-0-9966599-7-0

Contents

BULLDOG AND RATS

1. A Bluff

"Juve?"

"Fandor?"

"You heard?"

"Yes, I heard this much—that I couldn't hear."

"Our engine stopped."

"But it started afresh, Fandor."

"I know that, but there was a stoppage! Oh God, suppose the petrol runs out! You astound me, Juve."

"Really? Why, my lad?"

"Because you keep so abominably cool."

"Would you have me tear my hair?"

"I would rather have you devise something."

"Something, eh?"

"Something to get us out of the mess."

"You ask too much, Fandor."

"But, Juve, your ingenuity…"

"Don't mention it…"

"Your genius…"

"My genius won't refill a tank that's run dry."

"Done for, then? We're done for, Juve, eh?"

"What's the good of asking? You know that as mil as I do."

"True! But I think I'm more worried about it than you are"—and Fandor gave a nervous laugh. Yes, undoubtedly the opinion the journalist had just stated seemed justified by the facts. Finding himself along with Juve aboard an airplane floating above the stormy waves of the Channel, knowing that their stock of petrol was coming to an end, observing as he leaned over the side Fantômas' submarine waiting there for the fall of the plane that was bound to follow, Fandor might well assume that he and his companion were inevitably "done for."

Nonetheless he exaggerated in surmising that their appalling position affected himself more deeply than it did the police officer. The fact was neither Fandor nor Juve were susceptible to fear. Nor, indeed, could either one or the other be surprised at the tragic fate that manifestly threatened them both.

For years now they had fought the Lord of Terror; for years they had pursued the scoundrel at the peril of their lives. Obviously the struggle was bound to end in a decisive victory or a no less definite defeat. If Fate, then, declared against them, had they any call to feel surprise? Had they not themselves invited the dreadful doom that was about to overtake them?

"Juve," Fandor went on again, "I'm asking myself a question…"

"Yes, my boy?"

"Is Fantômas going to leave us to drown or will he rescue us to kill us by slow degrees?"

"A silly question, Fandor."

"Not it."

"But I say it is. To die in one fashion or another is simply to die."

"Agreed, but the circumstances *do* matter."

"The main point is that the villain will be triumphant, free and ready to commit fresh atrocities"—and for once Juve's voice trembled, betraying a trace of horror. Plainly enough, to die meant nothing to him; but to leave the victory to Fantômas was a torture beyond bearing.

"Well, think of something," mocked the journalist.

"I *have* thought of it," retorted Juve. "You're just clumsy."

"What say?"

"I repeat, clumsy. It's your business to save our lives."

"How, pray?"

"By planing down, Fandor. When the petrol's done, they plane down—so there."

"Devil take it, you're quite right. Only…"

"Only you don't know the trick, eh?"

"True for you, Juve. I don't know how; it's all I can do not to capsize the show."

"You're just a duffer, Fandor."

"You make me ashamed of myself, Juve... Whoa, the engine!"

"Leave the engine alone!"

"Oh, never fear, old man! It's the engine's going to leave us alone... It's stopping! Stopping dead!"

Indeed, the fact was beyond dispute. Bit by bit the motor seemed to lose its power. There were constant stoppages; the engine was, in pilots' phrase, misfiring atrociously. The level of the petrol in the reservoir being too low, the stroke of the engine was becoming more and more irregular."

"Going precious badly," observed Fandor with a smile.

"And you laugh?"

"My good man, it adds a certain grace; I take it we mustn't go crying at our own funeral."

"Very good... As a matter of fact, how long do you suppose we shall manage to keep up?"

"Five or six minutes, perhaps."

"Suppose you get a bit higher, for planing down?"

"How you run on!... Get a bit higher, eh? But I don't know how to set about it, not I... On the contrary, we're losing height all the time"—and Fandor spoke truly. A novice, an amateur of the moment, he was perfectly right in declaring his ignorance of how to manage his craft. To keep her on an even keel, to check her capsizing, to keep her going, was the utmost he could do. But any more complicated maneuver was beyond his power.

"You're a clumsy fellow," reiterated Juve quietly.

"Do better yourself, then, my fine friend."

"Not I. I prefer to keep an eye on Fantômas."

"He's still there, eh?"

"Yes, still there."

"Waiting for us, by gad!"

"Not a doubt of it; he has only to wait; he knows very well we're bound at last to fall into his hands."

Leaning over the edge of the fuselage, the police officer was gazing down at the surface of the waves, two hundred yards below the machine. Her long, black hull was almost indistinguishable amid the tumbling billows, but her position could yet be dimly made out by reason of the line of her foaming wake.

Alas! if marvels of courage, Juve and Fandor, in a few moments to meet the most terrible of deaths, had found courage to jest, what must be the joy of Fantômas, the cruel ruffian, the hideous torturer, who, risking nothing, assured of victory, was calmly awaiting the instant when his two most mortal foes would meet their doom! Juve! Fandor!—must he not at this tragic hour be tasting a horrid delight in watching their agony?

For Fantômas it was a triumph, certain and assured. For this monstrous criminal, who held the whole world spellbound under the glamour of his foul genius, the sure promise of immunity, the voice, calm and controlled, rose clear above the howling of the wind.

"Yes, done for! Goodbye, Fandor."

"Goodbye, my gallant Juve."

"To die together—a consolation that."

"Yes, Juve—and to know that we have done our duty."

After that, for some seconds, they said no more. Such was the fury of the wind that beat about them that both were panting, breathless, bewildered.

"About Fantômas," questioned Fandor presently; fully occupied as he was with the control of his machine, he could not turn round nor yet lean over to look.

But Juve had caught the words. "Still there," he reported; "partly submerged, that's all."

Whirled on by the blustering wind, the two men were now struck dumb, giddy, incapable of thought. Below them, meantime, making mock of the angry waves, rolling in mighty crests and deep hollows, the pirate submarine was steadily pursuing her course. She could be seen cutting through the mountainous billows, plunging into the whirling eddies, disappearing altogether, only to come to the surface again a little further on.

The very elements were Fantômas' allies. Aboard the vessel the arch-villain ran no risk. If the fury of the waves grew too violent, he could, of course, submerge altogether. Less than six fathoms beneath the surface the greatest storms are entirely unfelt. And what real need was there for him to keep watch on the shattered airplane, whose engine was now slackening more and more, stopping fitfully, then starting afresh, bound before long to come to a complete standstill.

"Juve!" bawled Fandor suddenly.

"Yes?" demanded the police officer.

"I can do no more… Suppose we dived too, eh?"

No need at this moment for Juve to ask an explanation of the young man's words. It merely meant that, beaten by the storm, Fandor proposed to end the useless struggle. Death was there—certain, inevitable; why prolong the agony they were enduring? Why not let the machine crash here and now and plunge into the waves that would inevitably engulf it in a few brief moments?

But thereupon Juve started to crawl to where Fandor sat in the cockpit, at sore risk of being pitched from the fuselage by some wild plunge of the machine.

"No, no!" he protested.

"Why, Juve? Why?"

"Struggle on; we must fight on to the end."

"We have no petrol left, Juve!"

"But yes—we have a few drops left."

"I cannot keep her going any longer."

"I say yes, you can."

"We are lost, Juve—lost!"

A silence—one of those silences that seem eternities… Then, in wild tones, Juve's voice bellowed:

"No, we are saved!"—and he pointed to a point on the horizon. "There!… There!…"

And Fandor, too, saw… There, in the direction Juve had indicated, away on the horizon, appearing and disappearing, smothered in the foam of the dancing waves, a steam vessel was fighting her way against the billows.

"Oh!" was all the journalist found to say. But all the same, his common sense realized how impossible it was this could mean safety. In such tempestuous weather was a rescue practicable, indeed, had they even been seen from the vessel? And for themselves, could they keep aloft till the steamer would be able to pick them up?

Simultaneously Juve likewise was reasoning in the same strain. Presently:

"Too late!" he groaned; "it is too late, Fandor. Have us down into the sea."

But this time it was Fandor who protested.

"Never, Juve, never!"—and he went on, in confident, ironical tones:

"Duty, Juve… To struggle on to the end, to fight to the last drop of petrol, to fight to the death."

The two men said no more. When the stormy elements are let loose against two stubborn wills, the battle is superb and tragic.

Half dismembered, the wings holed in many places, sundry of the controls torn away and broken, the airplane seemed quite beyond management. But by now Fandor was at grips with Fate, firmly resolved to win the day.

"We will fly to the vessel," he kept telling himself; "we will fly to the vessel, we *will!*" It was like a refrain, an imperative word of command he gave himself, an order he was resolved to obey, even if it meant fighting against the impossible. How glorious these last few moments of this tragic flight! As if bent on triumphing over this great bird of wood and canvas, the hurricane grew more terrible than ever. The machine reared and plunged and recovered its balance, tossed by the tempest every way, often half-overset, twenty times brought back to equilibrium by Fandor. Meantime, blinded by the hail, his hands bleeding and benumbed, the pilot hardly knew sometimes what he was doing. Then, from behind him, Juve's eager voice sounded:

"Hold on, Fandor! Keep a good heart!"

But the encouragement was hardly needed; Fandor was not the man ever to confess himself beaten. In spite of the wind, in spite of sudden squalls that now and again brought him to a halt, at times forced him backwards, Fandor was making his way towards the steamer.

"A ship of war!" sang out Juve. "A torpedo boat! A Frenchman, I think!" Then, before long, with a shout of triumph: "They have seen us! They have seen us!"

Flags were being hauled up along the mast, signals that unfortunately neither Juve nor Fandor could read, but which certainly signified offers of help.

"Oh, the gallant fellows!" Juve was now thinking. "Yet they themselves are in danger."

For indeed, in this heavy sea, the little vessel was rolling and pitching terrifically; at times she would disappear altogether amid the foaming breakers that broke against her hull. Yet she never failed to reappear, the black smoke pouring in torrents from her smokestack.

"They have seen us! They have seen us!"—but Juve had no time to add another word. Suddenly a yet fiercer blast of air struck the airplane, and the engine stopped altogether.

"Hold on, Juve!"

"Look out, Fandor!"

Now the machine, at the mercy of the winds, was falling, falling; then, spinning like a dead leaf, it crashed. Next second, with a stunning shock, it met the surface of the stormy sea. Another second and two panting voices could be heard:

"Juve?"

"Fandor?"

"Present—all present at the roll-call! But, oh God, this is a cold bath!"

The incorrigible journalist was mocking at Fate, when a wave tossed him over like a cork and cut him short. Still clinging to the wreck of their machine, the two men reappeared next moment on the surface.

"Hold tight, Juve!"

"Never fear, Fandor!"

"They must have seen us come down."

"Yes… but will they be able to pick us up?"

"And Fantômas, Juve?"

"A moment ago the submarine dived."

"Look out, Juve! Look!…"

They spoke in broken phrases, the angry surges interrupting

their words as they swept over them, rolled them over and over, dashed them against the wreck, which they seemed resolved to destroy and break up and tear to pieces.

No doubt Fantômas was no longer to be feared. Submarines are certainly wonderful craft, but, for all that, they do no while on the surface possess seagoing qualities of a high order. In danger, therefore, of shipwreck, or at any rate of suffering serious damage, Fantômas had been forced to make up his mind to submerge. And was he not convinced of the inevitable death of his two enemies? Had he for one moment suspected the presence of a ship of war capable of affording them help?

Then a huge wave broke. Buried under a mountain of water, the wrecked airplane disappeared, broken and shattered worse than ever. Yet, when it once more rose to the surface, when recovering breath a little, Juve and Fandor opened their eyes, they cried with one voice:

"There! Look there!"—and the agony of their suspense grew more intense than ever.

*   *   *   *   *

Still, neither Juve nor Fandor needed to exchange a word to tell each other the cause of their new excitement.

Defying death, scorning the stormy seas that seemed ready at any moment to swallow up the rescuers, a boat was pulling might and main in their direction.

How fine, how admirable, how noble the gallantry of sea-going folk, who never count the cost when it is a question of going to the rescue of fellowmen in danger! The boat carried half a score of stout mariners whose oilskins and sou'westers were dripping with seawater. Bending to the oars with straining muscles, confidently attempting the impossible, they were advancing inch by inch against wind and tide. Now a wave, more monstrous than the rest, would drive them back; now a clever turn of the rudder by the officer who took the helm would win them a few yards' advantage.

"Oh, the brave fellows!" sighed Juve hoarsely.

"They are sailors," said Fandor simply.

For sure he and his companion were in dire peril of drowning. It was indeed a miracle they had not already loosed their hold; but they forgot their own danger as they watched the efforts of the gallant rescuers risking their lives to save them.

At last, putting a speaking trumpet to his lips, the helmsman shouted:

"Stand by! I'm sending you a lifeline. Take it, first one, then the other"—and from the boat a buoy came drifting towards them before the wind.

"You first, Juve!" bawled Fandor.

"You're crazy! *You* first, Fandor!"

"No, no! Never…"

"Oh, well, if you don't do as I say, I shall let go my hold!"—and the police officer was just the man to do as he threatened. Fandor gave way and grabbed the line first, letting them haul him to the boat, where they soon had him aboard.

"In the bottom of the boat! Lie down in the bottom!" he was ordered.

"My friend! Save my friend!"

"Why, o' course! That's what we're here for."

After that the young man knew nothing. A lurch threw him on the bottom boards of the boat, and, exhausted as he was, he felt a numbness creep over his senses. It was not till some minutes later that he became aware that Juve had been got on board.

"Now for it, my lads!" cried a manly voice. "Pull hard! We've got to get back now!"

Then Fandor sprang to his feet. Doubtless he had every right to be worn out after the tremendous efforts he had had to make to keep the airplane flying. But, like his friend, Fandor was resolved to give a hand to help the men who had saved their lives.

"Give me an oar!" he demanded; "you'll see, I'm strong enough, I can do my share!"

Then all fell silent, Fandor, Juve, and all the crew. No one inexperienced in the fury of the ocean and the fierceness of the wind that blows on the open sea in an equinoctial gale can form a notion of the prodigious effort now called for. The boat had take three-quarters of an hour to come from the steamer to the wrecked airplane; for two whole hours the struggled lasted before they regained the vessel they had so courageously quitted.

Then: "You're sturdy lads, anyhow, the pair of you—scoundrels maybe, but brave fellows."

With one accord Juve and Fandor turned upon the officer at the helm.

"Scoundrels? We are scoundrels?" demanded the police officer. "Why so, pray?"

"Enough said. The Captain will tell you why. Now get aboard."

Lines had been thrown, and in a momentary lull the rolling, pitching boat was hoisted to the davits. On the deck, which was swept by the waves from stem to stern, Juve and Fandor scrambled to their feet.

"Oh God, I can't make it out!" growled Fandor; "they save our lives—and then they insult us."

"Hold your jaw, you rascal; and have a care you ain't pitched overboard."

Juve had not found his sea legs, while Fandor barely managed to get a hold on something solid. The former would inevitably have tumbled overboard had not a couple of sturdy deckhands dashed forward to hold him up.

"This way! The Captain's waiting to see you."

"So much the better… We are going to thank him"; and Juve, followed by Fandor, proceeded to climb down a steep stairway, not much better than a ladder, to find himself in a passageway so narrow that his shoulders touched either wall.

"Go straight ahead; the Captain's cabin is at the far end."

"Very good! Very good!"

Never could the police officer have imagined that the below-decks of a seagoing torpedo boat would be so utterly lacking in comfort. All space available was devoted to the powerful machinery and formidable armament. What heroism is demanded of the men forming the crew of these vessels to put up with such precarious conditions of existence! In storms, amid the tempestuous waves, the mighty billows that roll from one horizon to the other, how soon the frail craft begins to dance the wildest of dances!

"There, knock at the door; the Captain is within."

Juve knocked and entered, followed by Fandor, who looked curiously round the cabin hardly bigger than a closet. A sofa bed, a table, an armchair, a collection of nautical instruments comprised the whole furniture of this abode of a commanding officer. Clad like his men in an oilskin coat still dripping with seawater, the torpedo boat's commander wore the air at once genial and serious common to all naval officers who are responsible for the safety of their crew and of their ship.

"Sir," began Juve, "you have saved our lives. We thank you."

"No need; do not thank me; it was my men who risked their lives."

"Granted! But you gave the order."

"French sailors never refuse to go to the help of those in danger… No, I count for nothing in your rescue."

"But, sir, you maneuvered your ship…"

"That is my trade… But no more of this… Please give me your names, to begin with."

At this, Juve turned to look at his companion's face, doubting his own judgment. Doubtless the Captain, in refusing to be thanked and giving all the credit of the rescue to his men, was following the traditions that do honor to naval officers. Nevertheless, in spite of himself, Juve felt a trifle offended… How cold had been the welcome accorded them; how grave and chilling the other's manner! He had never even offered to shake hands—a natural action, surely, in the circumstances— or vouchsafed one smile of greeting.

Juve noted on his companion's face a like surprise to his own. Then: "Excuse me, sir," he said; "I was forgetting the necessary introductions."

A touch of irony was perceptible in his voice as he announced ceremoniously:

"I take the liberty to present Monsieur Jerome Fandor, reporter on the staff of La Capitale, whose name, no doubt, is familiar to you… For myself, I am the police officer Juve, Chief Inspector in the service of the Criminal Investigation Office."

"You have papers to show?"

Juve frowned; such a question was equivalent to an avowal of suspicion.

Anticipating him, Fandor replied:

"You must excuse us, sir… The fact is, after the bath we have just had and the adventures we have gone through, we have not so much as a visiting card upon us!"

"You do wrong to make a joke of it."

"Come now, sir! Pray, why?"

"Because, my men, your situation is not what you think."

"Which means?"

"Which means that it was not by accident that I sighted you."

"How so?"

"I was in search of you."

"In search of us!"

With one accord Juve and Fandor had taken a step forward. Well used as they were to the most alarming imbroglios, they were lost in positive amazement… Saved from drowning after falling into the sea from an airplane stolen from Fantômas, they now learned that they had been the object of a search by this ship of war! How was the thing possible?

"I can see you don't understand," resumed the Captain. "Well, I will explain. A few minutes ago I received a wireless message informing me of an abominable crime… A transatlantic liner had been sunk… A pirate had attacked her… Do you know what pirate this was?"

"Oh God, yes!" returned Fandor. "It was Fantômas!"

"So you know?"

"Obviously. We have just escaped from his hands."

"So you say; but can I believe you?"

"But, sir—"

"Let me finish… This radio communication—it was anonymous—informed me also that a flying machine had risen from the scene of the disaster, manned by Fantômas and his lieutenants…"

"Very good! So you ask us—"

"If one of you is not Fantômas, yes!"

The Captain spoke with the utmost gravity. Certainly his mistake was understandable, under the circumstances, indeed, inevitable. But that did not prevent Fandor instantly breaking into a merry laugh.

"Ho, ho!" he cried, "what a blunder! What a blunder! Juve and I mistaken for brigands! The more things change, the more they remain the same!"—and he was going on to renew his protestations and explain what had actually happened when Juve, with a peremptory gesture, enjoined silence on him.

"Sir," declared Juve instead, "I can now quite realize the doubts you feel… I would swear, in fact, that the message you received was sent out from one of the boats that had escaped from the disaster, the crew believing in all good faith that Fantômas was on board the airplane… But no matter; the point is of small importance… Fantômas or not, we are in your hands. So you can easily keep us under observation. On the other hand, we should have very little difficulty in clearing ourselves if we were going to France."

"If we were going to France?"

This time it was the Captain of the ship who started in surprise. The words Juve had used implied such a strange supposition that he added:

"We are not going to France, then?"

"No, sir," declared Juve calmly.

"And where are we going in that case?"

"To England."

"To England! And what are we going to do in England?"

"That I will tell you, sir, as soon as you are assured that nobody can overhear us."

"Why, what do you mean?"

"You are convinced that no sailor can hear us and gather the purport of our conversation?"

"I give you my word."

"Very good, sir; now I will speak… We are going to England because every second is of incalculable value… I am Juve, as I told you before. Very well, on my honor as a police officer I tell you this: If I am not in England before tonight, tomorrow His Majesty the King will be assassinated."

"What say? I'm going crazy!" stammered the Captain.

At the same moment Fandor was much inclined to make the same exclamation. Never had the police officer said one word as to any danger threatening King George V. Never had he made the smallest allusion to a wish to visit England!

But at that moment a vigorous dig in the ribs warned the journalist he had better hold his tongue. The Captain at the same time mastered his emotion, and, fixing his eyes on Juve's face:

"Come, explain yourself," he demanded.

"I cannot."

"But you must… You suppose that Fantômas is preparing an attempt on the life of the Sovereign?"

"I do not suppose; I know."

"Can you give me any proof?"

"Certainly not."

"And yet you require me to land you in England?"

"I simply give you this warning, sir: either you will land me in a few hours' time in England, or you will make yourself responsible for the villainy contemplated."

"But this is midsummer madness!"

"Just put yourself in my place, sir. What means have I to prove the truth of what I say? And, if I am sincere, is it not my duty to inform you of what I know?"

The officer looked down in doubt, weighing the amazing statements he had just listened to. To sail for England was to take a grave step; ships of war, such as this torpedo boat, have no right, except in cases of emergency, to enter the territorial waters of foreign countries. On the contrary, to refuse to satisfy Juve's wish, if it was really Juve, was to assume a terrible responsibility.

"Well," said the officer, "I am going to wireless to the French Admiralty and ask for orders—"

"In order to warn Fantômas, who will intercept the message?

I beseech you to do nothing of the sort."

"My message will be in cipher."

"There is no cipher, sir, for a brigand like Fantômas."

"Well, in my place, you yourself—"

"If I were in your place, sir, I should not hesitate a moment."

"Really?"

"Not a doubt of it. I should make for England, but meanwhile I should clap my prisoners in irons."

"What! You advise me—"

"To arrest us, Fandor and myself. You have saved our lives; it is the least we can do to realize your difficult position."

Again the officer paused. But, accustomed as he was to come to the grave decisions that are incumbent on every naval officer in command, he was too energetic not to make up his mind to adopt a course that it seemed his duty to follow.

"So be it, then," he announced. "I am going to steer for Newhaven—or, better, for some English port the name of which I shall not disclose to you. Once in harbor, I shall communicate with the English authorities, who will no doubt want to hear your story. If you are Juve and Fandor, I shall have done my duty by helping you. If you are a pair of scoundrels, the English police will likewise be doing *their* duty in arresting you. But, meantime, please consider yourselves my prisoners; this cabin will serve as your prison cell."

"Your cabin, sir?"

"Certainly. If you chance to be the two heroes you say you are, it shall at any rate never be said that on my ship everything was not done to soften the hardships involved in the measures circumstances force me to adopt"; and with a curt nod of the head, the officer left the cabin, bolting the door behind him and summoning a sailor, stationed him outside as sentry.

Hardly was the door shut before Fandor dashed to Juve's side, crying:

"Are you losing your senses?"

"Why so?"

"Why, my good man, the King of England has never been in any danger!"

"I quite agree with you."

"Then why this untruth, Juve?"

"It wasn't an untruth."

"But I say it was."

"Not it; it was a bluff."

"Well, but why this bluff?"

"Because, my young friend, I have sworn to overcome Fantômas. Because, Fandor, Fantômas is a terrible menace to all humankind, and that the use of any and every weapon is justified against him."

"But I don't see—"

"You're just a fool, Fandor, if you can't understand."

Juve spoke in a voice of agitation. It was evident that in lying as he had just done—for it *was* a lie, say what he might—the police officer had been hard put to it; but it was no less manifest that he was convinced he had done his duty, convinced he had acted as his conscience dictated.

"Still I fail to understand," the young man proceeded quietly. "May I know your game?"

"Certainly; this is how it is…" And, after a moment's reflection, he went on in brusque, downright tones.

"The Captain received the message he communicated to us… Now, do you imagine he was the only one to get it?"

"No, of course not."

"Fantômas on board his submarine intercepted it, and knows its contents just as well as the Captain. You agree with me?"

"Certainly I do."

"Then it follows logically that Fantômas knows for certain of their coming after us, knows they are going to carry us to France and hand us over to the police. You know, and he knows as well as you do, how things are managed. Then tell me how many days he will have calculated must elapse before our release from jail."

"Four or five, Juve."

"Well, my dear boy, it is precisely because Fantômas is going to suppose himself freed from our interference for three or four, possibly five, days, that I have resolved to keep my eye on him, to search him out, during these same days."

"But we are under arrest, Juve."

"Oh, for that…"

"But we are bound for England."

"Fandor, my lad, you can't see one inch beyond the end of your nose. See here, I say; think and you will understand. Now let me go to sleep; we shall have a hard night of it, no doubt. Best regain our strength… Good night to you!"—and leaving the journalist completely bewildered by his behavior, Juve, without a touch of compunction, planted himself in the one and only armchair in the cabin, shut his eyes, and went to sleep…

2. An Escape

Witnessing Juve's perfect self-possession, Fandor could not refrain from cursing. The police officer might indeed have such complete command of his nerves that he could go to sleep when he chose and whenever he deemed the time come for taking a nap, but he, Fandor, did not enjoy such a privilege. On the contrary, nervously constituted, quick-tempered, liable to sudden bursts of passion sometimes, the journalist was downright angry for the moment.

"The brute!" he growled, as he gazed at his sleeping companion; "there he is, already in the land of dreams! How the devil is the man made, to be always ready to weave the most intricate plots, and never lose his coolness and calm?"

Then, after a moment's reflection, he went on:

"At the same time, I know him too well to doubt him; if he has acted as he has done, it is because all-powerful motives have constrained him to behave like this… Still, all the same, he does go a bit too far!"

Grumbling and growling, Fandor went stamping up and down the narrow cabin, and as this was of the tiniest dimensions, he kept passing and repassing in front of Juve, looking down at him with eyes expressive of anything but goodwill.

"He wants to pursue the chase… Very good! And so do I, of course. But is this the way to do it, to get us arrested by the English authorities?… In France, if the worst came to the worst, we could make things clear—Juve is so well-known, so celebrated, that he can always manage to get himself released if he so wishes… But in England…?"

The young man left his sentence unfinished. He appeared to be thinking how Juve, for all his greatness, would be losing precious time in establishing his own identity and that of himself.

However, at that moment a more than usually violent roll of

the vessel almost threw the journalist into the sleeper's lap, who naturally woke up with a start.

"Oh, it's you!" he exclaimed.

"Yes, it's not the hangman come for you."

"So I should suppose… You're not asleep?"

"No, Juve, no!… I've no wish to sleep."

"Well, I have." And Juve reclosed his eyes.

Such consummate coolness brought Fandor's annoyance to a climax.

"No, Juve, you've got to wake up."

"Fandor, you're past bearing."

"And what about you, Juve?"

"About me?"

"You—yes, you!"

"But in what way am I past bearing, dear boy? I'm not stopping your sleeping, am I?"

"Yes, Juve; yes, you are."

"And how so, pray?"

"You make me boil with curiosity!"

"Curiosity, indeed! But you *will* say such things! However, to say no more of that, what is it you want? I have told you the truth. Fantômas will believe us to be in France; he will suppose us in custody. I have my reasons for thinking he is going to England—"

"Oh, you think—"

"Why, of course. Lady Beltham has started for London."

"Oh, good!"

"Therefore *I* prefer to go to London too—and to be at liberty there."

"But we're under lock and key."

"For the time being only, Fandor"—and throwing himself back in his chair, once more closing his eyes, Juve went off to sleep again.

"Nothing to be done!" the journalist admitted; "there's nothing to be done to extract a further explanation from him. I know the fellow; he has the most obstinate character I ever heard of!… He's worse than I am!" And so saying, he resigned himself a few minutes later to follow Juve's example. For all his pretended anger, he loved the police officer too well, and knew too well all he was capable of, to doubt for one instant that Juve was in the right; as his comrade had judged it was expedient to take some rest, was not the best thing just to do what he advised?

A quarter of an hour later Fandor, too, was dropping off to sleep. But between Fandor and Juve there was a wide difference. Whereas the journalist was soon buried in the sound, unbroken sleep that follows on great exertions and profound exhaustion, no sooner had the police officer noted his friend's unconsciousness than he rose quietly, a smile on his lips, so wide awake as to leave no doubt that he had never been asleep at all.

"So there," he muttered to himself, "the confounded fellow needed rest… If I hadn't played him a trick, he would never have closed an eye… And now to take advantage of this quiet moment to set about some some necessary business." And he did not waste a second before getting to work. Unlike Fandor, *he* had no need to be forever on the move—far from it; he could remain for hours perfectly silent and perfectly still, as though plunged in some sort of deep reverie.

But this in no way prevented him at other times from showing a capacity for a consuming activity; of this he gave good proof on this extraordinary occasion when he found himself a prisoner on board a French torpedo boat.

"The lockers," he growled, "I must search the lockers; that is of the first importance."

No sooner said than done. Necessity knows now law, we know, and, whatever his plans and projects, these once fixed upon, the police officer felt no scruples so long as he was acting in a way to ensure success. He now proceeded to open the Captain's lockers and searched them minutely, giving from time to time a little chuckle of satisfaction:

"Very good… excellent! A dandy officer this… Equipment number one, I take it… And a second uniform, quite presentable… Come, we mustn't complain… Now, where are the caps kept? Then we must have oilskins—or a mackintosh… Mustn't ask too much, though; never look a gift horse in the mouth, as they say." And Juve kept laughing little smothered laughs to himself as he went on with his task.

Alas! if the Captain could have seen his prisoner at that moment he would have felt no hesitation about proclaiming that Juve—was not Juve! Only a brigand, a scoundrel, he must have concluded, could behave with such shameless effrontery. Without the smallest hesitation, in fact, Juve had just extracted from the open locker two suits of officers' uniform—two complete suits—which he proceeded to fold up with the greatest nonchalance, like a man who cares nothing for the causes he makes in the garments and the inevitable crumpling to which he subjects them.

"Devil take my clumsiness!" he swore from time to time. "I've no notion of how to tie up parcels properly… Well, they'll be strong enough, anyway—that's the main point… Now then for string…"—and to procure this string, on the strength of which he insisted, Juve now cut down the cords of the curtain that masked the captain's bunk.

"So there," observed Juve. "I think that, so far as the needful costumes for the part are concerned, I am provided." And with a smile broadening into a grin, Juve went on:

"Let's slip them into a corner; no call to run the risk of a surprise."

The two suits he had selected Juve had made up into two separate parcels carefully wrapped in one of those waterproof oilskin overalls all naval men possess, and these he pushed away under the Captain's writing desk.

"And now for the mechanical side," he resumed; "that's all-important… Hang it, the portholes are closed, eh?"—and Juve gave a look of consternation at the sort of shutters they fasten up the portholes of a ship with in heavy weather to save the thick glass of the scuttles being broken by the seas.

But next moment he added: "Bah! that makes no matter; it's the brass mounting that concerns me…" And two minutes later the police officer was busy on a very remarkable piece of work. Using the blade of a penknife as a screwdriver, he methodically unscrewed one after the other the brass screws of the mounting that framed the cabin portholes.

"Very good! Excellent!" he chuckled. Then suddenly he gave a start. "What! the engine has stopped! I've just finished at the right moment then."

He listened, and then smiled again.

"Yes, there's no doubt," he proceeded, "we're in the roads all right; there's the anchor chain rattling through the hawsehole." The sound was unmistakable, and Juve recognized it instantly. The Channel is not broad; for a vessel of the speed of a seagoing torpedo boat the passage could not take long. The steamer carrying our two friends had just reached the English coast and was anchoring.

"And the sea is calmer," Juve went on; "there's no doubt about it... Now, will the Captain be coming to pay us a visit before going ashore?... Hmm! I hardly think so, after all; he's bound to be in a hurry to go to the authorities..."

A few more minutes and the police officer felt sure he had been right in believing in the Captain's speedy departure. A slight shock had jarred the light iron hull, followed by the sound of loud voices giving orders and the whistle of the bosun's pipe.

"Excellent," Juve told himself again; "the skipper is stepping into the ship's boat, which proves we are not at the quayside... But no, it's of no importance... What o'clock is it, by the by?" And Juve glued his ear to a crack in the scuttle and gave a sigh of satisfaction. "I don't know the exact hour," he went on, "but, anyhow, it's a dark night, and that's all I care about... Come, to work!" And after listening a moment or two to the comings and goings of the crew, and having convinced himself that nobody was concerning himself with anything but the anchoring operations, Juve softly awoke his companion.

"Wake up, lazybones," he said in a low voice, and, starting half up, Fandor demanded:

"What is it?... Why, are you awake?"

"Yes, my boy—wide awake."

"We have arrived, haven't we?"

"Arrived?—why, no! We shan't have arrived till we've started."

"Come, Juve, more enigmas?"

"Enigmas a child of three could solve. But you're still half asleep."

"I'm not, Juve."

"I say you are. Well, the cold bath will do you good."

"What cold bath?"

"The one we are going to take."

"My good Juve, I like you very much, but as I don't want to go mad guessing your conundrums, I warn you once for all I don't mean to cudgel my brains trying to understand what you mean."

"Very good! I won't say another word. I have a horror of explaining obvious things. Look and you'll see what I mean," and, as he spoke, he stepped calmly up to the porthole, the mounting of which he had unscrewed:

"Well, look!" he said. "Do you see, I'm taking this parcel… But there's another just like it for you… And now…" Juve left the sentence unfinished. Indeed, his actions sufficiently explained what his words failed to explain. Seizing hold of the framework of the scuttle, dragging it out with a vigorous pull and depositing it on the bunk, he mounted on a chair and drew himself through the hole thus opened in the vessel's side.

"What a man it is!" exclaimed Fandor. "What a devil of a man!"

But he showed no more hesitation than the other. Holding securely under his arm the parcel he had just picked up, but the contents of which he did not know, Jerome Fandor in his turn leaned for a moment out of the aperture, made sure no sentinel or guard boat was anywhere about, then let himself slip lightly down into the muddy waters of the roadstead. He was an exceptionally fine swimmer, and in two seconds reappeared on the surface and struck out with a strong, capable stroke. Next moment he caught sight of Juve, who was making good progress, swimming sturdily and well.

"Ho, there, Jove!" he hailed. "A fine thing, a cold bath at ten o'clock at night!… But where the devil are you taking me to?"

"Straight ahead!" panted the police officer.

"A trifle vague," grumbled Fandor. "It's an escape, then, you're after trying?"

"Why, certainly!"

"You might have told me… And all this is to put us on Fantômas' track again?"

"Yes. But hold your tongue, do!"

"Why should I?"

"Water carries sound… You'll be having us arrested again!"

"Oh God, that's not a thing I want!" And he obeyed orders.

Still he failed to understand what his companion was after. However, he felt such confidence in the police officer's combined cleverness and audacity that he was not over and above amazed at his friend's extraordinary proceedings. So for a good ten minutes the pair swam on in silence. The waves ran high, in spite of the fact of their being in a sheltered roadstead. Before them the coast was barely visible.

"You're not tired, Juve?"

"No; are you?"

"I'm getting along, getting along. But I ask you again—where are we going?"

"I'll tell you that later on."

"So you don't know, eh?"

"My dear boy, if I did I should tell you."

"Not so sure of that, Juve; not so sure," retorted Fandor in a tone of good-humored raillery—and once more the two men fell silent, swimming on side by side.

There is an end to everything, however. After a good half-hour's steady going, and when even Juve admitted he was beginning to feel some fatigue, Fandor, rising on a wave, gave a cry of joy.

"Land!" he shouted; but, immediately correcting himself, "Wrong again!" he added; "it's not 'land'; I should have said 'stone.'"

"What do you mean?"

"We are coming into a harbor, Juve. I caught sight of a quay."

"The devil you did!"

"You don't like that, Juve?"

"What I don't like, Fandor, is the prospect of coming face to face with inquisitive folks."

"I see that," declared Fandor calmly, "and the more so as we are hardly presentable objects."

"Hold your tongue, chatterbox! It's no time for ill-placed jokes."

"Right, Juve! Right!" And the young man stopped talking. But a few minutes more and he began again:

"A ladder, Juve! Are we to go up it?"

"Yes… yes, we'll take the risk."

It was one of those iron ladders fixed in the stonework of quays in harbors to give access to boats in spite of differences of level due to the rise and fall of the tide.

Going first, Fandor climbed nimbly up the rungs.

"Nobody about!" he announced, putting his head cautiously over the edge. "Solitude, and some old derelict boats."

"The very dressing room we wanted," was Juve's reply.

"So we are going to dress, are we?"

"Oh God! I don't suppose you wish to march through the town in the state you're in, eh? Undo your parcel, my lad!" And with no small curiosity Fandor opened the parcel he had been carrying ever since leaving the torpedo boat.

Finding therein clothes in it as good as dry, he could not help smiling.

"First rate!" he cried. "Only, to dress up as a naval officer without any right to wear the uniform is to be guilty of a breach of the law."

"Yes, my young friend; but it is likewise to get oneself warm again."

"You are right, Juve; so let's break the law."

The journalist's scruple, however, had arisen from a purely abstract punctiliousness; he was not likely to bother his head about so venial a misdemeanor after his complicity with Juve in acting just before in the outrageous way he had. Ready presently, he merely demanded:

"A dandy officer am I not?"

"As smart as they make 'em," Juve declared; "and I?"

"You too, my dear Juve… But that coat is a bit tight for you, isn't it?"

"No matter for that, Fandor; that's a trifle. But oh God! I'm asking myself where we are. I shouldn't be a scrap surprised if we found ourselves inside the walls of an English arsenal."

"So, Juve? And in that case, how are we to get out?"

"Bah, one can always get out!… The only difficulty is not to meet anybody… Come, let's be off"; and with the calm audacity he knew so well how to display when it was impossible not to trust to luck to solve the most difficult problem. Juve unhesitatingly quitted the sheltered corner where he had just changed his dress in company with Fandor.

Before them lay the darkness of night, dense, mysterious, and threatening. Where were they? Where were they going? Impossible to say.

"Look you, if we meet nobody—" Juve was beginning, when suddenly the light of a lantern pierced the blackness and a peremptory voice demanded in English:

"Halt, there! What name, gentlemen?"

"A sentinel!" exclaimed Fandor.

"We are French officers," said Juve politely, and he continued to advance without a moment's hesitation.

3. A Council of War

Juve appeared in no wise disturbed in mind. Just when everything combined to render the situation in which the police officer and the journalist found themselves precarious, when they were, strictly speaking, escaped prisoners and wearing uniforms which they had no right to assume, which, indeed, they had stolen. Juve's face wore an agreeable smile as he stepped forward to meet the unknown who was staring at him by the light of the lantern.

"Yes, French officers!" he repeated. "You are an official, I gather?"

"I am."

"Enchanted, my dear sir! Enchanted to meet you! Where are we exactly, please inform us? Our boat landed us rather at random."

"South jetty of the arsenal," announced the Englishman laconically. "I was on my way to meet you, gentlemen."

"Really?"

"Yes, to conduct you to the Admiral."

"Oh?"

"Where your Commanding Officer is waiting for you."

"Indeed?"

"The Admiral invites you to dinner, gentlemen."

"Very amiable on his part… Well, lead the way."

Juve continued to manifest the utmost calmness; not a quiver of the voice, not a sign of agitation betrayed his anxiety, not to say his bewilderment. Lost in the shadow, meantime, Jerome Fandor, on the contrary, was biting his lips to check himself from cursing.

"Charming!" he growled. "Here we are, Juve and I, involved in a truly delightful adventure!… The Admiral, of course, has kept our Captain of the torpedo boat to dinner. Nothing more natural!… He has likewise invited all the superior officers of the ship. Most polite of him!… But what will he look like when the Captain declares we are—Juve and I—his two prisoners escaped from custody?"

It did, indeed, seem that the imbroglio was getting more and more serious. By bolting from the French vessel, swimming ashore, and dressing up in stolen uniforms, surely the unlucky pair had aggravated their case disastrously.

Meantime Juve went on talking to the sailor, who was now, lantern in hand, walking by his side, showing him the way to the Admiral's house.

"Have we far to go?" he questioned.

"Oh no, not far," replied the Englishman with the curt brevity of his nation. "About two cable lengths from here."

"Within the walls of the arsenal, then?"

"Yes, sir."

"So much the better."

Juve certainly did not lay bare his thoughts. Nonetheless, Fandor was regaining his spirits little by little; he saw this friend so calm and unruffled, so perfectly master of himself, that he began to share the other's confidence. With that confounded chap was any case ever desperate?

"Here's the house," broken in the sailor.

"Ha, excellent! The Admiral is very polite to ask us… But tell me, my man…"

"What, sir?"

"My comrade and I would just like to wash our hands and do a bit of toilet before meeting him."

"But, sir!"

"I know, I know!" persisted Juve; "you are going to say they'll take us to a dressing room. No doubt they will.. But it was such heavy weather outside, we look like a couple of ragamuffins… You couldn't, could you, give us a brush down here, before we go into the house?"

The sailor seemed a good deal embarrassed. But every Englishman values the importance of correct dress, and he could not but feel the demand was natural enough.

"That is to say," he stammered, "I don't know… If you so order, gentlemen, I could ask at the kitchen door…"

"That's the ticket. Off with you; we'll wait for you here."

Juve still displayed such calmness it was really impossible to distrust his good faith. Indeed, how could any sort of suspicion have entered the head of the English sailor? He had been sent to meet two French officers who were to arrive at the south jetty. He had actually met two officers and was guiding them to the Admiral's house. Was it not simple enough to suppose they desired a brush-down before presenting themselves at the big man's door? With a hurried salute he started off at a run. "I shall be back in a second, gentlemen."

"Oh, no hurry! We have plenty of time."

This last sentence Fandor had spoken in his broken English on his own responsibility. He had, in fact, tumbled to his companion's plan. To get rid of the sailor was so much to the good; to take advantage of his absence to make a bolt for it was better still. Hardly had the man turned the corner of the house before Juve and Fandor were off.

"Best leg foremost, Fandor!"

"Same to you, Juve!"

"By the time he's back we shall be two hundred yards to the good."

"And he won't give chase just right away?"

"Of course not. Run, run!"—and the pair shot off with all the speed they were masters of. But where were they going? An arsenal—and above all an English arsenal—is more or less one great manufactory. Defended by walls, guarded by sentries under the strictest orders, patrolled night and day, no place is under closer surveillance.

"For sure we shall be copped," thought Fandor as he ran. "It's going to turn out a bad business, this."

"Look out!" came a warning cry from Juve at the same moment; "you're going to tumble into a dry dock!"

It was pitch dark. The two men, running at top speed, were skirting a series of great black holes, basins for the repair of ships, into one of which Fandor had all but fallen.

"A bad look out!" panted the young man. Then he added: "Say, Juve, I'm getting blown! What about you?"

"Right you are. Walking pace now; we must just take the risk."

But only Juve was capable of the bold trick he was already planning. Less than three minutes later—and poor Juve was panting still—they found themselves at one of the entrances to the arsenal. There, in front of an imposing iron-bound gate, was a guardroom, brilliantly lighted, before which two armed marines were stationed.

Juve marched straight up to them. "Your officer in command," he demanded.

At the same moment a sergeant came out of the guard-room and, seeing the two French officers, saluted with an air of surprise.

"Attention, sergeant!" Juve addressed the man at once. "We have just come from the Admiral's. Have you been warned? Two escaped convicts are at large in the arsenal. Let nobody there-fore go out without first giving you the password—nobody, I repeat! And now, where is the telegraph office?"

"Just the far end of the street, sir."

"Very good! You will receive further orders… Meanwhile, keep your eyes open… What! is not the gate open yet?"

"I didn't know you wanted to go out, sir."

"You should have guessed as much, my lad!… And your men, they look half asleep! Pull yourselves together, by God! The thing's serious… Good night to you"; and taking Fandor by the arm and assuming an air of dignity, Juve stepped through the great gate of the arsenal, which two men had just thrown open, and a minute later the police officer gave a sigh of relief.

"But I was in a stew! Fact is, I don't know a thing about English military ways. At the very moment I spoke about the password, I was asking myself if there was any such thing in the United Kingdom!" And he went off in a great peal of laughter.

"Juve, I'm surprised at you," broken in Fandor. "Upon my word, you're laughing like a madcap girl! Do you think our affairs are in such fine trim now?"

"By God, my boy, I think we have no cause to complain!"

"Why?"

"Because only five or six hours ago we were expecting to be drowned, now we only risk being hanged for high treason. We're getting on, eh?"

"Granted. Remains to find out what we are going to do."

"Cut our stick, my boy!"

"And how?"

"The quickest way possible."

"But again, how?"

"Oh, what a wet blanket you are!… Come, patience! I know what is troubling you… But you are wrong; I am not forgetting, any more than you… I can even promise you you're not far from getting what you're wanting…"

"That means?"

"Means that in a few hours from now we shall be on Helene's track."

Juve's voice as he spoke the name had trembled slightly, while Fandor's face paled as he heard it… Assuredly Juve had divined the truth; if Fandor failed to share his companion's gaiety it was because he had always on his mind the hideous lot of this charming creature, now fallen into the hands of her villainous father. How cruel the destiny that had willed that Helene should owe her existence to the scoundrel who held the whole world spellbound under the terror of his abominable crimes!

However, Jerome Fandor was not the man to let himself be mastered by gloomy thoughts. From the moment Juve declared all was going well, did he not know he would be doing wrong to go on troubling overmuch? For was not his friend the oracle that could never be mistaken?

"Juve," said Fandor simply, "you know I would give my heart's blood to save Helene?" But he little expected the answer he received.

"All I ask you for is your coat," announced the police officer.

"My coat?"

"Exactly… Anyway, I am sacrificing mine for the same

purpose. Then, look, I am arranging our suicide"—and as he spoke Juve stripped off his uniform jacket and, after dragging it in the mud, ended by throwing it down at the edge of a basin in which the water was lapping gently.

"You do the same," he directed. "Tomorrow morning, finding our duds, they'll think we have fallen in… Forty-eight hours gained… They'll drag the dock… they'll try to recover our bodies… Nothing like it to get ourselves left in peace."

"I agree with you; an excellent notion! But what are *we* to be doing during those forty-eight hours?"

"Getting to London, my dear boy."

"By what means?"

"By this means."

At that moment the two friends were following a road that ran along the seafront, while below lay a rough beach where boats lay drawn up on the sand.

"We're going down onto that beach," Juve proceeded. "We have one of those boats down to the water… We hoist sail. By-the-by you don't know where we are? We are in the Isle of Wight, Fandor… And we are going to Southampton… You'll allow that, once at Southampton, landing at some likely spot, we shall find it easy to get to London."

"Without coats?"

"Not so! We shall buy coats. I have money in my pocket."

"Then I'm ready, Juve… Away we go for London."

Fandor's confidence was restored. He was well aware that in police engagements victory always declares for such as never shrink, who unite audacity with perseverance. Was he going to show himself at this crisis less daring than his comrade? Springing down onto the beach:

"Now, Juve," he cried, "what say you to *this* fine clipper ship?"

"I say it will suit our little game first rate."

"Bravo! Let's shove her into the water"—and a few minutes after the modest skiff he had dubbed "this fine clipper ship" was afloat. Juve and Fandor climbed aboard, and while the former hoisted sail, the latter took the helm.

"Let go everything, Juve. I've done something in the sailing boat line in old days at Meulan. Never fear! With a good wind the passage won't take long."

"I trust so."

"Unless, of course, they come after us. This time it's a serious theft we're committing, for, after all, this boat—"

"Hold your tongue, Fandor. It's only a loan… We're not going to eat the blessed boat, and we're not going to smash her up… All in good time we'll tie her up securely where we land, and all her owner has got to do is to come and recover her and pocket this hundred-franc note we shall leave to pay the hiring."

Then Juve altered his tone.

"But we'll leave that. The first thing of all is to hold a council—a council of war."

"I'm all attention, Juve."

"My boy, it won't take long. We are entirely of one mind, are we not? We must have done with Fantômas?"

"Why, surely!"

"And to have done with him, we must first deliver Helene?"

"Why, Juve, you know very well what I think."

"Why, yes. I know quite well… So, then, Fandor, let us come to a clear understanding; this time a battle to the death is going to begin; let us have no hesitation in fighting it with all our might… We have an advantage on our side; let us make the most of it."

The police officer seemed to be talking to himself. Perhaps he had some extraordinary plan in his mind which he did not see fit to communicate to his companion.

"We have an advantage, you say?" questioned Fandor. "I don't understand…"

"Why, yes, you do. Think: Fantômas believes us dead, or prisoners. It is not he, therefore, who will open the battle. It is ours to conduct the campaign, to have the initiative. Don't you call that having an advantage?"

"Surely. But what are your plans, Juve?"

"Ah, you ask me too much, Fandor! First and foremost I am an opportunist. We must wait and see; we must have patience."

Juve was laughing to himself as he spoke… For sure he knew

well enough that what he had resolved to attempt to triumph over Fantômas. But this did not hinder Fandor from persisting in his questions.

"What a queer character you have, Juve," he said crossly. "One can't get a word out of you once you've made up your mind to say nothing."

"Which shows a fine, obstinate will, Fandor."

"And when you announce a council of war, you hold that council all by yourself."

"So as to be always in the right, Fandor."

The journalist had succeeded in getting nothing further out of his companion even by the time they had made a landing on the outskirts of Southampton and found themselves in the train on the way from that port to the English capital.

There, too, Juve was no less enigmatic.

"Let us avoid the fashionable districts," was all he vouch-safed. "I am pretty well known here since the days when I formed part of the Council of the Great Ten. No, it won't do to risk meeting…" And on very modest terms—it was on the con-fines of Whitechapel, in one of those poverty-stricken streets in the neighborhood of the Docks—the police officer hired a lodging.

"So there!" he declared. "Here we are at home!… These three rooms will be quite sufficient, don't you think so?"

"Why, yes!" Fandor agreed. "But my own opinion is we are wasting our time."

"Because?"

"Because we have now been three hours in London and have done nothing in the way of search."

"You think so?"

"Naturally!"

"Well, you are mistaken, my boy. I have done something of vital importance."

"Nonsense!"

"Without your noticing, I have sent a postcard…"

"Who to?"

"To a Press Agency."

"To say what, I should like to know?"

"Go out and buy the papers, they are selling below our windows, and then you'll know."

Fandor did not need to have such a suggestion repeated. He knew too well that Juve never spoke a word at random not to guess that the newspapers the police officer had told him to buy must contain some sensational statement. Three steps at a time, the young man scurried down the two flights of stairs leading to the little flat Juve had rented, and, dashing up to a newspaper boy, bought three papers at random.

"Let's see!" he said to himself as he unfolded the printed sheets. "What the devil are we going to find?"

Then he very nearly dropped the paper. On the front page in enormous capitals was a heading:

"ARREST OF FANTÔMAS, THE BRIGAND!"

"Good Lord! I'm losing my wits!" growled Fandor.

Lost in amazement, he read the article. It was only a brief statement, and read as follows:

> At the moment of going to press we have received over Juve's signature and in the handwriting of the famous detective, in one word offering apparently unmistakable signs of genuineness, a postcard containing this startling announcement, which we here reproduce for the benefit of our readers: 'I am in London. I have been fortunate enough to arrest Fantômas on the point of assassinating H.M. King George V.'

"By God, is this a silly hoax, or is the news authentic?"

> By tomorrow, no doubt, we shall be in a position to publish the results of the inquiries we are at this moment instituting.

"God Almighty!" stammered the journalist, and dashed up the stairs again.

But in the humble lodging where he had left his friend a few seconds before a fresh surprise awaited him. Juve was not there! The man had disappeared, vanished in the two or three instants of the journalist's absence.

4. Juve and His Friends

At first Fandor was so amazed that the journalist seemed to lose his head altogether.

"Good Lord!" he stammered. "Good Lord!"

What had become of the police officer? How could he have got away so quickly, without a word of warning to his friend as to the motive that constrained him to take his departure?

Rapidly Fandor posed all sorts of questions to himself and indulged in a string of incoherent conjectures—or so it seemed.

"Fantômas," he stammered in a voice of fear, "can it be that Fantômas has been here and attacked Juve?"

Only Fandor, who knew what prodigies of reckless audacity the brigand was capable of, could have conceived such an idea. He had not been five minutes away… Of those five minutes he had employed two in going down the stairs, another two in going up them again, and it was only for the remaining minute that he had actually been outside the house; and he had never left the pavement in front of it—he had never been ten yards from the front door.

"Come, come!" stammered Fandor, still talking to himself. "I'm going dotty. If Fantômas had come here to attack Juve, if he had spirited him away, I must have seen him go into the house and come out again."

But at the very same moment that he was convincing himself, or trying to convince himself, that an attack by Fantômas was out of the question, he was bound to conclude that it was equally impossible to understand how his friend could have disappeared without apprising him and without being seen by him.

"Juve never left the house," Fandor summed up with an oath. "There's no room for arguing about that."

The lodging, in fact, which the police officer had rented was very unpretentious and very small. It consisted simply and solely of two rooms furnished as bedrooms and another, such as in London they call a parlor, which Juve had immediately constituted his future working room. To make a thorough search of these sumptuous apartments could not occupy any length of time. In three minutes the young man had searched every corner, even looked under every piece of furniture and turned over the bedclothes.

"Dust," he grumbled. "Plenty of that for sure, but no trace of Juve. The walls are solid, no doubt; no secret passages. It's impossible…" He broke off abruptly. In the parlor that served as vestibule to the furnished lodgings the good landlady had taken care to install a little table covered with a clean white tablecloth of American cloth, intended evidently for five o'clock tea—an invariable and traditional rite in London. On its immaculate surface Fandor had just caught sight of a couple of lines of penciled writing.

"By the Lord!" shouted the journalist.

Bending more closely over the table, he exclaimed with another oath:

"Juve! It was Juve who wrote that!"

But, after reading the message, he felt bound to admit that he was no wiser as to the means whereby the police officer had managed to leave the flat unseen. To make up, he was pleasantly relieved of all suspense with regard to his friend's safety.

> *If you don't find me here on your return, as is possible, have no anxiety. All you've got to do is to take post at Piccadilly Circus and watch the passersby. Though I have arrested Fantômas, so the papers say, it is possible you may see someone interesting. If not, come back about eight o'clock.*

"The confounded fellow!" Fandor growled. "He's always at it! He's really more mysterious than is quite fair!"

But he was smiling at the same time. No doubt Juve's disappearance was extraordinary; no doubt Fandor could not understand by what means the police officer had managed to slip away in this fashion. But his mind was now at ease about the matter. Juve had gone—gone because he chose to go. Need his friend be surprised or disturbed by the fact that he had not gone in the same way anybody else would have done?

"In fact the surprising thing would have been if he had," Fandor told himself. Besides, he had something better to think about. The paper announced Fantômas' "arrest." Juve, on the contrary, gave it to be understood that the brigand was still at large. Undoubtedly the police officer was better informed than the newspaper; then he it was who had sent the famous post-card which the latter had turned to advantage.

"It is bewildering!" exclaimed Fandor. "So he has been bluffing again. Yet that's not generally his way... Now what is his object?"

Moreover, he was pondering over the order Juve had given him. But there the journalist had no real reason to feel any surprise. Was not this merely the putting into action of a favorite police theory of Juve's, one that the latter had many a time expounded to him?

"In every town in the world," the police officer used to explain, "there is one spot where all the inhabitants, with a few rare exceptions, go by at least once a month... When you are on the lookout for someone, therefore, all you need do is to take ambush at the said place and wait patiently. Inevitably the individual wanted will go by before your eyes." And he would name the places in question. These were: in Paris, the carrefour of the Rue du Havre and the Gare Saint Lazare; in New York, the vast open space at the intersection of Broadway and Fifth Avenue facing the "Flat Iron"; in London, Piccadilly Circus.

"Therefore," concluded Fandor, "it is only logical of Juve to send me to mount guard at Piccadilly Circus."

Indeed, the journalist could feel no hesitation about adopting the plan advocated by the detective. Juve was precision personified. A man who never spoke at random or acted at a venture, he had for certain some scheme in his head that called for collaboration and blind obedience on his friend's part.

"Let's be off, then," Fandor decided. "Perhaps, as he foresees, I shall see something interesting there." The door of the flat banged behind him a few seconds later, and Jerome Fandor set off to take up the duty assigned to him.

But no sooner was the journalist gone than an individual came quietly down from the third floor and, without a sound, reached the landing outside the flat Fandor had just left. It was Juve and no other. It was simple enough, the way he had managed to slip away unperceived; its merit, in fact, consisted in its extreme facility of execution. Counting on Fandor's surprise, on the amazement the young man would feel on missing his friend after he had been away for so short a time, he had simply walked out of the flat and gone upstairs to the floor above. He felt sure Fandor would never think of that.

"A scatterbrained fellow!" muttered Juve, opening the door and re-entering the flat. "Without two penn'orth of logic to bless himself with! Why, the thing was obvious—as I wasn't able to go downstairs, I just went up instead… Obvious to the meanest intelligence!"

Juve sat down and remained absolutely still; anybody seeing him would surely have supposed him asleep. Nothing of the sort—far from it; the detective was listening hard, alert to catch the faintest sound coming from the street outside.

"Let's think it out," he told himself. "Ten minutes to read the paper; another ten to decide on his line of action; five minutes to call a taxi; say, on average, twenty minutes to get here. Come, things can't be long now in happening."

But still he never moved. Whatever the happenings he expected—and it was plain these were of grave import—the police officer sat awaiting them with absolute imperturbability.

"By-the-by," he observed again to himself, "I haven't even a weapon. "Bah, if he has one, I'll take *his*… Ah!…"

He interrupted his reflections to listen harder than even.

"A cab!" he noted presently; "few and far between in streets like this. Can this be the visitor I'm expecting? Yes, I think so… Now, counting three minutes per floor, the time an excited man would take—I shall have him here in six minutes"; and calmly, methodically, he counted the seconds and added up the minutes he gave his hypothetical visitor to arrive.

"One… two… three… four… five," he told them off. "He must be near by now… Three seconds left"—but hardly had he said "three" when a ring came at the door.

"Here he is!"—and Juve sprang up.

For sure those who spoke of Juve as a genius were in the right. Whoever the visitor ringing at his door, be sure the detective had foreseen his coming, made ready to receive him with admirable address. Above all was it sure that at this critical moment he experienced no visible emotion, displayed no trace of agitation. For was not an absolute, perfect control of his nerves in the eyes of the detective an indispensable qualification for every police officer worthy of the name?

With an even step Juve traversed the rooms and made for the door. Halfway there, however, he halted, thinking:

"If it is he… hmm! I'm not badly prepared. But if it is she… Well, it must be she!"—and moving forward again, he laid a hand that never trembled on the latch, and opened with a determined gesture.

But next instant all doubt was removed; it *was* she! Through the half-opened door Juve saw the figure of an elegant and very charming woman, a being worthy of all admiration, of a pure, blonde beauty set off by an air of supreme dignity, of sovereign distinction.

Clad in black and heavily veiled, she stood with downcast eyes, visibly trembling.

"Monsieur Juve?" questioned the visitor.

"My name is Juve. Pray come in, Lady Beltham. I was expecting you."

"You were expecting me?"

"Certainly. I was sure you would come. Will you sit down?"

Juve was doing the honors of his home with perfect self-possession. Yet that name—Lady Beltham, the sight of that superb creature with the queenly carriage, how they must have stirred him! Was she not now Fantômas' wife? Did she not love the monstrous criminal with a senseless infatuation? Was she not devoted to him with a passionate ardor?

Yes, indeed, Juve well knew the tragic history that had

brought about this amazing marriage. Belonging to the highest English aristocracy, widow of Lord Beltham, she had met and loved and married one whom it was only much later, on a day of horror and tragedy, that she had known, poor woman, to be in reality Fantômas, the appalling, abominable Lord of Terror.

Lady Beltham! When Juve saw her, all the sad story of the past revived in his memory. He told himself that the unhappy woman, faithful in her love and her marriage vows, was not really blameworthy. Was it her fault if she loved a villain? Had she not again and again endeavored to divert Fantômas from his tragic and murderous career?

But the police officer found little time for reflection. Dropping into a chair, overwhelmed apparently by emotion, the noble lady only roused herself on hearing the detective's last word:

"You were expecting me? You knew that I was coming?"

"Yes, madam. After I had read the evening papers it was only logical you should come."

"Oh, Juve, have pity on me! That announcement?…"

An agony of apprehension was betrayed in her gentle voice, all the terrible anxiety of a woman tenderly attached to her husband.

"Certainly, madam," he declared, "I do pity you. Take courage; I never arrested Fantômas; my statement was false."

"Oh, thank you, Juve, thank you… But in that case, why?…"

"Why did I say the opposite? For the express purpose of bringing you here; it was my only way to induce you to come."

"Oh, sir, is it possible? But you did not give me your address."

"True, madam. But I thought that was needless. And this point also I wanted to make sure of."

"I fail to understand you."

"Yet it's perfectly simple. I was not sure Fantômas was to come to London, and I had to make certain. Your presence here, your anxiety, at once provide me with the information… But there is more than that. Fandor and I arrived by the express from Southampton… Now I felt certain that if Fantômas was coming to London he was having the railway stations watched.

I was equally certain that his spies had seen us, Fandor and myself, and had followed us… In a word, you were bound to know his address. You see I was not mistaken?"

Without a word Lady Beltham stared at the floor. Alas! she had had so many proofs already of the great detective's perspicacity that she was incapable of further surprise… But she was afraid.

"There was nothing else you wished to see me for, Juve?"

The police officer's face hardened for a moment. "Yes, there was," he said grimly. "I also wanted to tell you this, that I have made up my mind at all costs to end it all… at all costs, I say… You can repeat this"—and the detective got up and made for the door. "We have nothing more to say to each other, madam. I have learned, if only by your being here, all I wished to know. Goodbye!"

But Lady Beltham never stirred. While Juve seemed to be dismissing her angrily, the wretched woman was wringing her hands in despair.

"Sir," she panted, "one word more!"

"Speak, madam."

"A confidence… a secret… Yes, I have a right to reveal it to you, I think."

"I am listening."

"Juve!… Helene… Fandor… it must never be!"

But for once Juve lost his imperturbability. Little was the police officer troubled when he alone was concerned, when he alone had to enter the struggle. But it was easy to see how strongly his feelings were moved the moment the name of Fandor was uttered.

Eagerly he interrupted:

"Fandor? Helene? Well, these two are betrothed. They love each other. They are going to marry."

"No, no! That is impossible!"

"Impossible? And why, Lady Beltham? If Helene's father is a scoundrel, a brigand, an outlaw, the odious villain the whole world fears and abominates, is Helene to be held responsible?"

"It is not that," put in Lady Beltham with another deep sigh.

"Great heavens! What is it, then? Do you suppose that, in pursuing Fantômas at the peril of his life, Fandor is not doing his duty?"

"Juve, let me speak…"

Lady Beltham's face had turned deadly pale. Slowly she brought out the words: "Juve, you must hear the truth… If Helene cannot marry Fandor, it is because she is bound by an oath to her father… to Fantômas."

"Tell me, what oath?"

"Fantômas has taken an oath to his daughter Helene that, should she not become Fandor's wife, he would refrain from killing you, Juve, and him—Fandor—except in lawful self-defense, when he would have to destroy you to save his own life… Now do you understand?"

Paler than death, Juve dropped his eyes to the floor. Be sure he understood all the horror of this bargain the scoundrel had imposed on the gentle girl his daughter, giving her to understand that if she refused to take the oath he demanded he would annihilate Juve and Fandor. For had he ever hesitated to attempt the destruction of his two enemies? Again, supposing Helene, faithful to the pact, refused to become Fandor's wife, had the miscreant ever yet recoiled before any vile trick of a sort to deliver him from his two determined adversaries?

The detective turned scarlet now under the lash of a storm of mad fury.

"Madam," he said, "I thank you for your confidence… But you will be seeing Fantômas again soon? Oh, never deny it! I know you will. Well, you will give him a message from me. Tell him I, Juve, have sworn—and he knows I keep my word—tell him I have sworn that Fandor shall marry Helene."

Juve had spoken in a tone of violent emotion, and it was under the like stress of overmastering agitation that Lady Beltham left the room—slowly and as if reluctantly.

Well she knew, the unhappy woman, that Fantômas, on hearing of Juve's oath, would hasten to take up the gauntlet thrown down by his enemy, and that a campaign more ruthless than ever would be undertaken.

*   *   *   *   *

After Lady Beltham had gone, Juve seated himself again in the armchair he had quitted to conduct her to the door. Consummate as was the mastery he possessed over his nerves, a gift of which he was justly proud—for self-government is always a fine thing—the detective for the moment was strongly moved.

"Poor little Helene," he murmured; "and poor Fandor!… The two children are made for one another, to love each other and to be united… And Fantômas bars their happiness, simply out of jealousy, simply because he hates Fandor."

Juve heaved a deep sigh, and went on: "But the scoundrel's will is not all-powerful, thank God! I am here to combat him… So he would balk Fandor's happiness? Well, it is betwixt you and me, Fantômas. This time it is a personal interest that stirs me to vanquish you," and Juve gave a laugh that was half expressive of pain.

Surely if anybody in the world was of a strength to fight the brigand, who for years had defied all attacks, that someone was Juve. Turn and turn about calm and passionate, turn and turn about capable of the most subtle machinations and the most reckless acts of bravery, he, and he alone, was the man to triumph over the arch-criminal.

Now, pacing the little London lodging where he had taken covert, he was already pondering a plan of campaign.

"Come, come, let us keep calm and cool," he admonished himself. "Let us examine the situation and see clearly how we stand."

But it was no long or complicated task to sum up what Juve knew of Fantômas and of the way to attack him… The villain was certainly in London, or, if not there already, about to arrive from one moment to the next. Lady Beltham's presence in the capital of the United Kingdom, her distress on reading the newspaper, everything clearly proved as much.

"Therefore," concluded the detective, "it is in London the battle will be fought out. So far, so good; but who will open the campaign?" And on this point Juve was bound to confess he had no answer to give. Had he known where or how to attack

Fantômas, be sure he would not have hesitated. But that was impossible.

"It rests with him to show himself by committing one of his many crimes… Then I throw myself on his track. That is how things always go. So, by the Lord, I am reduced to hoping he will commit some fresh delinquency!"

Juve hated the thought of it. Heart and soul he was a police officer, "born a police officer." He possessed all the qualifications required for the practice of a profession that demands for its adequate exercise wide knowledge, the highest skill and intelligence, and an undaunted courage. At the same time, if he had the qualifications of men of his trade, he showed also sundry of their disqualifications. Apt to fear compromising himself, apt to dread putting himself in the wrong, rules and regulations often assumed in his eyes an exaggerated importance.

"Oh, if only we were in France!" he sighed. If he *had* been in France he would not have hesitated one minute as to the course to pursue. Once face to face with Lady Beltham, he would there and then have arrested her, assured that Fantômas would at once have adopted every possible means to set her free.

"Yes," pondered the police officer, "that is entirely illegal. Lady Beltham has never personally been guilty of crime. She defends her husband, but she cannot, properly speaking, be called his accomplice… To arrest her here in England, where personal liberty is thought so highly of, the thing simply cannot be done. So—"

But what particular conclusion Juve was about to draw will never be known, for at that moment a hesitating ring made itself heard—the timid ring of someone who is far from sure if he has any right to be received…

"Why, what now?" exclaimed the police officer with a start. He had stopped dead in his pacing of the room and was thinking hard.

"Who the devil can be coming to see me now?" he asked himself. "I hardly know a soul in London… My acquaintances here are in strict fact limited to zero… Apart from Lady Beltham and Fandor…"

There came another pull at the bell, but Juve never moved.

"Now, Fandor," he proceeded, "has a key and would not ring. Lady Beltham has just gone, and is not at all likely to be coming back… I really cannot see…"

The bell sounded again.

"But," Juve went on, "the strangest thing of all is that Fandor and I came here incognito… The communication I sent to the papers gave no address; so how can people know it?"

But suddenly he caught himself up. "Bah! what an ass I am! Perhaps it's just someone who has made a mistake."

For the fourth time the jarring note of the bell disturbed the quiet of the flat.

"Well, better open without more hesitation… Either it is He—He, Fantômas—or it is nobody!"

Once again Juve stepped quietly to the door. He fully expected to come face to face with the brigand. Knowing Fantômas' audacity, deeming capable him of the most reckless acts of imprudence, he felt sure it was the terrifying figure of the arch-criminal he was going to see. But surprise, sheer surprise, drew a half-stifled exclamation of "Man alive!" from him. "Man alive!" he cried.

And it was a man, a queer little odd creature, that stood revealed, the strangest-looking being ever seen. What Juve saw was a sort of dwarf, almost a hunchback, with long ringlets and a red beard covering the upper half of a waistcoat splashed with dirty spots and stains. A perfect caricature, the fellow carried a wide-brimmed hat in his hand as he asked deferentially:

"Is it Monsieur Juve himself to whom I have the honor to address my tribute of admiration?"

"Yes, sir—monsieur…?"

"Signor Santa-Cabaleri—at your service, Monsieur Juve."

"An Italian, sir?"

"My accent in speaking French is proof enough of that, Monsieur Juve… But will you deign to receive me?"

"Be so good as to come in," and preceding his unexpected visitor, Juve led him into the parlor and pointed to a chair.

"I am all attention, sir. To what do I owe your visit?"

"I am desirous, most illustrious of police officers, of appealing to your talents."

"You appeal to me to help you?"

"You, and only you, can save me."

"But save you from what, signor?"

"Why, Monsieur Juve, to save me from a villain who is ruining me, torturing me, overwhelming me with hideous misery."

"Sir, I do not understand you in the least. Will you be so obliging as to quit compliments and tell me in two words what it concerns me to know of you?"

"Monsieur Juve, if I come to you it is because you have arrested Fantômas."

"Come, come! You found that out from the newspapers?"

"Precisely, Monsieur Juve... By reading your splendid missive."

"My postcard had nothing splendid whatever about it. But another question..."

"Speak, Monsieur Juve."

"How did you discover my address?"

"By asking for it."

"Evidently—but asking whom?"

"A journalist I know—a reporter on the *Evening Journal.*"

"And how did this journalist come to have it?"

"Oh, for that, I don't know, Monsieur Juve. Didn't your postcard give it?"

"Certainly not," Juve replied in a thoughtful tone. In the eyes of a police officer indeed there is nothing that can be called unimportant. On the contrary, it is the most petty details, such as appear to the run of mankind the most commonplace, the least interesting, that lead to the most surprising discoveries.

Juve had given nobody his address. Yet it seemed it was known to the newspapers! Then who could have communicated it at this moment if it were not Fantômas?

"I wager," thought the detective, "the wretch has sent to the Press some solemn contradiction of my statement... Possibly, indeed, he has informed them of my address to lead to an investigation being made. That's what it is; it must be that."

At the same moment the Signor Santa-Cabaleri was making a thousand apologies.

"Most illustrious and most sagacious of detectives, I trust I do not put you out by my inability to inform you?"

"Not at all," declared Juve. "Go on with your story."

But suddenly he frowned in perplexity. "Had Fantômas," he reflected, "protested against his pretended arrest? He was quite likely to have done so; the arch-criminal was entirely capable of committing such an act of imprudence, or even of having denounced Juve as an impostor. But at the same time there was one point—a small detail, but of much significance—that suggested that any such supposition of the sort was unfounded: if the newspapers knew the police officer's address, how came it no reported had yet presented himself at Juve's lodging; how was it not journalist had arrived to interview the man who claimed to have arrested Fantômas? Fandor himself would tell me the thing is impossible."

And simultaneously another obvious "impossibility" occurred to him. If his address was known to the newspaper editors, it was hardly to be doubted that the English police, the best organized, the most well-informed, the most energetic in the world, would also be aware of it. Juve knew their abilities too well not to be sure of this.

"By now," he concluded, "the detectives would be here, I cannot but remember I am an escaped prisoner, a man who has stolen a naval officer's uniform; who has 'borrowed' a boat; who has spread false news—all of them things that could hardly be passed over lightly."

However, Juve had not the time to reason it out clearly. His visitor was again speaking.

"Knowing your address, dear Monsieur Juve, I could feel no hesitation about coming to see you; you alone can relieve my distressing situation."

"What is your distressing situation, then?"

"I am the plaything of a vile brigand."

"Oh, ho!"

"A brigand I should have suspected to be the terrible Fantômas, had I not known you had arrested him."

"Forget about that, sir, and tell me how your case stands."

"Monsieur Juve, I am a collector, and it is my collections they attack."

"Your collections?"

"They are my life, my soul, Monsieur Juve, my beloved prints."

"You collect prints, then?"

"Yes, Monsieur Juve—prints, engravings, all the precious unique productions of the artists of the eighteenth century."

"I congratulate you."

"I thank you, sir, I thank you; I see you are an amateur too. I have some superb Fragonards and Boilys it is a joy to look at, and Moreaus—Moreau *fils*—that make me pale with delight."

"Be brief, sir, be brief. So then…?"

"Well, then, all my prints are together in one room… in a cabinet… and others on the walls… and others in portfolios… And one and all I love them. I have prints to the value of hundreds of thousands of francs, sir."

"Yes, I understand. Well?"

"Well, sir, it is my prints, my beloved prints, they are slaughtering for me!"

"Slaughtering for you?"

"Yes, slaughtering—there is no other word for it. Think of it, Monsieur Juve… I have had a letter. I have been ordered to put an envelope under my door containing a hundred thousand pounds… or else my prints would be ruined, slaughtered, massacred."

"And you didn't do this?"

"And my poor prints have been murdered."

"In what way?"

"Oh, if I knew that, how the villain sets about it—"

"I'm not asking you that. What I ask you is, what damage have they done to your collection?"

"Every day, Monsieur Juve, I find one of my poor pretty darlings half burnt, stained and torn in holes, as if someone had thrown an acid over them."

"And no one has been in?"

"Oh, but, Monsieur Juve, the door is locked and double locked, and I keep the key always on me. The windows are barred."

"And the police? What do the police say?"

"Monsieur Juve, I haven't wanted to tell them about it yet… I don't care!"

"But why not?"

"The villain told me if I called in the police he would kill *me*."

"So you appeal to me?"

"Yes. But you, monsieur, you don't belong to the London police… I hope the scoundrel will not know… You will save an old man from this torture?"

Juve made no immediate reply. He seemed lost for the moment in perplexed thoughts. How odd this adventure, the particulars of which he was hearing under such surprising circumstances!

"Monsieur Juve," the Italian resumed, "you don't refuse me your help?"

The police officer started up. "Certainly not," he cried, in a voice of friendliness. "Prints they succeed in destroying in a room hermetically closed—why, this promises to prove interesting—the more so as the business is further complicated by an attempt at blackmail."

"Oh, most illustrious of police officers, how can I ever thank you adequately if you succeed?"

"Pshaw, no more of that!… Perhaps I shall not succeed. Let us go to your house, sir."

"To my house?… Hmm… The fact is…"

"Well?"

"It is late—it is nighttime."

"So it is; but I don't see…"

"I am an old man, Monsieur Juve. If I'm attacked, I shan't be able to defend myself."

"Oh!… I understand… you are afraid?"

"Afraid? Great heavens, no! There's no braver man than I.

But I prefer…"

"You prefer not to expose yourself to danger? I understand. And you are your own master. Now where do you sleep?"

"At a hotel; I have been sleeping at a hotel since these adventures."

"Better and better! So your tormentor has a free field. Upon my word, sir, I am sorry to break my word, but you force me to do it. Unless I can spend a night on the lookout in your print room, I fear I cannot be of any use to you."

"But it's all right, most illustrious sir. I perfectly understand. Go there by all means! Here are my keys."

"You wish me, then, to go to your house without you?"

"Certainly. In fact, I should only be in your way."

"Then that's settled. Will you give me your address?"

"Here is my card, Monsieur Juve."

"Good! So keep your mind easy; I shall go this very evening to take stock. Will you call round here tomorrow?"

"I shall be here punctually. And about your fees?"

"We will talk about that later on," Juve answer dryly. Did this mean that he had no mind to discuss questions of money payment? Anyhow, the Italian did not seem to notice his reluctance. He bowed again profoundly and took his departure.

But hardly had he disappeared though the door before Juve's face changed suddenly.

"By the Lord!" he growled, his eyes flashing fire, "can this be a defiance? An ironical challenge? An insult?"

Then rapidly he went on:

"An Italian? Not a bit of it! My visitor is no Italian… He pronounces his 'u's' too correctly. Just as an Englishman never succeeds in articulating clearly the French word *'huit,'* just as a Frenchman is incapable of aspirating properly the English 'h,' so the Italian can never manage to say the vowel 'u' distinctly, he always makes something like 'oo' of it."

"Halloa! What's that you're muttering to yourself about, eh?" a cheerful voice broke in at that moment. "I find your door wide open and you gesticulating like a jack-in-the-box—with all due respect to you be it said. Why, Juve, old man, what's up now? I've been mounting guard—pure waste of time; not a suspicious face anywhere to be seen!... And you, you've been out? I tell you I've come home in a very bad temper."

It was Fandor, who, in spite of what he said, was laughing and chaffing in his usual way, for the journalist was never really put out.

But in another second his face fell. Juve had caught sight of him and was coming towards him, declaring in a voice of decision:

"I have not been out, Fandor, no!... But I am going out... You've come too late; five minutes sooner, my boy, you'd have found here..."

"Why? Who?" panted the young man, surprised at the other's tone.

"Upon my soul! I don't know the gentleman's name. But I do know his profession. You would have found here, my boy, a messenger of Fantômas'—his first lieutenant, no doubt; a lad of eighteen or twenty... who doesn't understand the way to disguise himself—not an Italian at all, but a Maltese... And it's to Fantômas' I'm going! Never look at me in that amazed fashion. I tell you, I'm going to Fantômas'. He has challenged me to a duel—a duel and no mistake... And I've taken up the challenge, of course I have... In two hours from now, he and I, one of us will in any case have won the day over the other."

5. An English Colleague

No sooner had Fandor heard his friend's surprising statement than he, too, was strongly moved. At the same time, so unexpected was the startling news, he could not easily make up his mind to believe it true.

"Impossible!" exclaimed the journalist. "You're joking!"

"Do I look like it?"

"Why, no, Juve! But with you one never knows."

"As you will. Best listen."

Juve had the secret of precise statement, clear and succinct sentences that in a few words explained the most complex problems and made them intelligible. He quickly put Fandor in possession of the facts regarding the visit he had just received.

"Do you understand?" he concluded by asking.

"Not very well," the young man protested. "Or rather, if I gather perfectly well what occurred, I have to ask myself if the conclusions you draw from them are correct."

"You mean?"

"Whether this Italian is really an envoy from Fantômas, whether Fantômas really wishes to challenge you—of this I'm not sure."

"Ta! ta! ta! how simpleminded you are!"

"No, no! I don't think I am."

"But I say you are; it's obvious."

And in a voice showing positive annoyance he went on:

"Why, see here, the trick is childish! Don't you understand that Fantômas has had recourse to it only because he guessed quite well that I should not be taken in by it? Just think for a moment. Everything in the business goes to prove that I am right in my conclusion. The Italian, to begin with, is not an Italian—his pronunciation proves it. Then why this bogus nationality, if not meant to inspire confidence?... Secondly, the fellow professes to have learned my address from the papers. But that is clearly a lie. If my address had been known the reporters would be here to interview me—the reporters and my colleagues the detectives. We are getting on now. A mysterious attack is referred to—engravings destroyed in some odd way. There you have the detail purposely intended to draw my attention, to pique my curiosity… Say at once the affair is Fantômas' work."

"But can't it be genuine, this affair? Supposing Fantômas concerned—and nothing proves the contrary, seeing he is at large and free to act—is he not capable of this ruse?"

"My dear boy, if this affair were genuine, the means adopted would be more mysterious."

"That is to say?"

"That is to say the method chosen to destroy the prints would not be so puerile…"

"Puerile! you say puerile! Do you understand, then, how prints can be destroyed in a locked room which nobody enters?"

"Undoubtedly I do."

"Juve, you amaze me. Tell me the way you mean." But Juve only shrugged his shoulders.

"What!" he jeered, "the celebrated Jerome Fandor doesn't understand how it's done?"

"Not a bit."

"Yet, my child, it's perfectly simple. You merely take a good magnifying glass and a mirror. You wait till there's a strong sun. Then you concentrate the rays, and throw the beam onto the print you wish to burn… Every schoolboy knows the trick."

"The devil!" was all Fandor found to say. Once more, in fact, the journalist was astonished at the sure and swift way in which Juve resolved police mysteries apparently the most incomprehensible and difficult. Two seconds' reflection sufficed the detective to guess what other men would never have dreamt of; he went by instinct straight to the truth with a certainty that was positively amazing.

"Are you convinced now?" he demanded.

"By God, yes!" Fandor admitted.

"Then you understand Fantômas' terrible game?"

"Almost."

"My good Fandor, here you have it in two words: Fantômas has the railway stations watched. He learns of our arrival. Possibly, indeed, from his submarine he had already seen us picked up at sea. In a word, he knows we are in London; he knows our address."

"We ought to have concealed it from him."

"By no manner of means! Eager as he is to come upon *me*, I am every whit as eager to fight *him*… No doubt of it, he wants to make an end of it—and so do we! To make a long story short, he reads the papers; he sees my announcement of his capture; he feels that such a piece of news may dishearten his accomplices… Now tell me, Fandor, is it not natural he should pick up the gauntlet thrown? Is it not logical he should contrive, clumsily, a mysterious affair that is to entice me into a trap? Look you, I would take my oath Fantômas has acted under the stress of anger. I would swear the scoundrel didn't take two seconds for reflection. He wants revenge; he wants it at once. He summons me to his house; he summons me there to kill me… Just think of it! What a fine revenge! The newspapers announce his arrest. True; but next day the very same journals will have to eat their words—Fantômas is at large and has just killed Juve!"—a sardonic peal of laughter concluded the sentence. All the same, beneath his forced gaiety it may well be Juve concealed a painful wound to his self-esteem. It may be he was piqued by this clumsy trap the torturer was laying for him!

Not pausing to think these questions out, Fandor sprang up briskly.

"Well, Juve, forward's the word in that case."

"Forward, eh?"

"Why, surely; we're to go there, I suppose?"

"We?"

"Evidently! You don't imagine I'm going to leave you to go alone?"

"'Evidently,' you say. No, I don't think it is evident."

But his voice shook as he spoke. How well he knew that Fandor was a brave man; and, above all, he knew the deep affection the young man bore him. Nor could he fail to experience a fond emotion, an intoxicating feeling of pleasure, as he saw with what eagerness the journalist volunteered to share the danger.

"You know the risk we run?" he asked.

"Pretty much. But victory…"

"Or defeat, Fandor."

"Bah! We must never think of that."

"We may be murdered. To go there is almost certainly to fall deliberately into a trap."

"My dear Juve, we are wasting time."

The police officer did not insist. Without a word he gave Fandor his hand and the two men exchanged a clasp that expressed all the depth of their ardent affection. What need of any further discussion? For sure Juve would in any case have done what his friend desired; to lavish praise on him was only an offense to his gallantry.

"Well, Juve," Fandor resumed, "you have thought out a plan of campaign, no doubt?"

"On the contrary, my boy, I have made none. The best thing in a case like this is to be an opportunist; we must act as circumstances dictate. To form projects based on mere surmises is to walk blindfold."

"Maybe so, Juve; but nevertheless, if we are going to face Fantômas, it would be well…"

"To do what? To be armed? Why, yes, I am with you there. We're going to provide ourselves with a brace of revolvers of a good make."

A quarter of an hour later the two might have been seen coming out of a gunsmith's in the Strand—one of the best known shopping streets in London—and making at a leisurely pace for the address given by the self-styled Italian.

"Two Brownings of heavy caliber… sixteen shots to fire. With these playthings in hand, I think we hold the trump cards. You don't agree with me?"

"But I do, Juve… Only that doesn't prevent my heart beating a bit fast."

"Nonsense!… I know you; that's not going to make your hand tremble when you have to take aim."

Neither of the pair in fact failed to realize the seriousness of their undertaking. Everything pointed to the fact that it was Fantômas they were about to confront, and how, then, could the battle be anything else but terrible, desperate to the last degree?

"Moreover," Juve observed, "we are in a foreign country, where, very rightly, the police have no notion of taking matters as a joke. If we cause a scandal without showing we had good reasons for acting, we shall be making ourselves liable to some unpleasant punishment."

"In France, Juve, it would be sufficient to mention your name."

"We are in London, and don't let us forget it, my boy."

Juve was not really anxious, but he realized the seriousness of the situation. He professed, indeed, for the English people sentiments of respect and admiration, arising no doubt from his knowledge of the degree to which, in that land of liberty, the great principle of the respect due to the liberty of one's neighbor was rigorously applied. Juve proposed to act without any warrant whatsoever; he was going to intrude into a private house, to make an arrest there, to use firearms there, perhaps, without having, in the eyes of the laws of England, any official capacity. It was a grave matter, and he realized this to the full.

Fandor, on the contrary, felt no scruples of the sort. Was not Fantômas, enemy of the human race, as formidable a foe to Londoners as to Parisians? The former, no less than the latter, would rejoice at the downfall of a wretch who deserved to be looked upon as the scourge of all mankind.

"Let us keep our eyes open, Fandor, and be prudent," the police officer admonished his companion.

"Keep our eyes open, yes!" assented the journalist. "But a fig for prudence; you can't make omelettes without breaking eggs."

On coming out of the gunsmith's shop the two friends called

a cab and were driven to a spot not far from the address supplied by the sham Italian. Arrived there, they made their way on foot to the house indicated. The very look of it sufficed to arouse feelings of excited anticipation in the two adventurers. It was a small private dwelling, in itself harmless enough in appearance, but surrounded by extensive gardens and great empty spaces of wasteland. A church clock nearby had struck eleven, and nobody was abroad in the neighborhood at this late hour.

"A cutthroat place, truly!" Fandor described it. "One could be murdered here in all peace and quietness. Let's be going in, Juve."

"No, no! Best inspect the ground first."

Thereupon the two proceeded to make a leisurely circuit round the building. Nothing, however, seemed to call for remark. The front was closely shut up; not a spark of light filtered through the shutters; not a sound was to be heard. There was nothing whatever to call for special notice.

"Result nil!" remarked Fandor.

"Even so," agreed Juve. "Another proof my visitor lied."

"Proof, what proof?"

"Not a house anywhere near, Fandor; not a house from which anyone could throw a beam of sunlight. It proves never a print has been burnt in the house here."

"Unless, Juve, you have made a mistake? Unless the miscreant denounced by your Italian adopts some other device?"

"There is no other way. However, we are going to find out."

Back again outside the front door, the two friends had halted for a moment. But now the detective was drawing the keys from his pocket.

"Careful!" he cried. "No silly rashness! Revolver in fist, and keep behind me."

"Go ahead, Juve, go ahead, and never you worry about me!"

Without deigning to reply, the police officer inserted the key in the lock, turned it rapidly and pushed open the door.

"Very good!" he observed; "a passage… two doors. Can you see the switch? Then turn on the light"—and next moment the dazzling glare of a big electric lamp blazed out.

"Nothing out of the ordinary," Fandor was saying, when Juve interrupted him.

"Nothing!… barring this…"

The detective had taken a step forward and, stooping, caught sight of a small object of brass. His piercing eyes at once discerned what it was.

"An empty cartridge case," he remarked quietly. "Decent people evidently, who are fond of firearms… To proceed"—and next minute he was throwing open the door on the left. It revealed a modest dining room, the furniture of which was thick with dust.

"So," observed the detective again, "my Italian has told me another lie; if he lived here the place would be in order… To go on…"

Fandor meantime had pushed open the door on the right.

"That must be where he keeps his collection," said Juve.

"Wrong again; there's not a print to be seen. It's a smoking room."

"Yet another lie in that case."

"Yes, Juve, another lie. But—"

"But, what?"

"You didn't hear?"

"No."

"A sound of breathing."

"You're dreaming."

"I am not dreaming."

The two men looked at one another in strained suspense, nervous and anxious to the last degree.

Those who do not realize the superb courage of the men who devote their lives to the pursuit of famous criminals will surely never know what tragic moments have to be faced in the performance of police duties. In this lonely house to which both had come fully convinced they were about to meet Fantômas, the arch-criminal of criminals, face to face, Juve and Fandor lived a thousand lives in one moment. Was not the torturer capable of any and every atrocity? Was not the dread Lord of

Terror a mastermind for the invention of any and every foul machination? What was to be the next step in the tragic drama?

"My heart is thumping in my chest," Fandor confessed breathlessly.

"Hush! don't talk… Listen again… I thought…"—and both stood silent for a moment. Then: "You are right, Fandor… I heard too…"

"Someone breathing, eh?"

"Perhaps… it seemed to me—"

But Juve never finished his sentence. A half-stifled cry of surprise had broken simultaneously from both. The electric light had suddenly gone out in the room, then next instant been flashed on again.

"Stand by to shoot!" ordered Juve.

Fandor had his Browning already in hand. At one and the same moment the sharp click of the two safety-catches pulled off could be heard.

"Stand by, Juve!"

But the police officer had no time to answer. A footstep approached, and framed in the doorway the figure of a man stood out.

"Good day, gentlemen!" said a voice—and before Juve had recovered from his surprise, Fandor was lowering his weapon.

"By the Lord!" thundered the journalist. A young man had entered the room. He was tall, decently dressed, and held a paper block in one hand.

"Good day, gentlemen!" repeated the unknown. "Allow me to introduce myself. My name is John Graham, reporter on the *Evening Journal*. Your brother, Mr. Fandor—"

"My colleague."

"Precisely so. Ah! Monsieur Juve, I presume? Enchanted to meet you. And… you have not seen Fantômas?"

But this last question filled the detective with such amazement and surprise he could find no answer to make. He was ready for anything was Juve, but not for this.

Fandor, for his part, burst out laughing. Then:

"Well, now, my dear colleague, will you tell me how we come

to have the pleasure of seeing you here?"

"Gentlemen, it is quite simple. I have come to interview you."

"Interview us, eh? But how did you know?"

"Monsieur Juve, it is exceedingly simple. Indeed, I'm surprised to have to explain it to you. Your perspicacity—"

"Say no more of that. To go on?"

"You played off a fine trick, Monsieur Juve, on Fantômas by writing to my paper to the effect that you had arrested him. Well, not to put too fine a point on it, Fantômas has paid you back in the same coin… Why, yes, this afternoon our news editor received a hint that you would be here… armed… ready for anything… here, where, of course, there would be nobody. Fantômas further added that he was much annoyed by your persistency… and that he intended once for all to break off all relations with you…"

"You are poking fun at me, sir?" was Juve's only answer to this, spoken in a voice shaking with anger. This bitter humiliation was reserved for him, then; after so many dangers run, so many perils faced—to be made a public laughingstock!

"There, there, don't lose your temper!" expostulated the journalist from the Evening Journal. The story will never get about. My paper pledges itself not to publish a single detail, if…"

"If?"

"Upon my word, gentlemen, we can talk more at our ease once we are before a counter. Will you allow me to invite you to a drink?"

"No!" said the police officer in the same hard voice.

"But why not?"

"Because I don't choose to listen to you."

"But, sir—"

"Good night to you, sir. Publish whatever you will… Publish that I am a fool… that I am an ass!… Say they ought to shut me up in an asylum! I don't care; when a man is called Juve he can despise such little pleasantries. Good night!… Ah! but I was forgetting… Anyhow, here's a great piece of news for you. You may announce that Fandor, my friend Jerome Fandor, will

be married before three weeks are out. Yes, Juve pledges you
his word it is the truth!... To whom? To Fantômas' daughter.
Till we meet again, sir. Come, Fandor, we must be going"—and
Juve carried off Fandor dumbfounded by his friend's fury.

6. There Are Pleasantries *and* Pleasantries

After leaving the house where he had suffered so painful a blow to his self-esteem, Juve set off at such a pace that Fandor had almost run to keep alongside his companion. But the journalist all this time was laughing in his sleeve. Without feeling any excessive surprise at Fantômas' audacity—he had long known the fellow to be capable of anything—Fandor was in truth a bit amused at his friend's discomfiture.

"That damned Juve is always for riding the high horse; a little lesson will do him no harm. He'll prove a trifle less presumptuous for the the future"—and at the thought he could not check himself from breaking into a peal of laughter.

"Oh, ho!" thundered Juve at this. "So you find the whole thing highly diverting, do you?"

"Upon my word, yes, Juve! Why, of course, what would you have? We must have looked such a pair of fools, with our revolvers in our hands! I'm only putting myself in my fellow-journalist's place"—and Fandor was going on to explain why his mirth was so strongly stirred, when suddenly he noticed what Juve was after, how he was actually trembling from head to foot, while his face was almost livid in its pallor.

"Why, Juve, old man, I'm not making you really angry, surely?"

"Not at all."

"You know very well I should be truly sorry if you took my merriment ill."

"I'm not taking umbrage at that."

"Then why are you so desperately upset? I don't know you anymore."

"Because…?"

"Because, my good, my dear Juve, modest-minded as you are, I am asking myself if a mere trifling wound to your self-respect can hurt you so abominably?"

In so speaking, Fandor was expressing his real thoughts. He was well aware how simple-hearted the police officer was, how genuinely he despised fame, what real horror he felt for the celebrity attaching to his name. How, then, came it he was so mightily upset by an incident that, after all, was of small importance?

But Juve, on hearing the young man's remonstrances, came to a sudden stop, and, turning to his friend:

"You are right," he said. "I am a fool. What is past is past… Besides, who laughs last laughs best… Come, my boy, let's waste no more time… Go back to Piccadilly."

"To Piccadilly? At this time of night?"

"Yes. The time makes no difference. Fantômas may go by there in the middle of the night… Besides, we are going to change our lodging. Stay there till I come and fetch you. I am going to remove our modest belongings, give back the keys to our landlady, and look for a new lodging… Upon my word, we'll simply go to a hotel… Is that all right, Fandor?"

"Agreed, Juve, if you give me your word of honor you are not going to do something else, that you are not planning some dangerous expedition."

"Bravo, Fandor! No, never fear; I'm not going to do anything else but what I told you"; and Juve was speaking the truth; he was not planning any new enterprise. Only he was in a hurry to be alone.

A few moments before, in fact, the police officer had had a startling surprise. No sooner was he in the street than, putting his hand mechanically in the pocket of his overcoat, he had felt in this pocket, empty only a second before, a paper, an envelope.

"No need to open it before Fandor," was his immediate thought; "best not worry him to no purpose."

But no sooner had Fandor walked away than Juve naturally enough stopped underneath a streetlamp and drew the document from his pocket.

"A letter!" he exclaimed. "It is evidently a letter. Who can have slipped it into my pocket? Who could have done it?"

Alas! he knew the answer he should have given, but had not had the strength to articulate it... With a trembling finger he tore open the envelope and read the mysterious letter at a glance:

> *Juve, I cannot congratulate you! Juve, my dear fellow, you are losing your usual perspicacity... How came you not to guess that the bogus reporter was I?... I have had a fine laugh at your extreme simplicity.*

The letter was shaking between Juve's fingers.
"He!" groaned the detective in a broken voice; "it was He!"
Then he went on reading:

> *I did not get you to come, Juve, simply to make a mock of you; that were unworthy of both of us... I had a serious motive for teaching you this less. You guess what it was, I imagine. Anyway, here it is. As a reporter, Juve, when I cajoled you so easily, I could have made an end of you, you and Fandor, without running the smallest risk... I did not do it. If I did not do it, it was because I respect the pact I have made with Helene... Now you understand, I take it?... Let Helene not marry Fandor, and I let you live, you and him. On the other hand, let the marriage take place, I swear to you both of you shall perish!... No need to say more, I think!*
>
> > *Fantômas.*

Again Juve could not repress a shudder. Was not this letter the definite, brutal, terrifying answer the Torturer made to his challenge? But quickly the police officer recovered his calmness. Doubtless it was a defiance in reply to his—it was an ultimatum he had just received. But was he going to let himself be intimidated by boastful rodomontade?

"Beaten twice over!" thought Juve. "Beaten when I mistook the sham reporter for a real journalist; beaten again when I never suspected it was actually Fantômas cleverly disguised. But the game is not finished; on the contrary, it is only beginning." And he added aloud in a determined voice: "Fandor and Helene love each other. They shall marry. I will marry them as

I have sworn—in spite of Fantômas."

Then the police officer walked on, but he was no longer in a hurry. He had torn up the insulting missive into a thousand fragments and tossed them in the gutter. But, despite himself, he was thinking of the grim Lord of Terror. What was the real power of this villain that he dared the outrageous deeds he did? He was everywhere; he assumed all aspects, all forms, all faces. Minute by minute he knew all his enemies were doing. Always he dictated his orders to them, as an absolute autocrat sure of being obeyed.

"Oh, but for all that," thought Juve, "I have an ally more powerful than he—the loving hearts of those children."

*   *   *   *   *

At that same moment, searching the spot Juve had assigned him as post of observation, Fandor, on his side, never ceased thinking of Helene. He loved her with all his heart; he knew that she would be for him the lovely and devoted wife who would make his home happy beyond all compare. Why, then, must Fantômas, yielding to his implacable hate, pitiless towards his daughter and her love, have sworn to prevent the marriage he longed for?

"Juve declares he will checkmate the scoundrel. But is he not perhaps deceiving himself? There are times when I lose heart…"

The you man spoke his true feelings. So long had he, with Juve at his side, waged an unceasing war against the enemy that sometimes he found himself yielding to an overpowering weariness. No, assuredly the young man was not prepared to abandon the struggle! Far from it—he would gladly have sacrificed life itself to triumph over the brigand. But for the moment he was asking himself if victory were possible.

Like Juve, Fandor evoked the image of the Lord of Terror. Like the police officer, he pictured the villain coming and going, a free agent, in London, a city twice as big as Paris. How he mocked at the efforts of his pursuers! How clearly he showed by his audacity the small account he made of the adversaries who dogged his footsteps, foes whom he overthrew so easily at every one of their encounters!

"He is stronger than we," Fandor muttered. But to have spoken so filled the young man with a passing feeling of shame. What, had he come to this? Was he giving way in this feeble fashion?

"I am losing my common sense," he told himself. "How many times has not Juve, too, triumphed? How many times has he not reduced him to flight?… No, no, we shall win the day, I am convinced of that."

Behind him a voice mumbled:

"Joking apart, M'sieur Fandor, what is it you're so blooming sure of?"—and so characteristic was the said voice, Fandor recognized its owner instantly.

"Bouzille!" he cried. "Bouzille here!"

Yes, at his back stood the old tramp looking at him with roguish eyes. Yet nobody but Fandor would have known the ancient vagabond in the startling figure he now beheld. Verily Bouzille showed no trace of his customary look of some disreputable ragpicker. Not, indeed, that he had acquired the special elegances that mark the English "swell" since he had come to live in London. Far from it; but still, his appearance was profoundly changed.

Clean-shaved—which gave his face a strangely unfamiliar look—he wore for head covering a gigantic top-hat that might have been the trade sign filched from a hat-maker's shop. Provided, moreover, with a monocle that contorted his visage with a perpetual grin, he was clad in a very long black coat that had evidently once formed part of an English clergyman's wardrobe. By way of contrast, no doubt, he sported a red necktie tied in a monstrous big bow and very wide flapping trousers. In his hand he carried a swagger-stick, while his feet were encased in top-boots.

"Why, yes, for sure," he declared; "it's just me, no use denying of it. You knew me by my photographs, eh? And I told myself right away as how it was you."

"But whatever are you doing here, Bouzille?"

Struck dumb at first by surprise and astonishment, Fandor presently recovered presence of mind enough to question this amazing figure of fun.

"So you are in London?" he asked.

"In London, yes, M'sieur Fandor. Here I am and here I stay."

"But since when?"

"That I can't just say. Postman ain't never brought me no almanac, seeing as how I ain't just in the way to get birthday presents."

"How do you live? Come, tell me. I thought you were in Belgium."

"You were thinking wrong, then, M'sieur Fandor—no offense meant."

"I see I was… But answer my question. What are you doing here?"

"I have turned gentleman."

"Gentleman?"

"A 'swell,' too, I tell 'ee, as they say in English. But mayhap you don't speak English?"

"No, not I… And you?…"

"No more don't I, o' course… To start with, that's all to the good; it would be agin me in my trade."

"So you have a trade, have you?"

"A profession, M'sieur Fandor—a profession. It's not with my hands I earn my crust; it's not a trade."

"Bouzille, you take my breath away. Have you been made an ambassador perhaps?"

"Next door to it. I am a guide—a guide for foreign gents."

"A guide? You are a guide? But you don't know London?"

"No matter for that… My clients don't know it no better; so they can't object."

"But you don't speak English?"

"For sure! If I talked English, folks would understand what I said… That would be a nuisance o' course; but seeing as nobody twigs what I tell 'em, I've naught to worry me. Say, shall I show how I do it? Now listen."

Bouzille took two paces forward on the pavement, then in a

ringing voice began:

"Ladies and gentlemen, allow me the honor and privilege to inform you as how this here is a public square, this is… Look about you and you'll see… There's houses all round it, and a statue in the middle… There's folks on foot go by, and carriages drive by. This here square is called—I don't know just what it is called. But there, you'd be none the better for knowing; you'd only go and forget it… So now let's get on; there's more to see… Follow me, ladies and gentlemen, follow the guide!"

Then, resuming his natural voice, Bouzille concluded:

"That's five bob, M'sieur Fandor, five shillings. I know the English money, you see. 'Twas the first thing ever I learnt."

"Bouzille, you amaze me!"

"Good! good! But come, pay up; you'd never have the heart, M'sieur Fandor, to refuse me five shillings… In France, look you, I'd ask you to stand me a glass, but here…"

At that very moment Fandor was searching through his pockets. He had known Bouzille so long, and was so well aware how the old chap was always without money, that he made no difficulty about offering the little contribution he begged for with his usual plausibility.

In fact, to tell the truth, Fandor was much exercised in his mind. How ever came Bouzille to be in London? What motive exactly could have induced him to expatriate himself? He had taken good care not to say, and the journalist, for his part, was careful not to insist on the point, which might well be a delicate one. Bouzille, in fact, was a man to be treated warily. Without positively and entirely belonging to the group of accomplices Fantômas gathered round him, he nevertheless gravitated about the Lord of Terror, not, strictly speaking, in his service, but not betraying him either. Was it mere chance, then, that decreed Bouzille should be in the English capital at the very moment the brigand had taken up his abode there?

"Here, Bouzille, here's half-a-crown for you; see, I'm in a generous mood."

"You're not ill, M'sieur Fandor?"

"I've no taste for irony, Bouzille. No, I'm not ill, but I'm not in good spirits."

"It's not M'sieur Juve by any chance has been annoying you?"

"Nothing of the sort!"

"He's so worrisome, that man is. 'Bouzille,' he's forever telling me, 'all this will end badly.' I don't like that sort of talk, I don't."

"I can understand that, Bouzille. But it's not Juve is to blame for my melancholy."

"So you're melancholy, M'sieur Fandor?"

"I've just told you so."

"I wasn't just attending at the moment. But true it is you did seem to be in the dumps when I came upon you."

"Where were you off to, Bouzille?"

"I was looking for clients."

"At this time of night?"

"There's no particular times in my trade, M'sieur Fandor."

"But come, Bouzille, tell me: you don't take visitors round London at this hour, I imagine?"

"I show 'em a curiosity."

"A curiosity? What do you mean?"

"M'sieur Fandor, if so be you like, I can show you this here curiosity. Entrance two shillings each person. Guide extra, as is only fair. But it's up to clients to give what they choose."

"No doubt. Well, I won't say no. But I should just like to know what it all is."

"A theater, M'sieur Fandor."

"You want to take me to a theater at midnight?"

"Why, yes, a theater—call it a circus if you like"—and once more adopting his tone of a professional cicerone, the old fellow sang out:

"Oyez! Oyez! a battle of gladiators, a spectacle of ancient days, that's what I'm a-going to show you. A sight Julius Caesar and Napoleon would have loved!… Gladiators, yes, real, live gladiators!… Kill each other as soon as look at you—one, two, three, claws and teeth!… The survivor eats him as is done in… Great applause!… And there's no law to stop a bit of betting…" Then the old fellow resumed his ordinary tone of voice to ask:

"Don't that put you wise now?"

"I don't understand one word of what you've been saying," Fandor confessed. "Who the devil are these gladiators that eat one another after the combat? Aren't you drawing the long bow a bit?"

"Not a scrap! It's rats, M'sieur Fandor."

"Rats?"

"Why, o' course. It's a specialty of the place, you see, these rat fights… You ain't never seen one before? Yet all the fashionable folks go there; it's only the cream of Society's to be seen there… Must see the thing, M'sieur Fandor, no mistake about it… Come along, only costs a crown a head. Guide extra…"

"Beg pardon, but you said two shillings."

"Two shillings? A slip o' the tongue M'sieur Fandor. A crown *and* two shillings, that's the tariff… Guide extra."

"Never mind the guide. I'll pay the guide afterwards."

"Before, M'sieur Fandor!"

"Before—why?"

"'Cause you might die o' delight at the fine sight; then I should be robbed o' my money."

"Well, so be it. Now let's be off. Here's another half-crown for you… Is it far to this theater of yours?"

But Fandor hardly listened to Bouzille's answer. For some little while he had been feeling a strange presentiment. What was the meaning of this encounter with the old vagabond? What lay beneath this proposal to visit a place that could surely be nothing else but some thieves' den frequented by the vilest ruffians in London? The journalist reflected.

"A trap? Could it be a trap laid by Fantômas? After all, why not?"

But he felt his trusty Browning weighing down his pocket, and he longed with all his soul to relieve the strain of his nerves in some dramatic and decisive encounter.

He actually urged his guide to hurry. "Come on," he said, "don't let's waste more time."

There are occasions when courage is near akin to the most reckless imprudence.

* * * * *

A quarter of an hour later Fandor would have been sore put to it to say precisely where he was. Not only was the journalist ill-acquainted with London—a city of such great size that it takes years to learn the intricacies of its endless districts—but Bouzille seemed to be doing his best to confuse the route followed. He turned and twisted up and down an infinity of mean streets, hesitated, and declared he had lost his way, reversed his direction, then started afresh, swearing the famous theater was just five hundred yards away.

"Don't 'ee worry, M'sieur Fandor. All roads lead to Rome," he declared. "The great thing is to have a sense of 'lucality'"—and he proceeded to bewilder his companion by all sorts of ridiculous protestations.

"To begin with, and first of all, you'll o' course understand as how I can't just take you there by the straight road, seeing as how after that you'd be setting up in the same trade and turning guide. I've no notion of handing over my customers to you."

But Fandor never thought of protesting. Well versed in police investigations, the young man was drawing some very shrewd conclusions of his own, following out a train of reasoning not unworthy of Juve himself.

"Bouzille is no scoundrel," he told himself, "*but* he is a simpleminded fellow… You may employ him on any job you choose, so long as he is paid for it… Best keep a sharp lookout, therefore; best be suspicious. Fantômas may very well have entrusted him with the task of enticing me into a trap without the old man's having the least idea of what it all meant."

Fandor was indeed displaying admirable prudence. But there was one defect about it: the journalist was too wise not to decide when it was advisable to be distrustful; but he was far too daring, on the other hand, really to act in accordance with this distrust when the critical moment arrived.

"M'sieur Fandor, we are close by the place," suddenly announced Bouzille. "The palace is in this here neighborhood."

"You're sure of that?"

"Sure and certain! I can see the door from here. You can be getting out your purse."

"I'll pay at the box office, Bouzille."

"At the box office! Why, whatever are you talking about? There ain't no box office, M'sieur Fandor… And a word of advice to 'ee: don't let the folks admire your pocket-case… You see, there's chaps as slips their hands by mistake like into other people's pockets, and who like to find summat there… No call to put temptation in a body's way."

"I understand, Bouzille, and I'll hide away my little fortune, eh?… It must be a pretty kind of place you're taking me to."

"Bah! everybody knows you, M'sieu Fandor; when there's a bit of pleasure to be had, you don't care a damn where it be or what it be… It's a set of jolly good comrades goes there."

Fandor said no more. He knew now whereabouts he was—in a low district in the Whitechapel neighborhood, an ill-famed locality where even the police hardly dare to trust themselves, so rampant are vice and crime there.

"Come on, let's have a look at your jolly good comrades," the journalist agreed for all that. "This is the place?"

"This and other places… Stoop your head a bit; the door's not over high, seeing as how it's the sort the police can't rush in over much of a hurry."

"Charming!" ejaculated Fandor, finding himself before a high moss-grown wall, with something that looked more like a hole than a door in it. A man must bend double to pass in, and it was, in fact, not difficult to understand that it would be anything but easy for the police to slip through an opening that allowed only one person to enter at a time.

"I'll go first," Bouzille proceeded. "On second thoughts I'll do the paying, I can trust you; you'll give me back the two crowns when we come out."

"Bouzille, you're for swindling me; it doesn't cost ten shillings!"

"Oh, M'sieur Fandor, you'll never be asking for change!"

The vagabond spoke with so much assurance and seemed so sure of himself that Fandor could not help smiling as he heard the fellow's impudent reply. But had the journalist any true cause for smiling?

The low door opened upon a corridor, a dark, narrow passageway that sloped gently downwards and apparently led to some sort of underground cellar. It smelled vilely; a heavy, fetid odor of alcohol, tobacco, and general staleness filled the place.

"Truly a delightful spot!" thought Fandor. "Bouzille is taking me to a fine 'palace,' as he calls it."

But the young man's reflections were suddenly cut short, his attention absorbed by the sight he now saw. The corridor ended in a sort of hall, low-ceilinged and badly lighted by smoky candles; there was a confused buzz of talk coming from a score or so of persons hanging over a rough balustrade above—he could not tell what.

"My God!" was all Fandor found to say. One glance had told him the character of the audience. Drinking, smoking, applauding something the nature of which Fandor could not yet realize, the fellows' oaths and vociferations told the journalist plainly enough the sort of company he was in.

"Oh, ho!" he muttered to himself, "something more than a shady hole. These folks are not mere scamps and beggarmen; they are brigands pure and simple; thieves and robbers without a doubt. Moreover, very few of them English."

Indeed, all the languages of the world could be heard in this Babel—all except English.

"Come on, M'sieur Fandor," Bouzille was urging him, "push your way to the front, onto the balcony; it's down below the fun's a-going on... Must see that... I'm off now to pay up for our places."

The tramp's last remark was drowned by a storm of shouts and cries:

"Bravissimo, Sultan!"

"Viva, Sultano!"

"Hoch! hoch!"

"Very fine!" thought Fandor; "the audience is nothing if not enthusiastic."

But he declined Bouzille's invitation. "I don't know a soul. I'll wait till you come back."

"As you please, M'sieur Fandor. I shan't be away long... Is it ale for you, or whisky?"

"Ale."

"I'll tell 'em to bring it you… But it ain't good… Better let me order two whiskies… I'll drink 'em…"

"Do as you like, Bouzille. Another bit of your sharp practice, eh?"

Bouzille wasted no time in protesting. *He,* for certain, was a regular frequenter of the place. He pushed his way through the crowd, plying his elbows and fists freely and shaking hands with one and another; then presently reappeared after a short absence with a very red face.

"Here's the stuff, M'sieu Fandor… It's paid for… a crown and a half a head. That's the regulation price."

"I don't believe a word of it, Bouzille."

"Say at once I'm robbing you… But there, I don't care. You can pay me what you likes—with the usual tip, o' course… But get to the front—must see the sights."

"Very well, Bouzille."

Nobody so far had paid any attention to the stranger. So fascinated were all present by the spectacle they were watching that not a man had turned his head to look round. Fandor, on the contrary, had found time to scrutinize faces and costumes. All races he could see thronged the hall—all races and all ranks of society. There were poor Spaniards, their clothes still white with plaster from the images they hawked about the streets; Italians smelling of vanilla from the sweetmeats on their barrows; clumsy, fat-faced Germans; Serbians; Arabs. There were dreadful-looking paupers, half naked under their rags, and elegantly-dressed men of fashion, whose very elegance gave a more sinister impression than the tatterdemalion attire of their poverty-stricken neighbors.

"All the riffraff of London!" thought the journalist; "from the pickpocket who frequents the fashionable resorts down to the low-class sneak thief…. Bah! I've seen worse in Paris; and every big town has haunts like this. Not a face I know, all the same…" As a matter of fact, not a soul there had evoked the smallest recollection in Fandor's mind. Nor, indeed, was this at all surprising. If Fantômas had accomplices in London, as he had in Paris, it was very certain these accomplices would not be the same in the two places.

"I was wrong to distrust Bouzille," thought the journalist. "Nobody here is paying the smallest attention to me."

So far this was quite true. But when Bouzille, going on in front of his companion, began to push and shove in order to secure a place for him at the barrier, protests became audible.

"No, no! Don't go hustling us; have a care, do!"

"Make room! Make room!" Bouzille kept repeating. "Room for the guide! Let me pass, gentlemen… I'm bringing a stranger…" And now Fandor felt himself the object of peering eyes and curious looks. No doubt the crowd there could trust Bouzille not to bring into the place a stranger suspected of belonging to the police, but they were by no means averse to a personal investigation into the unknown newcomer's *bona fides*.

"Go to, my friends!" Fandor was thinking at the same moment. "It isn't you I'm interested in… Pray look at me… I shall never trouble your lordships…"; and to show how unaffected he was by their scrutiny, he dropped his eyes, and, avoiding all appearance of examining anybody, pushed his way behind Bouzille up to the railing about which all were pressing.

"Mercy on us!" exclaimed the young man; "What an abominable sight!"

And he was well justified. Certain countries are reproached for their love of cruel sports. Spain is criticized for her bullfights, Northern countries for their horrid cockfights. But who can describe the hideousness of these battles of rats that are the favorite amusement of the riffraff of the London population, and which, alas, threaten to spread to France, where they are tolerated—it is difficult to say why?

Immediately below the railing over which Fandor leaned was a sort of wide cistern or tank, at least twelve feet deep, shut in by perfectly smooth walls without the smallest projection anywhere, the floor of which was made of hard, beaten earth. In this tank or pit a dog—a bulldog—was fighting savagely with six great sewer rats. Matched against their hereditary enemy, these were leaping furiously upon the animal, biting him, trying in vain to find a way of escape, returning to the charge—brave creatures, say what you will.

An abominable sight in truth, a spectacle of ignoble and repulsive cruelty! The dog, streaming with blood and growling savagely, defended himself with clumsy fury. Jaws foaming and flanks panting, the animal was uttering hoarse growls, darting round this way and that, springing to right and left, opening his formidable jaws to clash them to again with the rending, crushing force of some terrible machine.

As sure as fate, one after the other, the rats were snapped by the dog, their throats torn open by a fierce bit, or hurled half-dead with broken backs on the floor of the arena, where their bodies could be seen quivering convulsively in the death agony.

"Bravissimo, Sultan!"

"Hurrah, good dog!"

The crowd, spellbound by the atrocious spectacle, applauded frantically at every bit, exchanging oaths, cries of encouragement and disappointment, laying bets on the result.

"A bob on the rats!"

"Taken! A bob on Sultan!"

Calmly an official with a stopwatch recorded the times.

"You twig the game, M'sieur Fandor?" Bouzille explained. "The point is to learn how long the tyke will take to kill all the vermin… If he's over time, he's taken out beaten, and another dog is put in… But it's always the rats pay the piper… You're not betting, M'sieur Fandor?"

"No, this horrid massacre turns me sick!"

"Don't speak so loud, M'sieur Fandor… Look, you're scandalizing the chaps."

Jerome Fandor turned round and saw that Bouzille was right. It was surely because he was shocking the audience by his lack of enthusiasm that he was being stared at like this? What other reason could the wretched creatures have for watching him with those looks of hate, their faces contorted in ugly grimaces of fierce menace? True, till then scarcely anybody had noticed him; now, on the contrary, the whole attention of the crowd seemed concentrated on the newcomer.

"Damn it!" thought Fandor, "it seems as if they didn't much like my looks!"

However, he was well used to suchlike emergencies. How many times, with Juve or by himself, he had risked his life in dubious resorts such as this, where the frequenters, failing to recognize in him a chum familiar with the place, had been ready at a moment's notice to fly at his throat.

"Things are getting warm!" he told himself—"decidedly warm!"—and slowly and stealthily, so as not to attract attention, he slipped his hand into his pocket, desiring, should it come to a fight, to have his Browning within easy reach.

But no sooner had he done so than a cold sweat broke out on his forehead. The weapon had disappeared! Since his arrival in the hall, without his noticing anything wrong, his revolver had been spirited away.

"The devil!" he thought; "this is getting serious!"

At the same time he realized with perfect certainty what exactly had happened, what must have occurred. On plunging his hand into his pocket the journalist had immediately felt a hole, a slit that instantly explained how the theft had been worked.

"That's how it was done," he told himself. "A slash with a razor, while someone hustled me to distract my attention, and my pocket was cut open. Good! So I'm defenseless now; must get out of this."

But Fandor was well aware that the least movement, the slightest gesture indicating his wish to escape, would start the battle, and he never stirred. What, indeed, was he to think? Had they robbed him because his weapon had a value sufficient to tempt the cupidity of one of the "gentlemen" surrounding him, or had he been disarmed simply to put him at their mercy, so that they might attack him without risk to themselves?

"I don't know, but I am going to know soon. In five minutes the fellows will be on me."

Then, feigning a still greater calmness, he leaned once more over the tank in spite of an involuntary shudder that shook him from head to heels. Yes, there was going to be a battle. Alone—for Bouzille had prudently slipped away—he must meet the onslaught of a score of desperadoes, who, no doubt, judged him to be a spy, some detestable emissary of the police.

"Why, yes, there's going to be some fun," he told himself.

But next instant he knew better; in a flash he realized the truth; the appalling suddenness with which events may occur that paralyze the senses and leave the mind a hideous blank.

There was a sharp, shrill whistle. Instantly, with one and the same movement, all the spectators had taken a quick step to the rear and made a rush to a table—and this with such a concerted unison of purpose as made it impossible not to divine that the maneuver had been resolved upon beforehand.

"Now, blackguards!" yelled Fandor. But already it was too late to make any effective resistance. Lifted by forty strong arms, the table, making a sort of shield behind which his assailants were sheltered, was dragged athwart the cellar so as to separate the journalist from his enemies.

In a twinkle Fandor realized the horrid fate that threatened him, the trick his adversaries were playing him, simple as it was abominable. Carrying the heavy table that formed their protection, and pushing it before them, the cowards were advancing upon Fandor, driving him back to the barrier and forcing him against it.

"Blackguards!" he reiterated, and began to struggle with all his strength. Braced against one of the supports of the balustrade, he tried to press back this novel sort of battering ram.

But what could he do, one against twenty? Then he felt the barrier shake, yield, on the point of tearing loose its fastenings.

"The end!" thought Fandor. "If the railing gives way altogether, I pitch headlong into the cistern. I am at their mercy." But what could he do to avert such a catastrophe?

A voice sounded, very calm and composed:

"Come, come! Courage! It's of no use resisting, I take it."

At that the young man gave a yell of rage and detestation:

"Fantômas! Fantômas!"

No need to hear twice the calm, cold accents of that voice

to know whose it was. Fantômas was there! It was he who was hurling Fandor into the rat pit! It was he who, with his henchmen, was throwing him into the pit, where he would kill him at his leisure!

"Coward! Coward! Fighting twenty to one!" panted Fandor.

He felt the barrier giving way more and more, and knew that only for a few seconds could he retard the fateful issue of the struggle.

"Come! Come!" insisted the monster.

But now a lamentable voice was heard raised in protest.

"No, honor bright, master! No, it's not nice of you! You swore you would have no hand in the concern—and, look you, you're doing the very thing!… It ain't playing of the game, it ain't!"

"Bouzille!" thought Fandor, "Bouzille, who enticed me here!"

Then further reflection became impossible. At his back, with a sharp crack of breaking timber, the barrier had toppled over.

The end was close at hand. The victim felt his shoes slip under him on the cemented floor. In vain, in a futile effort that exhausted all his remaining strength, he strove to prolong his resistance. Then the ground suddenly caved in under one foot. His opponents yelled with delight… and the unhappy man fell, toppling over headlong, at the risk of breaking his skull against the walls of the pit or fracturing his limbs.

But Fandor was not the man to be knocked out so easily; he was of the sort who never own themselves beaten. Hardly had he touched the bottom before he was on his feet again.

Alas! on the edge of the pit, haughty and impassive, stood a figure—a figure Jerome Fandor, sublime in scornful defiance, greeted with the name of horror and abomination—the name that embodied all possible and impossible atrocities—Fantômas!

*　*　*　*　*

For several seconds more the scoundrel stood motionless, as if savoring an infinite pleasure in watching on Fandor's expressive face the emotions the mere sign of him evoked.

How terrifying, in truth, how nerve-racking was was the darkling figure of him men called the Lord of Terror! As always when he was perpetrating one of those sinister exploits that froze the whole earth with horror, Fantômas had donned his black hood, the loose folds of which entirely concealed his features; only his flaming eyes were visible, glaring through two eyeholes. Over the shoulders, over the whole stalwart, supple frame, was drawn a silken suit of tights, sheathing the whole body in black. A figure of darkness, a demoniac, fantastic apparition that seemed the very personification of crime!

No sooner, however, had Fandor set eyes on the Torturer than he began to reproach himself for a shameful act of cowardice for suffering his anguish to be visible. What! was he going to let the villain see him trembling? Must he not rather, if the hour of death had struck, prove to Fantômas that death was but a small matter for a valorous soul?

The young man drew himself up; following Fantômas' example, he folded his arms across his chest, then, leaning against one wall of the pit, he spoke:

"So, Fantômas, your vile treachery has carried the day? You hold me at your mercy. Kill me, then! Juve will avenge."

But the brigand deigned no reply, and Fandor went on:

"Oh, you may pretend not to hear me; but my words move you, I know… Juve has sworn to bring you to the scaffold. You will remember my farewell when the executioner stands ready to perform his office."

Still Fantômas spoke no word.

"So be it!" concluded Fandor. "You choose not to answer me. As you will; I have no wish to converse with you… You will allow me to smoke a cigarette?"

Supremely calm, genuinely contemptuous of death, Fandor drew a case from his pocket, rolled and lit a cigarette.

Then Fantômas seemed to wake from a profound daydream; he shuddered, seized with a spasm of rage.

"You defy me, Fandor!" he cried.

"Not at all! I despise you."

"Well, I shall yet force you to scream out in agony. That I

swear!"

As he spoke, Fantômas bent over the pit as if he would throw the threats that hung on his lips right in the other's face.

"You hear me, Fandor?" he asked.

"Perfectly, Fantômas… and I find you amusing."

"Well, well, you'll find it more amusing still when you hear what is to be your fate."

"So much the better! I am all attention."

Fandor smoked on imperturbably, without a sign of the anguish he felt. Was this a pose, an affectation? Not so, for at that moment the journalist was thinking of anything rather than what the brigand was saying. Face to face with death, well knowing that no rescue was possible, that no pity could be hoped for, Jerome Fandor was thinking of the only beings dear to him, the two he loved with all his generous heart, Juve and Helene.

Yes! Juve would bewail him with profound regret… But he would avenge him too; of that he had no doubt. But what of Helene on the other hand? What would be her grief when she learned this last crime of her father's and that the new victim was no other than her fiancé!

"Your fate will be a terrible one," resumed Fantômas. "You are to die, and you will die a lingering death."

"The headsman will be more merciful to you, Fantômas. No matter! Do as you think fit."

"You will remain all alone in this pit… Alone, do you hear? Alone with death for your companion!"

"Very good! I have no wish for the public to witness my death agony."

"It is no matter for jest, Fandor! You do not know yet… You have no inkling of how you will yell to demand help… how you will exhaust yourself with screaming… how you will suffer the pains of the damned… how you will die a living death!"

"Devil take me if I understand. Explain, Fantômas!"

"Delighted, Fandor!… Now listen. Into this pit, which a grating will close in, from which you will not be able to escape, from which no one could escape, I am going to let loose rats…

Do you follow me? Rats… famished rats… fierce, savage rats…
Ah, ha! you turn pale?"

"Really? I'm turning pale? You surprise me, Fantômas!"

"No, no, a truce to raillery! You are trembling. Hear the
rest… The rats will bite you… The rats will devour you alive…
You will die slowly, bit by bit… Yours will be a living death;
that's how it will be… Ho, ho! Fandor, this is my revenge.
You have robbed me of Helene's love, my daughter's love. It
is because she loves you that she hates me. It is because you
taught her what you call honor, duty, honesty, that she scorns
me… Ah, well! anyway, I am stronger than you; stronger than
you all. Yes, I am filled with chagrin to be an object of horror to
my own daughter. Yes, chagrin devours me. But, you, Fandor,
I shall have you devoured too—devoured alive!… And I have
not told you all yet. The cistern will be half filled with water,
the level will be only up to your chin… And the rats will have
to swim, and to rest. They will scramble onto your head, over
your face… It is your face they will attack. Perhaps they will go
for your eyes first… Ho, ho! Now tell me again that you are not
afraid!"

Breathless, panting, convulsed with passion, Fantômas broke
off. He counted for certain on an avowal of fear; he made sure
of a cry of despair from his victim. Was it not more than horrible this death he had contrived for the unfortunate journalist?

But Fandor was firmer in his resolve than ever. What!—
afford Fantômas the spectacle of his anguish? "Never!" he cried,
"never will I be guilty of such cowardice."

"Speak!" ordered Fantômas again. "To your knees; pray to
me for mercy! Perhaps I might do something to soften your
lot."

But Fandor refused to answer. Face to face with the most
hideous of deaths, he found himself in possession of all his
wonted calm and courage. No! Never would he condescend to
useless supplications.

"By God!" swore Fantômas in a sudden access of rage, "so
much the worse for you! Farewell! You are to die!"—and he
rose to his full height. Again the grim figure showed up at the

edge of the pit.

"The grating!" ordered the scoundrel in a tone of command. Then the journalist heard a heavy clash and he knew that his tortures were soon to begin. Without seeing the confederates who carried out the order, he beheld a ponderous iron grating pushed forward from either side of the rat pit, the two halves meeting in the middle and locking together.

Yes, this last obstacle made escape absolutely impossible, rendering the chain and the heavy padlock he heard snapped to an entirely needless precaution. Imprisoned as he was in a narrow space with walls of perfect smoothness any attempt to climb out was useless. Fandor was separated by a dozen feet of height from the grating, a space that in any case made escape impossible that way. And he laughed, the indomitable fellow, as he told himself:

"What a display of needless precautions to be sure! Surely they do me too much honor!"

But, undaunted as he was, nevertheless he shuddered presently, his face paling. Fantômas' footsteps had sounded in the echoing hall as the scoundrel walked away. A door shut and dead silence followed.

"So, then, the comedy is finished and the tragedy about to begin!" thought Fandor.

And so it was. Alone, as Fantômas had announced, alone in face of inevitable death, he was doomed to know the most hideous of dramas, at once tragical and farcical!

But already he was angry with himself for the shudder that had run through his limbs. Was not fear an emotion unworthy of him? Was not death itself a foe a man must look in the face with unflinching eyes? He told himself consolingly:

"Come, come, I am a fool, upon my word! Long ago logically I should have disappeared from the surface of the earth; it is sheer good luck that it is only now I am to die. Let's try to think of something else!"

Yes, it was typical of Fandor, this phase of indomitable, invincible courage. Knowing himself doomed to perish by a hideous death, he was all for thinking of something else! From where he stood in the circular space of the rat pit that formed his prison the young man gazed about him from right to left.

"Not much of a landscape!" he remarked. "However, the entire absence of furniture relives me of one worry at any rate. I have no need to cudgel my brains searching for a way of escape. It is sure and certain I can discover no road to safety"; and he took out another cigarette, lighted it, and began to smoke.

"Anyhow, it's very exciting to know which is to pay me the first visit—the water, or our friends the rats?"—and with a shrug: "The rats, doubtless," he went on. "Fantômas is the sort of man to wish to have me devoured more or less everywhere, without limited their attack to my face… Bah! seeing's believing. But no—I should rather say, dying's believing. In my plight it may well be allowed me to amend the proverb…" Who but Fandor could have found the heart to play with words at such a moment? But next instant the smile left his lips. For all his gallantry, a pang of anguish seized him.

"The water, eh?" he muttered, for at that moment a sound had reached his ears, the unmistakable noise of water issuing from a tap.

"Yes, the water first," he exclaimed; "no doubt of that! But where the devil is it coming from?"

He was soon to know. Under his feet the floor of beaten earth was liquefying, growing wetter and wetter every second.

"Very good!" he assured himself. "The bottom of a basin— the water's flowing in from there… Well, I'm going to have a bath, that's all."

But in very truth it was an appalling fate that threatened the journalist. At first the water was, little by little, absorbed by the soil; all that happened was an ever-increasing dampness. But soon the soaked earth could drink in no more, and the level began to rise steadily. The young man felt the icy fluid encircle his ankles, climb to his calves, rise to his knees, gain his waist. How long would it take to mount to his chest, to wash round his neck?

"Oh God!" he muttered, "it grows mighty chilly. A rare piece of luck it would be if only I could catch a good congestion of the brain! A quick death—I've nothing better to wish for than that!"

But suddenly a dreadful thought flashed across his mind. He desired a quick death in order to escape the abominable ordeal of the rats. Was it not in his power to end it all in a few seconds?

"I can stoop down, let myself go under… After all, drowning, they say, is an easy death!"—and he gave a wild laugh.

Alas! is it not prescribed by all religions, by all principles of morality, that suicide is an act of cowardice?

"I would like to see the authors of all these fine injunctions in my position. For my part, I think it allowable for me to kill myself."

But all the same a secret voice within him rose in protestation. To kill himself, was that not to shirk the battle, after all? To kill himself, was it not to confess himself beaten, was it not to ask for mercy, to beg for pity on his sufferings?

"No, never!" he cried, "not that! When a man is called Fandor, he stands up to face danger till the last instant possible!"

Then he broke into a laugh, without knowing why he laughed, laughing like a man going crazy, laughing because his willpower forbade him to weep or cry out and his nerves were strained to the breaking point.

A little thing had happened, trifling in itself, yet portentous. The water was rising very slowly; still it was rising. It reached his chin, wetted his lips. And lo! level with his eyes, a part of the wall seemed little by little to be crumbling over a surface of a few inches—exactly as if eaten away by the lapping of the water. There followed a shrill cry… then a second… then dozens more.

"Oh!" was all Fandor found to say. Instantly, without another thought of how he had hoped to escape, he had put his back against the wall opposite the part that was crumbling away and which now showed a hole. His eyes dilated with disgust and fear, Fandor gazed at this opening that had appeared in the smooth surface of the wall.

Yes, he understood this new danger. He saw this new horror. At first he could make out only two fiery points—points that moved and flashed in the dim light of the pit… Then the two points of fire became four… Then more and more appeared.

Soon Fandor's eyes grew accustomed to the half darkness, and he saw more clearly.

"The rats!" he cried hoarsely. "The rats!"

Marvelously well had the arch-plotter contrived the fearful death his unhappy victim was to die! Imprisoned in a cage fixed in one wall of the pit, with no issue save into the tank now brimming with water, the rats were beginning to stir uneasily, terrified at the encroaching flood.

Fandor could not take his eyes off them, the hideous, repulsive creatures, marveling at their size and terrifying activity. How many were they, struggling at their size and terrifying activity. How many were they, struggling in this cage from which the water was soon to drive them?

"Ten… twelve… fifteen? Oh! I cannot say!" groaned the miserable man.

Horror was mingled with sick disgust. To die was cruel; but to die bitten to pieces alive, his face mangled by these repulsive brutes, was appalling… Enormous beasts, sewer rats as big as small cats, with sharp pointed teeth that cause the most painful wounds… And hunger and terror had driven them half mad!

When the first of them, emboldened by Jerome Fandor's immobility, sprang into the tank and began to swim about, the journalist shuddered involuntarily.

"Oh, Juve, Juve!" he groaned, "unless you come!…"

But he spoke without knowing what he said. Was he not sure the police officer could not come? Was he not convinced he must even now be pacing Piccadilly in an angry fume, searching for his comrade, little guessing the dreadful plight in which the young man was? Genius as he was, Juve must needs have been miraculously inspired to discover his friend's whereabouts.

After that the wretched man fell silent.

Behind the first rat other rats had in turn taken to the water; almost touching Fandor's face, they were swimming about the cistern with the astonishing activity that makes these creatures seem almost amphibian.

Fearful moments when Jerome Fandor asked himself if he were not going raving mad.

To begin with, the rats had made the circuit of the cistern, trying to find some way out… But now they were panic-stricken, as they swam about frantic with fear, sometimes actually clawing and biting one another, and again giving the same piercing cries as they had at first. No doubt they were getting tired. Perhaps, too, instinct was telling them that they could not get away, yet that they must at all costs find some way of escape or somewhere to rest.

"What to do?" Fandor asked himself. "If I move, I draw their attention; if I keep still, they will come climbing over my face. Curse you, Fantômas! Curse you!…"

Then once more the power of thought left him. For a brief moment the unfortunate man seemed no better than a madman, a lunatic raving in an attack of acute mania. A rat, circling the cistern, had brushed past his face. In spite of himself, under an uncontrollable impulse, he had pushed the brute aside. But the animal returned to the charge. And now his fellows, squealing, fighting and biting one another, discovered Fandor, rushed at him *en masse*.

With both hands the journalist tried to defend himself, hitting out at the foul brutes, striving to seize hold of them and strangle them.

But what could he do against the host of his assailants? For two that he managed to grip, a dozen others sprang at him and bit him savagely. His blood crimsoned the water, and the hideous battle grew more desperate every moment.

As he struggled to drive off his ignoble foes, he had moved away from the wall. A score of rats took advantage of the opportunity… He could feel their little claws in his hair, he felt them clinging onto his head… He had the horrid presentiment they were going to gnaw his skull…

"Oh, God! Oh, God!" he screamed.

Then—was it madness complete and final?—he burst into a peal of laughter… he broken into words of triumphant joy.

"Saved! I am saved!"

7. Fantômas' Library

While Fandor, under Bouzille's auspices, was making for the infamous locality where he was to fall into Fantômas' hands and see himself condemned to the cruelest of deaths, Juve, on his side, had an evening of many adventures and dramatic happenings. While quietly making his way back to the lodging he and Fandor had hired, fully resolved to quit this refuge seeing it was now known to the Lord of Terror, sudden, within a few yards of the house, he saw a man confronting him, who in a peremptory tone ordered him:

"Hands up! Your money or your life!"

Instantly Juve dropped flat on the pavement. He was not a patient man, the police officer, for all his peaceable air, but he was very active, albeit he had the look of a man rather heavily built.

Nor was it long before his assailant had convincing proof of both these characteristics. True, at the summons to put up his hands he had let himself drop to the ground, but this was neither because agitation robbed him of the power to keep his footing nor because fear paralyzed his strength. No sooner was the detective down than he delivered so furious a kick at his adversary's ankle that the latter with a yell of pain incontinently toppled over too.

The wretch had but scanty time to recover his self-possession. In two twos Juve had thrown himself upon him, forced his hands behind his back, and clapped on the handcuffs. Then:

"Get up, you idiot!" cried the police officer, "and show me the way to the station. I am not an Englishman, and I don't know where the nearest police office is."

Juve was for scaring his prisoner, who could not but appreciate the ill luck he had had in attacking the most famous of all French detectives. But the effect intended did not follow. On the contrary, it was Juve who was dumbfounded, for the man was expostulating.

"Well, well, M'sieur Juve, you do have a funny way of taking a joke!"

"A joke, was it?... And you know who I am, eh?"

"No offense; but, upon my word, you didn't take long to tie me up—"

"Answer my question, fellow!" Juve interrupted. "Who are you?"

"Why, your colleague, to be sure... Simon... So you didn't know me?"

A peal of the frankest laughter was Juve's answer... Why, yes, he recognized perfectly who this gallant of the Paris Criminal Bureau was! Why, yes, he knew very well who it was he had to do with. Who else was it but Simon, now official chauffeur to the Department, the same who had driven him to Le Havre a fortnight ago when he was tracking down Lady Beltham, when he discovered the *Lotus,* Fantômas' private yacht, and embarked on the tragic enterprise that had subsequently led to his escaping with Fandor in an airplane?

Rapidly reviewing events, Juve recollected how he had left his humble colleague at Le Havre in company with a sailor, manifestly an accomplice of Fantômas'... How, then, and why was he in London?

Giving his hand to the agent:

"Anyway," he suggested, "you couldn't have chosen a better joke, eh?"

"Perhaps!" returned the agent. "Why! yes of course, I could... But, by your leave, M'sieur Juve, would it be troubling you to take the bracelets off me?"

This was nothing one way or the other to Juve and he quickly released his colleague; then, wishing to make amends for his roughness, he took the man home with him, gave him a cigar and a drink, afterwards questioning him:

"And now, how the devil do you come to be here?"

"Why, along of orders, M'sieur Juve."

"What orders?"

"Why, yours, to be sure! You told me, 'In a fortnight, if I'm not back, let your man go… and shadow him.' I have shadowed him… He led me to your house… to London."

"The devil!" muttered Juve. "A chance…"—and the detective continued his questioning.

"So he brought you here!… Excellent! But you lost sight of him afterwards?"

"Yes, but I know where to find him again."

"How so? Come, tell your story. Don't make me have to drag the words out of you by main force."

At Juve's words—for did he not revere the great detective as almost a god?—the man gave a little click of the tongue in sign of satisfaction. After all, when Juve showed an interest in the report of a subordinate agent, did he not always show symptoms of nervous irritation and excitement?

"For afterwards," resumed Simon, "here are the facts. At the end of the fortnight, as I heard nothing from you, I arranged to let my bird fly away… Of course I set off on his track… To be brief, he takes the boat for Southampton, and I stick to his heels… From Southampton he makes for London, and I follow… Once in London, without a moment's hesitation, he calls a cab—and I run behind…"

"Yes, yes, and then?"

"Then? Then he goes straight to a smart little house near the Park… Be sure I take post at the door. An hour… two hours… At last out he comes, hails another—a brand-new swift taxi, M'sieur Juve… Another gallop for me, a desperate race!… My legs are stiff still, I can tell you."

"Good! good! But go on."

"Don't be in such a hurry… Well, I stir my stumps all the way to Whitechapel."

"Still after our swell friend?"

"Oh, he was got up sweller than ever now, and the chauffeur was disguised, too. I saw 'em both as my man was getting out, and the driver never asked for his fare."

"Excellent. You're no fool, Simon… Go on!"

"It was at the entrance to a rum place, a sort of theater you might call it; it was written so in English outside."

"Proceed. Did you go in or wait at the door?"

"Oh, I waited. I didn't dare go in. The chap who'd come from Le Havre would have spotted me."

"Just so… And then?"

"Then I do sentry-go… An hour, and then the chap comes out again."

"Alone?"

"Yes, alone… Then I follow him up again—all the way here."

"Oh, ho!"

"No fear, I stuck close to his heels again. So there, he's prowling about here… loitering round… watching… All of a sudden, what do I see? Why, M'sieur Fandor and you coming out of a house… I tell you I had much ado not to spring into your arms. But that wasn't in the orders, eh?"

"No, you're quite right. But get on!"

"Well, I say to myself, they'll be coming back here presently… But I've got to see where my gentleman is off to. So I follow him up again."

"He was making for the 'theater' again?"

"No… first he goes back to the smart house I told you about, then from there to the 'theater.' There I left him not ten minutes after. You see, I was bound to let you know… A bit interesting what I'm telling you?"

The agent did not need to ask twice. Hardly had he done speaking before Juve had sprung to his feet.

"*Interesting*, you say! By thunder, don't you see who it is you've come across?"

"Who?"

"Fantômas, idiot!"

"Fantômas?"

"Oh God, yes, your swell, of course. It's plain as a pikestaff. Who was your runaway bound to go? Why, to his chief, surely. Well, who was his chief?"

Juve was rubbing his hands in evident delight. Yes, sometimes Providence was kindly disposed. An accident, one of those accidents that often put the police on the right track, had given him two pieces of information of the highest importance—Fantômas' address and that of the ken where he gathered together his accomplices. Verily Simon seemed to have come down straight from heaven! The thing was barely credible!

"You are pleased, M'sieur Juve?" the man asked.

"No, furious!… But… Ah, by the Lord Harry!…" Juve had lugged out his watch. He noted the time and muttered:

"Ten minutes to get here… A quarter of an hour talking… Allow another five minutes to make sure. Total half an hour since Fandor and I parted from the… journalist…"

Suddenly, quicker than lightning, Juve gripped his visitor by the arm and dragged him out of his chair.

"You are armed?"

"Why, certainly. But—"

"The house—the little house? You have the address?"

"Of course—No. 17."

"Let's be off"; and the agent had not yet recovered from his surprise before Juve was plunging down the stairs with a curt "Follow me!" to his companion that instantly brought the astonished Simon to heel. Outside in the street the detective signaled to a prowling hansom.

"Now, driver, quick's the word!… The address, Simon?"

"Victoria Avenue. Stop at No. 10."

"No. 5," Juve cut in, "No. 5. And five pounds for yourself if you drive like hell!"

It is true Juve spoke only rather broken English and sometimes founds a difficulty in making himself understood. Still, tonight he must evidently have pronounced the words "five pounds" quite correctly, for the surprisingly generous tip instantly had its effect, and in less than no time the cab was at the spot indicated.

"Here you are, driver… and good night to you!"

Juve was already on the pavement, and, turning to his companion:

"Simon, my lad," he said hurriedly, "revolver ready, and keep your eyes open! We're waiting here for your 'swell.' Tonight, I have to warn you. He is dressed as a common reporter on a newspaper—check lounge suit, yellow boots, a mackintosh. Anyway, I should know him, if you don't."

Decidedly events were going well for Juve's purposes. He and Simon had not been posted ten minutes on the watch a short way from the little house his lieutenant had pointed out when the police officer gave a low cry of satisfaction. A car had stopped at the door of the luxurious house and a gentleman, very elegantly dressed, was getting out.

"He!" muttered Simon; and "He!" echo Juve at the same moment. He felt no doubt whatever. True, it was not the humble newspaper reporter who now crossed the sidewalk, opened the door and disappeared into the little house. Was not Fantômas a Proteus who could at will assume all and every aspect and appearance? Already the car was driving off. How easy, thought Juve, for the Lord of Terror to have changed his costume inside the vehicle, probably driven by a confederate.

"He!" he exclaimed. "It was He! I recognized him by his walk. I cannot be mistaken…"

He was ready enough to take action, was the alert police officer. But what could he do? Inform the English police? But they would not believe him; he would have all the difficulty in the world to make them understand, to establish his identity, to get them to institute inquiries… Or wait till tomorrow? But did he not know how the brigand had a thousand places of abode if he had one, and was constantly shifting from one to another, and how every one of these resorts was contrived to baffle discover? To wait was to throw away a unique opportunity.

Juve decided on a much simpler plan. "Simon," he said, his voice hoarse with excitement, "the man who has just entered that house is Fantômas. To attack him means risking our lives. Are you ready? There are a hundred chances to one we never leave the place alive."

The agent never flinched. "No offense meant, M'sieur Juve, but do I look like a coward? Tell me that. Let's go for the hundredth chance."

"Come on, then!… Now, *you* are to take post in the vestibule;

all you've got to do is to watch the door… *I* shall go upstairs."

"But you know the place, then? You know there's a vestibule, and that you must go upstairs?"

"By God, of course I do! Look at the lights, man!"

These simple words were proof enough of the great detective's astuteness. However excited, he was invariably quick to observe whatever was worth nothing, to see whatever was worth seeing.

Yes, without doubt there was a vestibule. It was the room that had been lit up after Fantômas had opened the door. Yes, and it was manifest you had to go upstairs in order to follow the villain; small windows, one above another, had lit up in succession, thus betraying the passage of someone mounting the stairs, doubtless guiding himself by the flash of an electric pocket-lamp.

"I understand," agreed Simon, who had been gazing at the front of the little house. "But I would rather go up with you."

"No, you will stay below… And if I'm not the first to come down—if he is first—then… then don't hesitate."

"What am I to do?"

"Shoot!" replied the police officer laconically.

Then shuddering, as if assailed by some importunate thought of horror, Juve took his colleague's arm and drew him towards the house.

"Enough said! Forward!"

"And to get in?"

"Never worry about that… I shall get in"—and Juve seemed quite sure of himself. Had he not, in fact, for four years worked under an alias in the shop of a locksmith, learning all the secrets of the trade and mastering the intricacies of the most complicated safety devices?

"Come on!" he said again; and, keeping close under the house walls, avoiding attention as much as possible, Juve and Simon had in two seconds reached the door of the little house.

"No policeman in sight?" questioned Juve.

"No, not a cop to be seen. You can get to work."

But the police officer had no need for this encouragement.

Bending down, he was already examining the lock he meant to force with the eye of an expert.

"Ah, very good!" he muttered; "an electric contact. Not to attract attention the lock is quite an ordinary one, but it sets a bell ringing… Well, we're going to stop the bell ringing, that's all," and he set about the job with a cleverness that showed an extraordinary sleight-of-hand. Taking his tobacco pouch from his pocket, he tore out a leaf from his book of cigarette papers and crumpled it up into a ball.

"Nothing like it for breaking an electric contact," he declared with a laugh. "Now to copy the dentists!"—and, opening his penknife, he stuffed the lock with paper the same way dentists stop a decayed tooth. Then:

"A couple of turns of the picklock and the job's complete, and in we go"—and as he spoke he started operations. He was always armed with a supply of handy little tools. So often in the course of his adventurous life he had owed his safety to suchlike precautions that he was never taken unawares. Now the detective drew from his pocket his bunch of keys, and, selecting a tiny instrument shape like a hook:

"There!" he went on. "It's all a question of clever fingering… Bah! surgeons are successful in far more difficult operations… *I* run no risk of damaging the mechanism."

Such remarks at such a time surely proved that the detective was well pleased with himself and fully convinced of his success. For a moment he twisted and turned his instrument in the lock. Then came a little sharp click—and the door was open.

"Not a word now!" he whispered.

The door ld into a vestibule hung with sumptuous old tapestries, while thick carpets covered the floor.

"Stay where you are," he said, turning to Simon, "don't move an inch; there are sure to be hidden alarm bells." For his own part, he redoubled his precautions; far from treading where anyone would naturally have stepped, far from moving down the middle of the room to gain the staircase, he carefully skirted the walls, making a wide detour. He reflected:

"If the house is prepared with traps for the unwary, as no doubt it is, Fantômas is bound to have arranged for bells to ring at the first footstep of anybody invading his premises, and that's what I must guard against at all costs."… But would the police officer triumph over the countless snares the Monster was certain to have multiplied on the road followed by an undesirable visitor?

Juve at this moment was admirably calm, completely master of his nerves. Yet what was his excitement, his agonizing, maddening suspense! He knew that the Lord of Terror, not supposing he was being spied upon, had returned to his house entirely devoid of suspicion. Did this mean that fortune was turning in his favor at last? Was this the decisive moment when he might satisfy the chief ambition of his life—to clap his hand on the scoundrel's collar?

Juve reached the stairs without any interference. There he stopped. Truly he was gifted with admirable presence of mind. Even now, when his heart was beating with joyous triumph in his bosom, when a firm conviction of success urged him forward, he forced himself to halt and think.

"Have a care!" he warned himself. "The stairs may hold a trap—indeed, it is certain they do. Yet I must go up them… I am bound to do so, for He is there…"

Suddenly his eye fell on the balustrade… Perhaps Fantômas had not thought of it. There and then he mounted the banisters, gripped hold with both hands and, sitting astride, hauled himself up towards the floor above. In this fashion he made sure of not setting in action any electric contacts concealed under the stair carpet.

Alas! in this contest that brought to grips two superlative geniuses—the Criminal and the Police Officer—Fantômas had on his side the sure advantage that always belongs to those who defend over those who attack.

Just as the detective had reached halfway to the next floor, he suddenly felt under his fingers a thin thread of silk tied to the banisters.

But already it was too late. The thread, stretched across the stairway, had parted; a deafening peal filled the house—the alarm signal Fantômas installed as a matter of course every time he came home!

*   *   *   *   *

In such a case, however, Juve was not the man to waste one second in hesitation. The pealing of bells that still continued ringing rendered all precautions useless. Instantly the police officer grasped the situation, the more readily as hurried footsteps now became audible on the first floor.

"God's mercy!" he swore in a frenzy. The, jumping down off the banisters, heedless of any other alarm bells in the place, he dashed forward, mounting the stairs three steps at a time, brandishing his revolver as he yelled:

"Hands up, Fantômas! You are my prisoner!"

For reply, the instant the detective came out on the first floor landing, a door banged shut in his face.

"God!" he swore again, and hurled himself against the door. The fellow was there, caught napping in spite of all his alarm bells; he had taken refuge in the room behind this door. Between him and Juve were merely a few planks of wood.

"Hands up!" screamed the police officer a second time. But he spoke at a venture, hardly knowing what he was saying, his nerves quivering with such a fever of excitement he felt his strength redoubled.

"Oh, but I will burst it in, this door!" he cried, and fell to with shoulder and feet.

From below at the same moment Simon was shouting: "Am I to come upstairs?"

"No, no! Don't move! Fire, if you see him!"

For another five seconds, perhaps, the door resisted his efforts. Then suddenly, shattered and torn from its hinges, it gave way, one of the panels burst open.

"Do you hear what I say?" Juve demanded.

A kick or two more and the split panel offered the detective a passage… Revolver in hand, heedless now of all danger, never thinking how Fantômas was just the man to take cool aim and shoot him down the instant he was inside, Juve sprang into the room.

The next moment a cry escaped him: "Empty! Empty! There's no one here."

And so it was. Not a soul was to be seen; Fantômas had vanished… For a second Juve stood stock-still. Such frantic efforts, such reckless daring, to end in this anticlimax! The disappointment left him broken, struck helpless in sheer despair.

Then his spirit rose triumphant to meet this new crisis. Fantômas had disappeared? Be it so. But his hiding place could not be far off; in these few seconds he could not, in the nature of things, have gone far. He must search him out, get on his track, pursue him to the death.

"Calmness! Self-control!" Juve admonished himself, and at once he found himself in possession of his habitual mastery of his nerves.

Then with all his eyes he inspected the room he had entered. It was a very charming place—a library. Books in ordered rows and richly bound garnished the walls, rising from floor to ceiling, leaving not a foot of space unoccupied; books of all shapes and sizes, from tall folios down to lilliputian duo-decimos. At the far end, in front of shelves piled with serious-looking works, stood a writing desk on which lay a blotter, a chamber clock, and an inkstand. In full view, within reach of the hand, was a Browning of very heavy caliber and the safety-catch raised.

"Very good!" said Juve. "He was here, and now he's gone. It follows these bookshelves conceal a hiding place; one of them, no doubt, revolves on a pivot." No vestige of doubt remained in the detective's mind. Fantômas had left the spot within the space of a few seconds, and it was from here he had gone; a curl of bluish smoke, the smoke of a cigar, still hung in the air.

"Ah, well! I mean to find the way he went," the police officer assured himself, and darted to the bookcases, gripped one after the other the mahogany shelves and dragged at them with all his might. No use; nothing gave; the bookcases were fixed firmly to the walls.

"The desk, then?" And he shoved it aside, turned it upside down, sounded it; but it was just an ordinary piece of furniture.

"The armchair?"—but examination revealed nothing out of the common.

"He can't have escaped by the window, I suppose?"

Juve threw open the shutters, to find heavy iron bars solidly embedded in the stonework, making any egress impossible that way.

"Then?—then?" stammered Juve; but then a brilliant notion flashed across his brain. The door had been banged shut in his face; he had seen it shut. Might not this be a trick? Might not Fantômas have closed it from a distance by means of some secret mechanism with the very object of enticing him into the room, while he was all the while in another, ready to take to his heels at his leisure?

"Well, I mean to find out," he swore; and, quick as lightning, he left the room and returned to the landing outside. From below Simon was shouting:

"Is that you, M'sieur Juve? He has vanished, eh?"

"Yes! But he can't have left the house… Don't go away, but listen!… He is for sure on this floor." But the house was not large; three bedrooms and a dressing room made up the whole of the first floor.

"Now, can he have gone up to the floor above?" Juve asked himself, and hurried there, to find only a garret, a big room, quite empty. The floor was so thickly covered with dust that the moment the detective had entered this lumber room he stopped dead, thinking:

"No, he has not been here; if he had, his footsteps would have left marks as mine do," and he beat a hasty retreat.

He knew, of course, that in a house like this, arranged beforehand for emergencies, Fantômas would have every chance of making good his escape. Yet the escape had been effected so rapidly as to seem almost miraculous.

But when Juve returned to the first floor and re-entered the library a cry escaped him—a cry of rage and fury. Once more the smoke of a cigar hung about the room, slowly dispersing in the air.

"Damnation!" swore the detective savagely. "He must have left the place while I was in the garret! Alas! he is far away by this time..."—and he ground his teeth, his face livid with rage, as he wrung his hands in despair.

Fantômas' hiding hole, where with a sly chuckle the scoundrel had taken cover while the police officer was kicking down the door? Why, yes! He knew it now—he knew it beyond any possibility of doubt. From the bookcase he had examined to no purpose an enormous volume was now missing—volume one of fifty books all alike, ranged in order on the bottom shelf. The detective had only to look at the books to guess the use the arch-criminal had put them to. Backs and edges were intact, but the whole interior of the huge tomes had been cut out bodily. The bindings, all but the extreme edges, had been similarly sliced away and removed, while the pages had been reduced to mere borders, the size of the margins and no more. In this way, set side by side, packed tightly in their ranks along the shelf, only the backs being visible, the books formed a sort of tunnel, a long box into which it was mere child's play to slip and there remain hidden, unseen, baffling all suspicion.

"Choused!" Juve told himself as he noted this odd, ingenious adaptation of the Monster's library. "Choused to perfection!"—and he shrugged his shoulders. So many times before had Fantômas escaped like this from between his hands just when he deemed victory assured and certain, that his disappointment was unmingled with surprise.

"Choused!" he reiterated. "Nothing left now but to go away, to slip off as quietly as may be. The English police might very well come on the scene and arrest me... Let's be going"; and with dragging steps Juve crossed the room, casting a last look round this haunt of the Lord of Terror. Make a detailed search? Yes, he thought of that, but it meant mere waste of time and trouble. Fantômas was not one to leave behind him compromising papers or other evidence of his secret villainies.

"No, there's nothing for it but to go—never meaning to return. For certain Fantômas will never revisit the place...

High time to be off!"

Juve had no illusions, but he was profoundly chagrined. He threw a last searching look round the Monster's study, then down the stairs again, making for the ground floor.

"Well?" questioned Simon breathlessly.

"Dead failure! He's got right away."

"Good Lord!"

"Yes… not a chance left!"

"Still, I did think—"

"Never think, my boy! That's all there is to it… Ah, well! Fandor must be getting impatient. Let's go and pick him up before we start afresh."

"Start afresh on what, M'sieur Juve?"

"Why, on the pursuit, look you!" And, seeing the agent gazing at him with an air of stupefaction, Juve wound up:

"Fantômas must have been vastly surprised at our coming here. From that to gather that he will be fearing I know his secret is a short step—so short, indeed, that I'll wager that on leaving here he has gone to warn his accomplices… Well, ten minutes to pick up Fandor on our way… Ten minutes, or at longest a quarter of an hour, to get to Whitechapel. In half an hour at most we ought to join him at the 'theater.' One should never despair and never give up an enterprise once begun."

Juve, in fact, was one of those men who never abandon an undertaking once resolved on under the plea that they have met with a check. Scarcely had he yielded for a couple of minutes to a fit of despair before he was shocked at his own weakness and making up his mind to go on and renew the struggle.

Bidding Simon, who was looking spiritless and dejected at so serious a setback, accompany him, Juve called a taxi and told the man to drive him to Piccadilly.

"Fandor will be astonished to see me with a companion," he reflected; "and still more astonished to hear I have been within an ace of capturing Fantômas… and that the game is only beginning."

But once again Juve was to be the one to experience a startling surprise. Hardly had the taxi pulled up before the police officer's eyes assured him that Fandor was not there.

"By the Lord!" growled the detective, "can he have forsaken his post?"

But so unlikely was the supposition that he immediately rejected it.

"No, no, it isn't that… Or can it be that he has had some serious reason for going off? Can he have seen a face that looked suspicious?"

At his elbow Simon was suggesting:

"Maybe, finding how long you were in coming, M'sieur Fandor has gone to see what's doing at your lodgings."

"Impossible! He knew I meant to move house—"

"Nothing for it, then, but to wait… He'll come back… Perhaps he's gone to have a warm in some public nearby?"

But Juve shook his head. That, again, was not to be believed; Fandor was not the fellow to miss a rendezvous once agreed upon for any such futile motives.

"No, no! He has had some serious reason for deserting his post. That I will swear… But what reason?" And Juve frowned in perplexity, angry and as much dejected as his subordinate. Yet what was he to do? Wait for Fandor, as the latter advised? This was the course his growing anxiety suggested. Or set off instanter for the place where perhaps Fantômas now was? Yes, that was the course his conscience as a police officer told him was the right one to adopt, and Juve instinctively did what duty ordered. Long ago, from the very first, it had always been understood that neither he nor Fandor should think of themselves when they were following up a trail.

In a voice that shook a little with excitement: "If Fandor," he declared, "has left his post here, it was because he found something more urgent to do in the interest of us all than to wait for me. By staying on here ourselves we should only be compromising a serious undertaking without any certainty of being of use to Fandor. We must follow up our pursuit of Fantômas. So *forward*, I say again!"

The two got into their conveyance again, and presently found themselves at the entrance of a shady-looking street in a disreputable quarter of the town.

"It's within a hundred yards of the place," announced Simon. "Look, you can see the big wall from here… If only the nest isn't empty… If only Fantômas hasn't already come and gone…"

But Juve vouchsafed no reply. Again he felt himself overmastered by fierce excitement, his heart thumping feverishly within his breast in anticipation of success. Would luck favor him this time? Would the quest initiated by his colleague lead to some all-important discovery?

Five minutes later he had changed his tune. The door was tightly shut, and not a sound came from inside. It was very certain there was nobody there now.

"Juve, what a bit of bad luck!" observed Simon. "It's here for sure I tracked my man down… only, as might have been guessed, they weren't expecting us… We'll come back tomorrow, M'sieur Juve, eh?"

"Tomorrow, yes!… But before coming back tomorrow…"

"Well?"

"Suppose we make a try to visit the place?"

"Why, for sure, that wouldn't be a bad notion… We should at least find out how to get in without attracting attention, and if there are other exits to be watched… But as for getting in tonight?…"

"Simon, you hurt me! Haven't I shown you already my poor talents? All your business is to look out that nobody comes along."

Then, while the agent scanned the horizon of the shabby street, Juve once more set to work on a bit of housebreaking. His faithful picklock in his hand, he worked a moment or two at the lock. Two or three times he cursed under his breath, but nonetheless he won the victory. The door came open not less readily than that of Fantômas' house had done.

"Stand by," Juve now admonished his companion; "we must beware of possible traps as before… Then perhaps there's someone left in charge."

But no—no snare was to be seen and nobody could be heard stirring inside. The place was evidently well known, and thieves must be aware there was nothing there worth carrying off; nor, on the other hand, had the police any reason for making special investigations.

Juve and Simon followed a narrow corridor, which, after sloping downward for some yards, opened on what seemed to them a great hall absolutely empty.

"Can't see a blessed thing," observed the agent; "but to make up, I can hear something… something like a lapping of water."

"True!" agreed Juve. "I was just telling myself the same… Anyway, I'll light up"—and he drew from his pocket an electric torch, flashing the brilliant light in all directions.

"Damned queer sort of place!" exclaimed Simon. "Halloa! look there; see that great table? All broken to pieces, too! There's been a scrap here, perhaps."

But Juve was looking at something quite different. He had at that moment picked up some fragments of silk lying loose on the floor, in entirely good condition and without a stain on them.

"Oh, ho!" he muttered, "oh, ho!"—and the things dropped from his hand.

"A hood!" he exclaimed. "A suit of black tights! Fantômas' costume he has just cast off!… He has been here; the clothes are still warm… It's not five minutes since…"

But the detective's sentence remained unfinished. The sounds of water he had heard before had grown louder and more unmistakable.

"Good God!" swore the police officer, and he sprang forward. Beyond a doubt the noise came from behind the up-turned table. Juve ran to it and bent over to look. Then a cry of horror and amazement broke from his lips. Behind the table he saw a kind of circular pit, half full of water, in which rats were swimming, fighting and snapping at each other.

But now Juve caught sight of another thing more tragic still. In the brief moment he had bent over the table and thrown the beams of his torch forward he had seen through the water a human form that seemed to have fallen in or else to be crouching at the bottom of this strange tank, a form that never stirred.

"Ah!" he cried, as he started back. Yes, he understood—or thought he understood—in one second. It was Fantômas who lay there… it could be no one else! Caught unawares, no doubt, by the police officer and his companion's entrance, cornered in this place that gave no means of escape, he must have fled to this extraordinary hiding hole. He had plunged into the cistern and there remained motionless, only diving underwater when Juve approached, no doubt to emerge to breathe when the detective moved away.

Yes, Juve saw it all! What else could he suppose, what indication was there to make him think of Fandor? Not another instant did he hesitate; how could he hesitate, when at last the Monster was trapped, when at last he had the villain at his mercy, when at long last the hour of justice and expiation had struck?

Juve grasped his revolver, cocked the weapon, examined it to see that all was in good working order.

Then he stepped forward again, with stealthy tread, his face alight with savage determination.

How hideous are some mistakes!… It was Fandor fallen into the horrid trap. It was Fantômas Juve was making ready to shoot down!

8. Fandor Is Wrong *and* Right

Face to face with the most dreadful danger that had ever threatened him, on the point of being devoured alive by the foul rats Fantômas by a devilish inspiration had imprisoned with him, Fandor had uttered a cry that only sheer madness seemed capable of accounting for.

"Saved! I am saved!" the young man had vociferated.

Alas, was any rescue possible in the awful plight he was in? Yet at this atrocious moment, when already the rats were attacking him, when already he could feel the filthy creatures scrambling over his face and their sharp teeth gnawing his flesh, Fandor never hesitated a second. He had but one means of triumphing over his irresistible and numerous enemies, and he adopted it instantly—by diving underwater.

Unfortunately these animals have no fear of water and are by nature excellent swimmers. Whole troops of them are to be seen crossing swift torrents, and anyone living on the bank of a river is well used to seeing how fearlessly these voracious and repulsive beats dive and swim underwater.

Those attacking Fandor, therefore, were not at all frightened when they found themselves dragged below the surface. However, though they did not loose their hold and their pointed teeth remained fixed in the unhappy man's face, they left off biting, obliged like their victim, to hold their breath. Thereupon an extraordinary struggle began between the animals and the young man—which of the combatants would be the first to have to come up to the top to breathe.

No doubt rats can stay a very long time underwater without suffering inconvenience. But Fandor, on his side, was a first-rate swimmer who could endure a lengthy immersion without distress. So then, once underwater and certain that no more rats would start attacking him, he began to defend himself vigorously. To seize hold of the animals that had got their teeth in his face, to drag them off and strangle them was the work of a few seconds. Yet, if this action freed him for a brief while, if thereby he got rid of a few of his enemies, it was nonetheless certain that it could not in the long run secure his safety. Hardly, in fact, had he torn the rats from his face before he found himself obliged to stand up and breath, and he felt very sure that, no sooner had he done so than other assailants would again attack him. For how long, then, would he be able to repeat the maneuver? For how long would he find it possible to prolong a struggle the end of which was already a foregone conclusion?

But now it appeared Fandor was thinking of something else than repeating his dives underwater. His brain, in fact, was working at express speed, as happens in moments of extreme danger when one second suffices to call up the most remote and most varied recollections. Getting to his feet again, and rapidly inhaling a mouthful of air, then diving again and ridding himself of two fresh assailants that had seized the momentary opportunity to fix their fangs in his ears, Fandor thought:

"Fantômas one time at Neuilly saved his life in that way, making good his escape from Juve and me by staying underwater in a cistern. I must copy his example…"

The journalist's memory served him well. It was quite true that Fantômas on one occasion had baffled the police by plunging into a cistern and crouching at the bottom where they could not see him.

But in the present case the situation was not altogether the same. When he adopted this unexpected ruse, Fantômas had recourse, in order to breath underwater, to a dodge Fandor had no means of imitating. Just as he disappeared, the scoundrel had broken away the bottom of a bottle and, gluing his lips to the neck, while leaving the fractured part outside, had drawn in the air through this improvised pipe.

But Fandor had no bottle nor anything that might serve as a substitute. However, at his second dive the young man was feeling in his pocket. "My stylo!" he told himself. "I must unscrew my stylo… The stem will act as a pipe to breathe through."

A wild idea that seemed impossible of realization. Still, the journalist was of the sort that laughs at impossibilities. In less than no time the stylo was found and dismantled; pen, holder, upper stopped were torn off in an instant.

"Saved!" he reiterated. "I am saved!"

But was he really saved? True, he was for the moment secure from attack by the rats; true, by remaining underwater, breathing by means of the short, thin tube, the end of which he kept above the ripples on the surface, he could escape their cruel bites. But for how long could he maintain so distressful an attitude?

The rats meantime were tiring; some of the less vigorous sinking to the bottom from time to time, their paws cramped by fatigue. But these creatures are very hard to kill; their death agonies might be prolonged for hours. Could Fandor, on his side, last out for hours, crouching in one position, breathing, after all, with difficulty and already shivering with mortal cold? The unhappy wretch's wits began to wander as he fought thus with death that threatened to cut short the thread of his life from one moment to the next. Even if—and this was to the last degree improbably—he managed to survive till the last of the rats was drowned, would he be any better off then? Delivered from his assailants, from the rats that were to have devoured him alive, as Fantômas had reckoned, was he not inevitably doomed to perish all the same?

"To get out of the pit, no, that's past praying for!" the young man told himself with a groan of despair. "A man can't well jump a dozen feet out of the water to reach safety… Besides, it's safe to wager Fantômas will come back to see if I'm still breathing, or at any rate send somebody to verify my death, with orders to knock me on the head, if need be… It follows…"

This "it follows," which Fandor naturally failed to articulate as his head was underwater, was, in truth, an obvious conclusion. Yes, it followed logically that he was doomed to perish in spite of his ingenious device.

Then once more the thought of suicide began to haunt his

mind. What use in prolonging a struggle the issue of which was as inevitable as it was easy to foresee?

"I leave off breathing," he told himself. "I let myself sink under for good… In five minutes…"

A bright light, flashing over the surface of the water, then immediately disappearing, interrupted his reflections.

"What, already?" he thought, without the shadow of a doubt as to what this meant. For who else could be bending over the cistern that was fated to be his tomb if it were not the Lord of Terror, if it were not the Torturer who had hurried back?

Instantly Fandor forgot all the terrors of the death that threatened him. Believing Fantômas to be so near him, divining that he had come to end all by killing him, he felt such a frenzy of rage boiling in his veins, such fury awakening in his heart, that he longed passionately to live on to be able to avenge his death. Yet was he not, alas, incapable of doing anything whatever, of making any attempt whatever, to ward off the fatal blow that from one instant to another was destined to end his days?

Seconds passed that seemed to Fandor longer than centuries. "What is he after?" the young man asked himself. "Why has he gone away again so soon? What has he to fear? He knows I am unarmed…"

Still crouching at the bottom of the pit, still breathing through the stylograph, the top of which he held above water, Fandor could hear nothing, but, on the other hand, by keeping his eyes open, he could see quite well, though he found it difficult to make out quite clearly what was happening above the surface.

The light came again, and, shuddering, "Ah, this is the end!" he thought. Then he forgot the rats, he forgot the horrid presence of the odious creatures… If Fantômas was coming to deal him the fatal blow, he should surely find him on his feet ready to mock, to threaten, to defy his foe at the very moment of his triumph.

Jerome Fandor rose to his feet, while the rats, scared no doubt by the blinding light, desisted from their attack.

Then the wretched man saw a hand holding a Browning, a hand that never trembled; it reached over the edge of the pit, pointing the formidable weapon at him, taking aim.

"Done for!" he thought. "I am a dead man!"

No time even for one sarcasm, for at that moment, clear, distinct, authoritative, a voice rang out:

"Fantômas, at last I have you!… Hands up, or I swear I will fire without mercy or pity!"

Oh, the heavenly sense of relief and thankfulness that filled the journalist's heart at the sound!… That voice, why, he knew it!

"Juve!" he screamed. "Juve!" And instantly a startled voice replied:

"Fandor! Fandor! Merciful heavens, is it you, Fandor?"

An hour later, calmed, warmed and comforted by help of a wood fire which Simon, an old soldier and a handy man like every ex-trooper, had kindled with the remains of the barrier and the table, Fandor left the place in company with Juve, while the agent stood by himself on guard a short way down the street.

"A bit of luck!" Juve was saying, holding Fandor lovingly by the arm as they walked away. "A bit of luck I felt a scruple at the last minute!"

"A scruple, Juve? How so?"

"Ah, my dear boy, just this way. At first, look you, when I thought I saw Fantômas, I never hesitated. I said to myself, 'Come, no false generosity! Kill him!'… Then, my revolver cocked and ready, I thought better of it. Kill the brigand? Kill Fantômas? Oh, clearly that's no crime. It is serving him according to his deserts… But I am a police officer… A police officer's duty is to arrest criminals. The judges alone have the right to condemn them. The headsman alone is justified in executing them… Consequently…"

"Consequently you did what you deemed right, Juve. Yes, a bit of luck, I grant you that… All the same, for my part, if I had been in your shoes, I confess I should have fired… A fig for legality! A fig for morality! Why, yes! Don't look at me with those shocked eyes! At this moment, look you, after my prolonged bath, my soul is fierce within me."

"At this moment, Fandor, yes, but in half an hour?"

"Oh, in half an hour the same, Juve. I'll take my oath to that. *I* am not a police officer... And then I'm thinking if you had killed me, if you had persisted in your mistake..."

"Come now, Fandor, you're poking fun at me?"

"Oh, just a bit—just a little bit!"

"Ungrateful fellow! I saved your life, anyway?"

"In spite of yourself, out of a scruple!"

Fandor laughed as he made the retort, and, following his example, Juve suddenly relaxed in a sunny smile.

"So then, my lad, you do wrong to make fun of me. I tell you again... Yes, you do wrong because what happened is all your fault..."

"Really? How my fault?"

"Obviously if it had not been you, Fandor, it was bound to be He who was in the cistern... All you had to do, therefore, was not to be there!... At this very moment Fantômas would be in custody!"

Plainly there was no answer to be made to such a line of argument, in which the police officer's smiling illogicalness was perfectly manifest. So Fandor held his tongue with a pretense at a shrug of the shoulders.

A merry interlude in the lives of these two, so long vowed to face the direst perils, this joyous reunion in which they found so amply the delight of dangers avoided and the sweet satisfaction of meeting again safe and sound together!

But the interlude was of brief duration. They had walked but a short distance in silence, both absorbed in thought, when Fandor, suddenly turning to his companion:

"All said and done," he demanded, "how far has all this brought us?"

"Why, not very far," returned Juve. "It's plain enough... Fantômas has just missed killing you... and I have just missed capturing him!... You have learned that Bouzille is in London... and I know, thanks to Simon, that Fantômas has accomplices who used to meet in the den where you spent such a horrible evening—"

"Who *used* to meet, Juve?"

"Why, of course! Do you think that, after trying to murder you there, Fantômas will be so simple as to have his confederates return to a place he is bound to suppose watched by us?"

"You are right, Juve."

"So then, to sum up our position, my dear boy, the state of our affairs appears to me simple enough… Tonight we have had an Ariadne clue in our hand… But the clue is broken."

"You are not encouraging, Juve… And then there's another thing."

"Really? What's that?"

"My marriage, Juve," and the young man's voice trembled as he made the reply.

"Your marriage? Well, you are going to be married; by the Lord, you know I have proclaimed it publicly; I have dinned it in Fantômas' ears; I have promised you you shall be married, my boy… You have well earned the right to be happy."

Juve, too, had felt his voice tremble as he uttered the words. For did he really possess the certainty he was trying to instill in Fandor's mind? Henceforth the tragic duel with Fantômas would be solely concerned with Fandor's marriage. But the police officer was one of those men who never confess themselves discouraged. Devoted, heart and soul, to his task, he never allowed himself the right to be afraid. On the contrary, he school himself to a consistent optimism, well knowing that self-confidence possesses a hidden virtue, a mysterious strength that miraculously ensures success where success seems impossible.

"Be of good hope," he urged the journalist.

"Well, let's hope for the best," sighed Fandor.

Then in silence the two went on their way revolving a host of anxious thoughts. It was not that they were afraid; it was not even that the memory of dangers barely avoided, escaped by what seemed like a prodigy, always ready to recur, troubled these intrepid souls. Nor was it altogether that they had no illusions left as to the difficulty of the task they had undertaken and which their pride as men of their word forbade them to abandon. Many men, no doubt, were assured of Fantômas' power, few realized what activities the Monster was actually capable of. But they, the police officer and the journalist, they had no doubts—they knew.

Under the shades of night enveloping London in a dense cloud of thick darkness they went on their way with weary steps, firmly resolved on their work of justice, yet fully recognizing its difficulty. Yes, Juve had spoken the truth; the Ariadne thread that might have guided their steps was broken.

Somewhere in the vast city the arch-criminal was free, triumphant. Somewhere at his own good pleasure he had taken refuge. And he must be discovered in the crowd, he whose true face no man had ever seen. He must be hunted from his lair, forced into the open like a noxious wild beast the hounds pursue. He had his accomplices; he had his wealth; the villain had powerful engines of defense on his side. What arms had they who were vowed to the task of vanquishing him?

"We are alone, or as good as alone," reflected Juve; "the official police does not really support me…"

"Fantômas holds a hostage," Fandor sighed, "a hostage that renders me powerless; he has his daughter—Helene, my poor Helene…"

A sad reflection, the end of the cheerful interlude coming from the joy of having escaped an appalling catastrophe!

Presently the two men reached the house in which they occupied a furnished flat. On arriving there: "By-the-by, Juve," observed Fandor, "what of your plans for changing lodgings?"

"Abandoned provisionally, my boy. After all, why leave here? Fantômas knows our address. Well, so much the better; he will unmask himself if he attacks us… Come, go in."

"By your leave, Juve," said the younger man, and entered the house. But he had not taken one step in the hall before he stopped dead.

"Juve! Juve, I say! Look!"—for a light could be seen coming from the upper floor of the house.

"Well?" snapped the detective. "What is there surprising in that? A lodger coming back home like ourselves?"

"No, no! Don't you see? The light comes from our floor—and there's only one flat on each story."

"By God! Yes, you're right."

"It's at our door, Juve. They're ringing."

"That's so. But *who* is ringing?"

"That we're going to find out, by God!" And in one second Fandor had forgotten his fatigue. Dashing to the stairs, he flew up the steps at a speed that sufficiently testified to the eagerness of his curiosity.

At a more moderate pace, Juve, active enough, but still somewhat handicapped by his years, panted after his junior.

Next moment the worthy man asked himself if he were not dreaming. From above, by the cage of the staircase, Fandor's voice reached him, shaking with emotion, restrained yet threatening.

"What!" the young man was saying, "you here?… Ah! how did you dare?…"—and Juve for the moment sought in vain to conjecture to whom Fandor could be putting such a question in such an indignant tone…

*   *   *   *   *

The police officer was soon to know the truth. Hardly had he reached the landing outside his door before he saw with indescribable amazement the person to whom Fandor had addressed his angry protest at her presence.

"Lady Beltham!" stammered Juve.

It was indeed Fantômas' wife who stood there; it was she Fandor was addressing in passionate words of reproach.

"You are innocent, I grant you," the young man declared. "But you love, you persist in loving, the vilest of murderers, the wretch who overpasses the utmost bounds of villainy."

"Is a woman mistress of her heart?" replied the noble lady, who looked more than ever beautiful.

On the ill-lighted stairs, where the gas was turned down to the lowest point possible by the parsimonious landlady, her fair hair seemed even fairer than usual. Standing there in an attitude of proud disdain that matched well the haughty mien of the woman, whose grace showed something of the sovereign charm of a princess, she gazed at the journalist with eyes that burned with a feverish light, whether of indignation or of suffering.

"Madam," replied Fandor, very ill at ease, "I had rather not discuss such subjects with you… I simply tell you that your place is not here… seeing you are Fantômas' accomplice."

"I am not Fantômas' accomplice."

"Oh, his ally, if you prefer the phrase."

"You are pleased to play with words, Monsieur Fandor?"

"Nay, madam, it is you who play with facts."

"I defy you to prove it."

"Upon my word, madam, a bold challenge! How do you call the indisputable fact that you are aware of the crimes of that abominable murderer and you still hold him dear… and help him to escape us?"

No sooner had the young man said the words than Lady Beltham seemed more moved than ever.

"How do I call it, sir? You ask me that? I call it doing my duty."

"Your duty?"

"I am the wife, sir, of the man you speak of."

For once Fandor was nonplussed. He had too generous a heart not to understand and approve, no matter what he pretended, Lady Beltham's attitude towards Fantômas. He knew she felt a genuine affection for the scoundrel; he knew that if Fantômas was not without reproach in his dealings with his wife, at any rate he had never directly attacked her. Never yet had he discovered her in an actual attempt to betray him.

"You do not answer?" questioned the noble lady.

Fandor made a gesture of furious impatience. "Never force me to say what I do not think. The part you play with Fantômas only concerns yourself—that much is certain. But…"

"Not another word, sir!… I am here for a like purpose, Monsieur Fandor… We will resume the conversation when you give me time to speak…"

"But, madam…"

"Have done, Fandor!" Juve broke in. "When an enemy—I say an enemy, do you hear?—does us the honor to come and see us, trusting to our magnanimity, we owe the visitor all consideration. You do wrong to speak as you do to Lady Beltham… Will you follow me, madam?"—and Juve at last opened the door of the flat and stood aside to let the noble lady enter, Fandor following behind.

But the journalist was far from being satisfied. To begin with, the rebuke Juve had administered rankled. Yes, it was very evident they were bound to receive Lady Beltham with the consideration merited by the confidence she had manifested in coming to see the detective. Yet, after all, was it not to make themselves liable beforehand to defeat, to employ such chivalrous courtesy towards those whom Fantômas used as his agents?

In much ill-humor Fandor sank into an armchair and said no more, leaving it to Juve to continue the interview.

"I ask you a question, madam. You are come, you say, in the hope of averting a fresh crime of Fantômas'?"

"Yes."

"Then can you, without betraying him, inform us who is threatened?"

A smile thanked Juve for his tactful delicacy. "Yes, it must be without betraying my husband if I am to speak," replied Lady Beltham. "I am grateful to you for remembering that."

"Madam I understand that so well that I will refrain from insisting on a reply if any one of my questions must remain unanswered… The names of the persons or person threatened?"

"There are three people in danger!" returned Lady Beltham hoarsely.

"In danger of death?"

"In danger of a fearful death… in danger of torture…"

"Madam, I beg of you to tell me their names."

"I am here only for that purpose."

The reply was uttered in a voice hoarse with indescribable

emotion—emotion that could equally be read in her beautiful eyes as she proceeded:

"Fantômas, I must tell you, is in a state of passionate anger, of insane fury that terrifies me… He had mitigated his cruelty towards certain persons dear to him, for, as you know, there were some beings whom he still deemed sacred… Henceforth I think these persons themselves are in peril at his hands…"

A moment's silence; then she sighed. "I think he is afraid… yes, afraid. I think he lives in terror of those he loves, because he knows these are horrified at his atrocious repute."

"Madam," interrupted Juve, "if I understand you rightly, he would seem to distrust you? You would seem to be one of the persons in peril of his wrath?"

"Oh, for me, *I* do not count, I am of no account anymore. I hold my own life cheap. No, it is not I that am now in question."

"Who is it, then? The names? Give the names."

But Lady Beltham did not appear to hear the peremptory question the police officer was asking her. As if unable to drive away a terrible thought that haunted her mind, she resumed again:

"Yes, Monsieur Juve, I have made my sacrifice without a word to—you know whom I mean. I have left him… left him forever."

"Forever? You are leaving Fantômas forever?"

"If I can master my heart, yes, Juve… I am going away… going away on a journey this very evening."

"You are ill, madam?"

"I have always been ill."

Lady Beltham had spoken in a broken voice. But suddenly she shuddered, then seemed to regain her self-possession, as though escaping from a cruel dream.

"Oh, it is not only I, Juve, that am in question. What, call to trouble you with my personal affairs? I was telling you how Fantômas has reached the extremest limits of insane fury, how at this moment I believe him capable of atrocities before which he would have recoiled… You take me? You know why?"

"No, madam."

"Because he feels himself surrounded on all sides by hatred, because he cannot win over the hearts he longs to win... Fantômas has always succeeded in every enterprise he has undertaken; now he knows failure for the first time. There is one being in all the world whose affection he craved—and this being hates him... and loves his worst enemy!... You can guess of whom I speak, Juve."

The detective's face turned pale as death. Why, surely he realized perfectly what Lady Beltham's words signified. This one being the precious gift of whose love Fantômas could not win, who else was it but his daughter, Helene? Was it not she, the gentle Helene, who loved Fandor as fondly as he loved her, the creature of his ardent dream whom he longed to make his wife?

Yet he denied, the astute detective, what was so plain to see.

"No, madam," he declared, "I cannot guess the riddles you ask me."

"But, Juve, that is impossible!"—and the unhappy woman went on in a shaking voice:

"Juve, I beseech you, do not push to extremities one who is—"

"A brigand, madam!"

"A man whose reckless audacity you know... Oh, Juve, if you would avoid the worst disasters, if you would spare yourself the most terrible regrets, quit London; abandon the pursuit you are on; leave Fantômas in peace... Nay, I do not ask you impossibilities; I do not urge you to forget for always. No! But grant a respite to a madman whom each hour that passes you are driving into a wilder frenzy..."

"Madam," put in Juve, speaking with slow deliberation, "I understand perfectly what it is you ask me to do. But let me tell you this: madmen—as you will have it Fantômas is mad—must not be abandoned to themselves. That does not calm their folly, but the very opposite... More than that, even to save three persons' lives I have no right to leave off trying to rescue all humankind from a Monster."

"Juve, you do not know who it is that is in danger."

"I have asked you for the names, madam."

"I know, Juve, that two of these names would not stir your feelings… But the thought of the danger these persons run through Fantômas' hatred maddens an unhappy woman as much threatened as they are."

"Madam, I assure you I fail any longer to understand… You must name these persons who are in danger—or end this interview…"

Lady Beltham pondered a moment, then slowly, as though reluctant, she spoke at last:

"Those whom Fantômas has definitely condemned in his own mind are… Juve… Fandor… and…"

"And?" demanded the police officer.

"And… Helene!" concluded Lady Beltham.

But at that, Fandor, unable longer to endure the anguish he felt, sprang up from his seat.

"Helene!" he cried. "Fantômas would make Helene a victim—Helene, his own daughter! But the thing is impossible! He loves her…"

"He hates her."

"Why, what has she done?"

"She has admitted that she loves you…"

"But Helene is not responsible for our pursuit of Fantômas…"

"He believes the opposite."

"Oh, but if you would disabuse his mind of the idea…"

"You are under a mistake, Monsieur Fandor. I have done everything in the world to mitigate his fury, to induce him to think… I have failed… I have only made myself an object of suspicion… I am leaving him; I am bound to go."

"Come now, madam, do you hope to persuade us to renounce a pursuit that it is our bounden duty to persist in by telling us of Fantômas' abominable purposes? Nay, even that would not save Helene."

"Perhaps… it might! Knowing you no longer on his track, Fantômas might grow less furious."

"As soon hope for a tiger to lose his taste for blood"—and Fandor, carried away by his anger, turned to Juve.

"Tell her," he cried, "his conduct is shameful! Tell her her duty is to save Helene, that her duty is to ally herself with us to rescue her from the hands of the Torturer!"

The poor fellow stopped, breathless with fury. In his horror of the dangers Lady Beltham spoke of as threatening Helene, he was beside himself, ready to insult the noble lady who, while deploring Fantômas' wickedness, yet could not resolve to betray him.

Meantime Juve had merely given a shrug of the shoulders on hearing Fandor's recriminations; then, when the young man ceased speaking:

"You're losing your head, Fandor," he said. "You insult Madam… What do you think it's going to lead to?"

"To dragging out of Fantômas' wife the secret of where he keeps Helene confined"—and with a wave of the hand imposing silence on his comrade, he went on:

"Oh, never think I am afraid! Never suppose even that I tremble for Juve, whom yet I love like a father. *Our* lives are of small account… But Helene's life, the life of an innocent girl, is everything… You will have pity on her, madam?"

As she looked at the young man Lady Beltham seemed on the point of fainting… "Ah me!" she groaned, "the trial is above my strength."

But soon she conquered her weakness and forced herself to further speech.

"I swear, Fandor, I do not know where Helene is… I swear I can do nothing more for her than beseech you to go, to leave England."

"Never! never!"

"Would you condemn your fiancée to death?"

"Should I be worthy of her, madam, if I listened to your advice?"

"Oh, but it is your pride as a man that speaks!"

"Not so, it is my conscience."

A tense silence followed. All three taking part in this tragic scene experienced those painful feelings that wound the very soul and are an unbearable torment to remember. Juve was the first to find strength to speak again.

"You are wrong, Fandor," he declared afresh. "No man has a right to employ violent words where he has been honored by another's unfaltering trust. Lady Beltham came here of her own free will. She speaks as her conscience dictates. You have no right to hurt her with angry speeches."

"But, Juve, I *have* a right to beseech her pity."

"To what end? She can do nothing; she possesses no power to protect Helene…"

"You think so, Juve? But if this is untrue?"

"Fandor, you forget yourself… You are accusing Madam of falsehood."

"No, Juve, not at all! It is you who are mistaken."

"What, then, did you mean?"

The young man's eyes flashed fire. But for a second he stood motionless and silent, evidently thinking his hardest before speaking again. Then at last:

"Juve, I meant something different from what you thought. You say I am wrong. Perhaps I am. In any case, remember I am right at the same time… Well, you shall judge…"

As he spoke Fandor stepped over to a valise in which he had packed sundry articles bought since his arrival in London, and which the two friends, no great sticklers for tidiness, had left lying in the room.

"Yes," he said, "I think I am right and wrong at one and the same time… and… and I beg your pardon, Juve."

But very surely, if Fandor begged the other's pardon, there was a highly surprising reason for this. The young man had been stooping over the valise; now he stood upright again with calculated slowness and kicked it away from his feet. Then with amazing rapidity, bounding like a wild cat, he leapt at the detective. There was a sharp click.

"What now! you're mad!" yelled Juve.

"Not that I am aware of," retorted Fandor dryly.

"You're clapping the handcuffs on me?"

"Yes, Juve!… Because I know you would not think as I do. Deliberately I continue being wrong in order to be right"—and turning away from his bewildered companion, on whose wrists he had actually slipped the handcuffs, taking him utterly by surprise, he looked at Lady Beltham.

"Madam," he proceeded, "I sincerely ask your pardon for the angry words I permitted myself to use. They were more violent than I intended; they were cries wrung from me in my agony. But you are right; it is not for you to betray Fantômas, even to defend Helene…"

"I cannot understand," stammered the Englishwoman, who was staring at Juve with looks of bewilderment.

"You will understand soon, madam. But first I must ask you a favor. Will you of your kindness suffer me to put these bracelets, on your wrists too?"

"What, on mine—on mine?"

"Why, yes, madam, on yours… Oh, I beseech you to consent! Do not resist. If I should have to use force I would not hesitate."

The young man, in fact, spoke in such a tone that Lady Beltham dared not resist.

"Do as you will," she faltered. "You are the stronger… But it is an insult."

"No, madam, no! What *would* be an insult would be to force you to betrayal. But nothing of the sort is involved. Being my prisoner, you will only be the dearer to Fantômas… No matter; what counts with me is that you will above all else be a hostage in my hands… Madam, Fantômas loves you, say what you will; and when he knows that your life is my guarantee for that of Helene, he will hesitate to attack his daughter"—and quitting the noble lady's side, he turned again to Juve.

"You, my dear, my true, my loyal-hearted Juve, you are too magnanimous, you fight Fantômas with weapons of courtesy. Much good may it do you! *I* use the means I have at my disposal. The end justified the means for me… You still think me in the wrong?"

"Yes!" replied the police officer curtly. "Like Madam, I say your behavior is an insult. Why yes, you did well to handcuff me. Otherwise…"

"Otherwise, Juve?"

"I should have released Lady Beltham."

"Oh, Juve, Juve, you pain me to the heart!"—and swinging about on his heels, he left the room.

A strange being truly, this journalist! Had he really been telling Juve the truth when he said he proposed to keep Lady Beltham as a hostage?

No sooner outside the door, in fact, and back on the landing, than Fandor's look changed; something very like a smile appeared on the young man's lips.

"There," he muttered, "let's shut the door and leave Juve and Madam Fantômas closeted together. They understand each other perfectly… And now let's cut our stick."

Jerome Fandor clapped on his hat, lit a cigarette, and then, as he expressed it, "cut his stick." In another second he was out of the house, running at his best speed through the deserted streets, which the dawn was already filling with a pale, wan illumination.

And as he went, a faint smile at the corner of his lips, he was asking himself a question:

"After all, one never knows what Juve really thinks. When I handcuffed him he protested… Yes, that's true, but not very strongly… Can he have understood? Can he have fathomed my little scheme, I wonder?"

9. Fandor's Unscrupulousness

"Yes," pursued Fandor, as he went his way, still running at top speed, "Juve did not protest against what I was doing with all the indignation he should by rights have shown… Hmm, that means something! Juve is no fool; he must have known I am not the man to behave dishonorably."

For, to tell truth, Fandor was entirely of Juve's opinion, albeit he had seemed to hold a diametrically opposite view. After all, in coming to the detective's lodging and adjuring him to abandon all pursuit of Fantômas in order to avoid the villain's being carried away by his fury and avenging himself on Helene, Lady Beltham surely had in mind nothing but a very praiseworthy action. Under such conditions, to keep her in durance vile, to hold her as a hostage, was in the journalist's, no less than in Juve's, opinion to be guilty of an act of treachery, to behave like a coward.

Yet Fandor had been ready to commit this enormity. Could it be, as he had told himself, that he held that in certain cases the end justifies the means? Far from it, for the journalist was now acting in a spirit little in agreement with that immoral and unworthy doctrine. Redoubling his pace, and presently espying a taxi, he made all haste to hail the driver.

"Quick!" he ordered the man, "drive to the Whitechapel rat pit," and ten minutes brought him to his destination.

There, concealed in a recess of the wall, shivering with cold, but with the conscientious sense of professional duty common among police agents, who are all trained men, still obstinately mounting guard, Simon was already beginning to find the time long.

Seeing the journalist, who had left the place in company with Juve two hours before, he sprang to his feet and accosted the newcomer:

"What, M'sieur Fandor, you're back again!"

"Yes, I'm back again… I've come to fetch you."

"To fetch me?… Oh, but what about my job here?"

"A fig for your job here, my man. You've something better to do."

"Very well, give me your orders… It's M'sieur Juve sends you, no doubt."

"No, it's not Juve. It's I who've come—on my own."

"Then there's something new up?"

"Perhaps."

"And M'sieur Juve doesn't know yet?"

"Juve knows without knowing, yet knowing all the while."

"Upon my word, M'sieur Fandor, no offense meant, but you're not over clear."

"Because, my good man, you don't give me a chance to explain."

"Oh, so now you're going to tell me I chatter too much!"

"Not a doubt about that!"—and Fandor broke into a great laugh at the chagrined look on the agent's face. Taking the worthy man's arm, he drew him away.

"There, don't lose your temper. I was joking. I'm a bit of a chatterer myself. But we've got something better to do than idle talk."

"Well, speak plain, M'sieur Fandor."

"Here you are then, my dear chap. I've come for you to take you to Juve. He requires to see you…"

"Then it *is* M'sieur Juve who sends for me. You said just now it was you who—"

"Have done! let me finish… He requires to see you because you'll be doing an excellent piece of service… Only he doesn't expect your visit."

"Don't understand!"

"Of course you don't; you can't understand yet. Juve is in handcuffs, my dear fellow…"

"Eh? What's that you tell me?"

"Juve is in handcuffs—and I put him there!"

"Never?… I'm going cracked, for sure."

At that moment, so overwhelming was the worthy agent's stupefaction, he stopped dead, unable to take another step. Indeed, the thought that Juve was in handcuffs like a malefactor and that it was Fandor who had handcuffed the police officer, was so bewildering that Simon might well be forgiven for losing his presence of mind.

Without paying any attention, however, to his companion's state of amazement, the journalist added:

"Juve is not alone. He is with another prisoner—Lady Beltham, not to put too fine a point on it, who is likewise handcuffed."

"Oh, good! It was you again."

"Exactly so! It was I again who put the handcuffs on Lady Beltham…"

"But why? Why?"

"So there," Fandor replied coolly, "you ask me why I acted in this fashion. Well, my good Simon, I will ask your leave not to tell you that."

"M'sieur Fandor, saving your presence, you stir my bile…"

"Still, try to keep calm; I have more to say."

"I'm all attention."

"My dear Simon, if I have come for you it is because I feel complete confidence in you."

"You don't say so! But you don't explain…"

"I explain all I can explain to you… Well, I have come for you because I thought you would not refuse to do me a service. All you have to do is to go and see Juve under some pretense or other, and keep him in the dark about having met me and that I asked you to go to him. You understand?"

"Not one word!" confessed the agent, and he was only speaking the truth in this admission of his state of utter bewilderment. Juve was under arrest and Fandor was sending him to the prisoner! Undoubtedly the moment he set eyes on Simon, Juve would demand that he should remove his handcuffs. Ought he to refuse or ought he to obey his chief's order? And why was he not to tell him that Fandor had arranged the visit?

"Well, well," proceeded the journalist, "I'm going to throw a light on the subject; then you'll see all this is less complicated than it looks."

"Thank God for that!"

"My good Simon, here is the plain truth. I am anxious that Juve may have his handcuffs removed by you, but at the same time I wish him not to know that I so desired it… Naturally, you can guess now that Juve's apparent arrest was in my mind only a piece of playacting meant to impress Lady Beltham. Only, look you, I could not let Juve know beforehand, as all this happened before the eyes of the third party."

"Good, good, M'sieur Fandor! I am beginning to understand. You made a pretense of arresting M'sieur Juve; but it was only a pretense—only meant to frighten Lady Beltham. Well, that's all plain so far… Only, suppose I set him free, M'sieur Juve, the effect will be spoiled, won't it?"

"Not at all!"

"Come, that surprises me… And what's the object of all this to-do?"

"That's the one thing I can't tell you, my dear Simon. You see, I don't want Juve to question you and for you to be embarrassed how to answer him… Anyhow, you'll easily find some pretext to account for your coming, eh?… Well, now, what is there to laugh at, pray?"

The agent had in fact just broken into an amused peal of laughter. Now, in answer to the journalist's question:

"Oh, that, M'sieur Fandor—the reason why I laugh? Well, see here, M'sieur Fandor, that's the one thing *I* can't tell *you*. But no matter for that, it's of no consequence."

*   *   *   *   *

Nevertheless, if Fandor could have known what passed between Juve and Lady Beltham after his departure, he would have found no difficulty in explaining the worthy Simon's hilarity.

The fact is, he had no sooner quitted the room than, turning to Lady Beltham:

"Madam," the police officer had begged his fellow prisoner,

"you will pardon Fandor. What he has just done in arresting you is not to his credit. Again, what he did in taking me unawares and slipping the handcuffs on me was simply idiotic. But be sure of this: I believe it was his rage blinded him. He is afraid for Helene's safety, and his fear robs him of his wits…"

"I know that."

"Then you will forgive him. But I say, further, all this is of no consequence—for two good reasons…"

"And they are?…"

"Madam, I know Fandor. His impetuous nature may lead him to commit childish acts of folly. But he quickly recovers his calmness… Tomorrow, in an hour or an hour and a half, he will set us free, if we are not meantime to be released by someone else. I have an agent in London—one Simon. I left him on the lookout at a certain spot in the town which I deemed it important to have watched. However, he has orders to come here at daybreak, when his remaining on guard will be useless. You need feel no anxiety, therefore. In an hour or an hour and a half this man will arrive and set us free… Fandor knew nothing about this appointment—so much the worse for him!… Well, this little misadventure will be a lesson to us."

Yes, if Fandor could have heard this conversation he would have understood many points. True, Juve had made little protest at the pretended arrest he had been subjected to and the breach of good faith of which Fandor appeared to be guilty in detaining Lady Beltham as a hostage, but this was simply due to the fact that he had remembered Simon's forthcoming visit.

If, again, Simon had burst out laughing in the journalist's face on being asked to invent a pretext to justify his coming, this was because he was thinking how needless such a pretext was, seeing he had been directed to come by Juve himself.

A man of ability but of little education, the worthy Simon was a good deal alarmed at the complicated nature of the investigations in which he found himself involved and as to which he was beginning to feel himself utterly at sea. Juve had bidden him come to see him, at the same time charging him to say nothing about the appointment to Fandor. "He must get to sleep and secure some rest," the police officer had declared. But was that the true reason for the secrecy he insisted on? In like fashion Fandor was now asking him to visit Juve, making a point of his not mentioning that the journalist had sent him, in order to avoid Lady Beltham knowing of his intentions… But was this the young man's real motive?

"Juve and Fandor are devilish clever," Simon was saying to himself; "but they're mighty mysterious too… Bah! What's that to me, after all? *I'm* not leading the dance. *I've* only got to obey orders… Anyway, up to now it's all plane sailing. I've got to go to see Juve; very good, I'll go. I'm not to talk; very well, I won't."

Then, with the utmost gravity, but secretly much diverted at the imbroglio, he added:

"Never you fear, M'sieur Fandor; it's all going to happen just as you wish… No, I don't understand, but I obey orders; I always make a point of obeying orders."

And Fandor asked for nothing better. He accompanied the worthy man as far as Juve's door; then, after shaking hands with him cordially, he walked away quickly.

"Goodbye for the present, Simon," he called back over his shoulder. "Oh, one word more! Tell Juve not to be anxious about me. I may perhaps be away for some time, but I shan't be in any danger."

But, as a matter of fact, the journalist did not seem to have any intention of going far. As he bade farewell to his companion, he had set off at a rapid pace like a man bent on covering a great distance, but no sooner had the agent disappeared in the doorway than the young man turned back again, muttering to himself:

"What I want now is a dark corner, really dark, where I can hide easily… Ah! there's just the sort of thing I do want."

He had caught sight at the corner of a plot of waste ground of rows of planks, the timbering of a dismantled house, piled up at the edge of the pavement. Slipping behind these, he made himself as small as possible, and remained motionless, his eyes fixed on the door of Juve's abode.

"There!" he soliloquized, "I shan't have long to wait—a

matter of ten minutes or so… Simon will set Juve free. Juve will not fail to release poor Lady Beltham. Lady Beltham, once at liberty, will take good care not to linger on the premises. Ha! ha! ha! Fantômas makes his unsuspecting helpmate warn us to desist from our pursuit of him. Then, again—ho! ho!—Juve accepts her mission at its face value… Ah, well, for my own part, I reckon I'm going to give old Juve a fine lesson in police craft… So there!…"

As a fact, Fandor had not for one moment been under any mistake as to the attitude of their visitor, whom he had treated so cavalierly in making her his prisoner, albeit fully resolved to have her released by Simon at the earliest opportunity. For the journalist, on hearing Fantômas' wife assert how the wretch was beside himself with fury and ready to embark on the most abominable cruelties, had come to the deliberate conclusion:

"Lady Beltham is of good faith, no doubt of that… But Fantômas has made her his cat's-paw, without her suspecting it. It was he who cleverly persuaded her to take this step… He wanted to see the back of us. So he made use of her to convey his message to us, convinced we would attempt no violence whatever against the unhappy woman… Ah, well, it is betwixt you and me, Fantômas!"

And in truth the journalist's plan of action was as simple as it was ingenious. By throwing himself on Juve and Lady Beltham and handcuffing them, he was sure to mislead completely Fantômas' envoy as to what he really thought. Then, the latter's suspicions once dissipated, evidently it only needed to have her released by Simon to persuade her that an unexpected slice of luck had saved her from an imprisonment that otherwise would have been serious.

"And from this point on," Fandor proceeded, "it all goes like clockwork. No sooner at liberty than Lady Beltham hastens back to Fantômas to beseech him to be prudent, to tell him that I am firmly resolved at all costs to push things to the direst extremity. Obviously that is the way a loving woman would behave, one who desires to betray neither her husband nor honest folks, but who does desire to avoid any conclusive

course of action… Good! then, let her go to Fantômas. I wish
for nothing better!… At any rate, if I shadow her, I shall come
upon the villain."

Jerome Fandor, in fact, had pulled the strings with such
marvelous dexterity that he had secured for himself the chance
of tracking down his prey under the most interesting circumstances. Moreover, and to begin with, the journalist found
good reason to congratulate himself on the course of events, all
tending to confirm his anticipations.

Peering through the shutters, he could see the figures of
Juve, Lady Beltham, and Simon. He perceived that, following
the police officer's directions, the agent was removing the handcuffs he had so adroitly slipped on the other's wrists. Above all,
he noted how, after a few rapid sentences, Lady Beltham was
hurrying away.

"So ho!" the young man chuckled, "here's the little game
beginning!"—and a few minutes after Fandor could clearly distinguish in the faint light of the dawning day the figure of Lady
Beltham issuing from the house.

Once in the street by herself she made no attempt to mask
her movements, setting off with a hurried step, as if fearing to
be late for some appointment.

"What!" thought Fandor. "Can she be going back to
Fantômas straight away? But, after all, why not?"

The young man go to his feet. Then, letting the woman he
was shadowing get a few yards ahead, he followed on the opposite side of the street, the collar of his topcoat turned up, his
hands in his pockets, and deadening as much as possible the
sound of his footsteps.

"If she does turn round," he assured himself, "she'll never
recognize me at this distance. Besides, I may have time to hide."

Nevertheless, another anxiety still worried him. What was
he to do, supposing Lady Beltham was met by a motorcar, or
even supposing she hailed an ordinary taxi and he could not
find another at a moment's notice.

"By God!" the journalist swore, "that would be just maddening! But there's nothing I can do. I must bow to the inevitable."

However, Jerome Fandor was not destined to know such a heartbreaking disappointment as this. Was Lady Beltham's mind so preoccupied that she never dreamt of being followed? This certainly seemed likely. Anyway, she did *not* look round, but continued to hurry on at the same pace as at first.

"Where is she going?" Fandor asked himself presently. "I do not know London well enough to guess that… Ah! now she is taking a bus. Oh, well, I'll get up outside. That's all there is to it."

One of the earliest morning buses had just gone by, and Lady Beltham, stopping it, took her place inside. Without a moment's hesitation Fandor sprang on the same conveyance and, quicker than lightning, climbed on the top before the other had so much as sat down.

"She didn't recognize me; she didn't even see me!" the journalist thought. "I'll get off after her when she gets out… Hang it all! I never looked to see where the bus is bound for!"

But next minute his face fell. The motorbus had reached its final stopping place and was pulling up in front of a main line station.

"Hmm! Victoria Station, I take it… Why, the devil! She's going into the terminus!"

He followed, his heart beating hard. If Fantômas' wife was really going off by train it must mean she had told the actual truth? That she had given up all idea of seeing her husband. What use following her in that case?

Lady Beltham made straight for the booking office, and, judging by the considerable sum she paid over to the clerk, Fandor gathered she was taking a ticket for a long journey.

"What to do now?" he asked himself. But his hesitation was only momentary. Whatever happened, he must find out the truth. In one bound he was at the window where a ticket had just been handed to the lady.

"Same, please!" he demanded with his most engaging smile.

"Single to Le Havre, sir?"

"That's it!"—and he paid his fare and made his way to the departure platform.

Jerome Fandor was dumbfounded… What the devil was

Lady Beltham going to do in France?

10. On Board the *Volunteer*

In another ten minutes, if Fandor had not completely recovered his previous optimism, he was at any rate in possession of all his usual cool self-possession.

On reaching the platform he had seen Lady Beltham, after laying in an ample stock of illustrated papers, quietly take her seat in a first-class carriage. All this was the behavior of a woman having no suspicion of being obstinately pursued, and Fandor was fully justified in concluding that this unruffled confidence of the traveler was, after all, the most important factor for the moment in the situation.

"She doesn't know I am on her heels," he surmised, "and that's just as it should be… As to where she is going, and what she proposes to do when she gets there, that is precisely the thing I am here to discover. So let's watch what happens and take this journey as it comes."

Indeed, Fandor had no doubts whatever now as to the eventual outcome of his present proceedings. He had concluded at first that Lady Beltham had not spoken the truth when she announced her intention of leaving her husband, but now he was changing his mind, for was not the lady's departure for France the best proof of her veracity?

"True," the journalist summed up the situation, "but that don't hinder its being important to know the exact locality where she could be found… Fantômas loves her; hence to conclude that one day or another he will come for her is easy… Juve, no doubt, will be delighted to know where to arrange an ambuscade. Should my journey have no other result than to supply this information, it will not have been in vain."

Thus reassured, Fandor paid no more heed for the present to his fellow passenger. Once aboard the train that in an hour or two more would be standing on the quay where the boats on the Southampton-Havre service are moored, obviously Lady Beltham could not disappear or vanish into thin air.

"So," the young man told himself, "my time is my own till we get to Le Havre… There, of course, I must keep my eyes well open once more."

Accordingly the young man enjoyed a most comfortable journey. Tired out by the sleepless night he had spent, worn out—as he had every right to be—by the terrible experiences he had gone through, he took ample advantage of the good luck that he chanced to be the sole occupant of the second-class compartment in which he had taken a place. Lying full length on the seat, he waited quietly until the train got underway, then abandoned himself to slumber, and slept so soundly that a couple of railway porters had to shake him to recall him to a consciousness of where he was.

"All get out here!" the men warned him.

"Eh, what?" returned Fandor, still heavy with sleep. "Get out, did you say?"

Then, fully awake at last: "Southampton, is it? Capital! I'm for the boat, my men. I'm going on board."

He was the last to leave the train, and as it was raining, all the passengers had by this time quitted the deck of the steamer, the shore-ropes of which were now being hauled in.

"More luck!" he exclaimed. "Lady Beltham is certain to have gone below by now; so she won't see me come aboard"—and he stepped smartly across the gangway, reached the forecastle, and joined the crowd of third-class passengers.

"Not over-comfortable," he observed, "the 'tween-decks! But there, there's not a chance of Lady Beltham coming exploring this part of the ship. So everything is for the best…" and taking his cigarette case from his pocket, more and more well satisfied at the turn of events, he gave all his attention to watching the waves, through which the vessel was now plowing her way. He knew nothing of the tortures of seasickness that so many people endure at sea. Having always been a great traveler and accustomed to face all conditions of weather, he was, indeed, something of a sea dog.

"Fine weather and a fair wind!" he judged directly the steamer reached the open sea outside the Needles. "Going to be an uneventful crossing this time!" And so it proved, and the whole way across the English Channel Fandor never left his place—or left off smoking.

"If only I were sure," he sighed from time to time, "of returning with sensational news!"

But he was sure of nothing, and was incapable of any sensation whatever save a lively curiosity regarding forthcoming event.

Such, meantime, was the journalist's preoccupation that at the moment the steamer sounded a strident blast on her siren to notify her entrance into the Le Havre roadstead and her passage between the jetties of the *Défense Maritime,* he gave a start of surprise.

"What! Already?" he cried. "Why, I thought we were still out in the Channel!"

Then he turned round sharply, to see the passengers, roused by the siren, appearing one after the other on the promenade deck, busy with their preparations for disembarking.

"Hmm!" muttered Fandor, "so here's the chase starting afresh… But I'm too much in sight here. I mustn't let Lady Beltham slip away; but, above all else, I've not to let her see me."

This was an obvious proposition. However, Fandor was far too skillful in the delicate art of "shadowing" to be overmuch embarrassed by the problem offered him for solution. To see without being seen was not difficult in this case. He simply turned to the right about and took covert underneath the fore-deck. From there he had an excellent view of the passengers landing without the latter having any chance of seeing him.

"Keep your eyes open!" Fandor told himself again. "Lady Beltham can't be far off… Come now, she can't, anyhow, have gone ashore out at sea… And I can't have let her go by without recognizing her. Her fur-lined mantle is too unmistakable."

The speaker stopped dead. Mechanically turning his head, he had just caught sight of Lady Beltham, already far off on the quay on her way to the outer harbor.

"By the Lord!" growled the journalist, "so she has changed her costume? Now she's wearing a leather motoring coat!"

However, this was no time for troubling his head about such details of dress. Startled as he was by this change of attire, he remembered it was quite likely that Lady Beltham had found on board suitcases and valises she had registered in advance.

"After all," the young man reflected, "that is her lookout; she has a perfect right to dress as she chooses… Only it means something, this leather coat; evidently she means to go off in a motorcar. The deuce of it is *I* have no car to follow her in."

But once more he must leave this point unconsidered. It might well prove difficult to continue the pursuit begun in London, but for the time being the all-important thing was not to lose sight of his enigmatic quarry.

"I will go ashore," he decided; "that is the most urgent matter. Later on we shall see…"

A second or two later, having set foot on the soil of France, Jerome Fandor experienced a shock of still greater surprise. Far from bending her steps to a hotel or railway station, as would have been the natural thing to do midway in a journey, Lady Beltham was nearing the outer harbor, going in the direction of the semaphore that stands at the extremity of the north jetty.

"One would think she's just loitering about," Fandor now conjectured. "Can she be waiting for someone? But whom?"

However, he was soon to alter his opinion. Halting before the notice board where the arrivals and departures in the port are advertised, Lady Beltham appeared to be deep in conversation with an old sailor man, who, with sweeping gestures and puffing hard at his pipe, was apparently puzzling his head over a host of complicated explanations.

"I'm more and more at sea," Fandor confessed as he watched the pair. "Surely she's just killing time, lingering about, while waiting for someone to come or something to happen…"

But presently he was more at a loss than ever, unable to come to any conclusion whatsoever. Smiling at the old salt and still talking volubly, Lady Beltham was leaving the semaphore and moving towards the inner harbor again.

"Where the devil is she off to?" Fandor asked himself. "I don't suppose she means to make a trip on the sea?"

But what Fandor refused to believe as being too wildly improbably was the very thing that was coming about. On reaching the floating basin where a crowd of fishing boats are always moored, the Englishwoman's companion stepped onto a flight of narrow stone steps carpeted with slippery seaweed that led down to the level of the water.

"Don't move, lady!" the man directed in a voice the wind carried distinctly to Fandor's ears. "I'm getting aboard my boat. Soon as I've hauled her alongside, you'll follow me down," and in another five minutes Lady Beltham sprang lightly into a seaworthy but uncouth-looking craft.

"Well," thought Fandor, "that's the very last thing I looked for! Now what am *I* to do?" And he stood stock-still on the quay completely baffled.

Already Lady Beltham's ancient mariner, managing his sculls with all the dexterity of an old salt, was pulling out to the open sea; then, dropping his oars, he began to hoist sail to take advantage of the fair wind.

"What am I going to do?" Fandor questioned again. "Wait here? Yes, but suppose she isn't coming back?"

But he shrugged his shoulders at the bare idea. Where could this ill-found craft with the patched sails be going except to cruise about in the roads?

"I'm supposing impossibilities," reflected Fandor. "Bless my soul! Folks don't sail for the Americas in an old tub like that! All I've got to do is to stay here quietly. In three-quarters of an hour, or an hour at the outside, Lady Beltham will be back."

But if common sense dictated the resolution, the journalist could not somehow for all that make up his mind to abide by it. He felt a mysterious presentiment, an irresponsible impulse, entirely unreasonable but which nonetheless spurred him on to undertake a pursuit that was absolutely unjustified by any sort of reasoning.

Jerome Fandor went up to a group of sailors with the air of a man desirous of information.

"Well," he remarked, "there's a lady of some pluck, eh? It must be blowing hard outside?"

The question was received with looks of amused surprise.

"Not a bit of it, sir. The weather's as fine as can be."

"Fine, yes!… But the boat's not big, either… Can those small craft keep the sea?"

The young sailor he was questioning shrugged his shoulders. "Why, no," he admitted, "I couldn't swear to that."

"Yet I wager you have a boat yourself the like of her?"

"I? Not I!… And nobody else neither. She's not a boat from these parts, sir."

"What say?… But the man who sails her?"

"Why, he's a stranger. We chaps don't know him… It's bad luck, too, mind you, as how it wasn't a Havre man got the job; that would ha' brought in summat. But it's always the outsiders get the best chances!"

But Jerome Fandor was no longer listening. The simple statements he had just heard threw him into a state of indescribable surprise. The boat was from foreign parts; the old sailor was a stranger too. How fail to guess in that case that the meeting of Lady Beltham with the man was no mere matter of chance? Fandor concluded:

"Yes, it was a rendezvous. The woman is escaping under my very eyes… Oh, well! I'll play the stakes. Nothing ventured, nothing gained!" And turning to the sailor, he panted:

"*You* have a boat, have you?"

"Surely!… The little 'un yonder, painted yellow… Why?"

"And she's as fast a sailer as the other?"

"Faster… Time of the regattas—"

"To sea, then, my lad! And quick's the word! We've got to follow those two."

"But why?"

"Oh, I'll tell you that later on… A hundred francs for you, anyway, if we don't let them get out of our sight…"

Amazed at such an offer, the sailor still hesitated.

"Get a move on, do!" cried Fandor. "You don't understand, man!"

"Oh yes, I do. It's your lady friend, surely?"

"It's just anything you please! I tell you I'll explain. Only let's get going!"

"Lord, there ain't no hurry! The *Saucy Maid*'ll catch up his old tub, never fear. Don't you worry, sir!"

The advice was good, but Fandor did not follow it. While the *Saucy Maid,* hauled from her moorings, was coming alongside, and a bit later when the young sailor was sculling her from the quayside, Fandor was positively dancing with impatience.

In the distance, now almost clear of the jetty, Lady Beltham's boat had left off tacking and, catching the wind, was making rapid headway.

"Don't you worry!" Fandor's man was saying again. "Upon my honor as a sailor I tell you we shall catch him up. So, then, she wanted to leave you in the lurch, eh?—that good lady, and a charming wench, too!"

"Come, come," retorted Fandor. "Never you mind about that! Only let's be after them!"

Seated in the bows, his eyes gazing ahead, he was horrified at the slow progress of the chase. Was Lady Beltham's pilot even aware that he was being pursued?

Suddenly behind him he heard the young salt break into a guffaw. "Look there," he was laughing, "I'd have wagered as much! He don't know this coast, that land-lubber don't! There he is in irons; must have let himself be taken aback!"

A wrong turn of the tiller had evidently brought about the disaster. The sails, the wind suddenly spilled out of them, were flapping idly, and, barely carried forward by the way she had on her, the boat seemed on the point of coming to a dead stop.

"What did I tell you?" went on Fandor's pilot. "Yes, there he sticks, broadside on to the wind!… Why, the fellow sails a boat like a fool; he don't know how to manage a sail, the lubber!" And with a loud laugh, hugging the wind and hauling hard on his foresail sheet, the lad went about, maneuvering his boat with the marvelous dexterity that is second nature to all the marines of the Normandy seaboard.

"We've got him!" he vociferated. "We shall be into him in

no time."

It was quite true. Yard by yard, Fandor's boat was now making up her leeway. How the journalist's heart throbbed with excitement and triumphant anticipation! At last she must needs confess, this lady of mystery, where she was bound for, and her companion, that clumsy navigator, admit his lubberly mistake.

"There, we're not fifty yards off… Am I to lay you alongside… or will you have my speaking trumpet?"

But Fandor was struck dumb. His face had suddenly paled, his hands were clenched in a passion of mad fury, as he stared at the atrocious sight, the abominable vision, that met his eyes.

Lady Beltham's sailor man, letting go the helm, had stood up in the stern sheets.

And now with a rapid gesture he was tearing off the sou'wester and oilskin jacket he wore. Now, turning his back for a moment, he seemed to be removing some sort of mask, then slipping on an extraordinary costume.

For a second, one second only, Fandor failed to realize the dreadful truth. It was the appalling figure, the legendary form of horror he knew so well. The man was clad in a suit of silk tights closely clipping the body; he wore a black hood whose loose folds concealed the features; he was shod in black, gloved in black.

"Fantômas! Fantômas!" screamed Fandor in sudden terror.

Then came a cry—a cry of rage and pain. Fantômas had raised his arm, leveled a revolver and fired. Instinctively Fandor ducked his head… and could hear the bullet whistle past.

"A miss!" he cried. "And I…"

But there he stopped. The ball meant for the journalist had struck the sailor. With a broken arm, giving a yell of pain and amazement, the poor fellow dropped in the bottom of his boat, letting go the tiller.

"Murder!" he bellowed. "Help! help!"

But Fandor was in no condition to succor his unfortunate companion. Disasters at sea always happen when least expected. With no one at the helm, Fandor's boat fell off the wind and spun round on herself… And the journalist, never anticipating the sudden lurch, was thrown into the sea.

"Ho, ho!" cried a voice in sardonic glee. "Ho, ho!"

But Fantômas' triumph was short-lived. Pitched overboard, and like to drown, as he realized, Fandor gave yet another proof of his splendid courage and coolness. Far from swimming on the surface, he dived without a moment's hesitation and struck out underwater.

Was he for getting back to his own boat? Was he for hiding beneath the waves and so avoiding other shots from the ruthless Lord of Terror?

Not so! His purpose was the exact opposite. A miracle of intrepidity, he was actually heading for the enemy's boat.

It was not three minutes after his immersion before he came up suddenly alongside Fantômas' craft.

"Betwixt you and me! You and me!" he shouted in defiance.

And next instant, gripping a rope's end that hung over the side, he was trying to clamber over the taffrail and leap aboard.

* * * * *

No one but Jerome Fandor would have been found capable of so heroic yet deliberate an act of madness—for what else but sheer insanity was this attempt of a swimmer to lay hold of Fantômas' boat and hoist himself on board? Yet except this desperate expedient, what could the journalist do?

For an instant success seemed within his reach. Managing to swing one leg over the side, he made a final effort to struggle into the boat, in which he could actually distinguish Lady Beltham's agonized face.

"Betwixt us two!" he shouted again.

But already it was too late. With one bound Fantômas hurled himself at the aggressor. Blinded by the salt water, exhausted by the efforts he had already made, the journalist was hardly master of himself.

He felt Fantômas seize him round the body and strove to resist. But resistance was impossible. In his present plight, half underwater, clinging to the boat's side, surely he was at his opponent's mercy. A violent blow half stunned him; another bruised his fingers cruelly… He loosed his hold—and sank.

"Oh, have pity!" screamed Lady Beltham. "Do not kill him! You have no right to—"

"Enough, madam! Enough!" Fantômas' imperious voice interrupted her supplication. "The decisions I come to concern me, and me alone."

Meanwhile, thrown back into the water, Fandor struck out again manfully.

"Oh God," he thought, cool again as ever, "the bath has nothing very agreeable about it. Now where the devil do I mean to go?"

He had the more reason to ask the question inasmuch as the current had by this time carried him fifty yards from Fantômas' boat, on which it was manifestly impossible to get aboard… As for that in which the unfortunate young sailor lay, it was still at the mercy of the waves, and had drifted to leeward and was drifting still, already so far off there remained no possibility of getting to it.

"So, then," thought Fandor, "I am going to be drowned. The coast is far too distant for me to reach it. Besides, the tide is against me."

By this time the unfortunate fellow had partly lost his wits. Only instinct survived, prompting him to make the movements necessary to keep afloat and to indulge in certain remarks that forced themselves upon his semi-consciousness.

"Now how comes it," he asked himself, "that Fantômas has left off firing at me? I must be a first-rate mark."

Alas! he very quickly realized, poor wretch, the true reason for the indifference shown by his enemy… The revelation was sudden, startling to the last degree.

Some way off he saw that Fantômas had clewed up the sails just as if he had resolved to abandon all thought of flight, or as though the wind had dropped altogether. Then the brigand got to work, apparently dragging away a mass of heavy tarpaulins that encumbered the stern sheets of his boat… Then next moment a loud roar and rattle broke out.

"A motor!" faltered the journalist. "He has set a motor going!"

There could be no doubt about the matter. Moreover, to an experienced motorist like Fandor, it was manifest that the engine was a powerful one, both strongly built and sensitive.

These facts sufficiently explained all that was previously incomprehensible, and in particular how Fantômas came to be at Le Havre. That night, that same night, or, to be more precise, on the evening of yesterday, Fandor had been at the rat pit in the presence of the Lord of Terror. Yet the latter, aboard this craft got up to look like a common fishing boat, but which was in reality a swift cruiser, had had all the time necessary for crossing the Channel. No doubt he had found it an easy matter to overtake and pass the steamer making the passage on behalf of the Southern Railway Company.

The journalist, however, had little time to weigh these circumstances that explained what would otherwise have been inexplicable. No sooner had Fantômas started his engine than Fandor was asking himself:

"He's abandoning me to my fate, is he? He knows I cannot help myself and simply leaves me to drown?"

But next moment he had altered his view. Fantômas had thrown the screw into gear. Bounding forward like a live thing, the boat darted ahead, cutting her way through the foaming water… And almost instantly Fandor felt a shock, a sharp brutal tug. Then he felt himself being dragged helplessly along in tow of the swiftly-moving boat.

No need now to trouble his head about the reasons for his enemy's apparent carelessness as to his fate, for was he not now absolutely sure of having his victim at his mercy without giving him the smallest chance of resistance?

A minute before, in fact, when he pushed Fandor overboard, the villain had seized the opportunity to pass round his body a slipknot at the end of a long hempen rope… And now the rope was running out and the slipknot tightening more and more, half strangling the unfortunate journalist.

"This time I am done for indeed!" Fandor told himself. And

he in no wise exaggerated the danger. So fast was the motor-boat towing him—she was heading for the open seas—that the young man was dragged through the waves with head under-water and utterly unable to do anything to save himself from a slow and cruel death.

Yet for a moment more he struggled, fighting to free himself of the rope… Then, while a red mist floated before his eyes and he felt his reason tottering, Jerome Fandor faltered the two names:

"Juve!… Helene!"

They were the names of the two he loved above all others… It was his last conscious thought, his last heartbroken cry of despair—and he lost consciousness without uttering another word—a beaten man.

But Jerome Fandor was not to die so. The hatred Fantômas cherished against his daughter's betrothed could not rest content with inflicting so simple and so comparatively painless a death.

Within a very short time of losing consciousness the young man came to himself under the shock of a bucket of cold water thrown in his face. Alas! almost before he had opened his eyes he could conjecture what his fate was to be.

Fantômas stood before him, wearing the costume so many tragedies had made notorious, and which rendered it impossible to recognize the scoundrel's features.

"Capital!" the villain mocked. "This is very reassuring. Jerome Fandor is a hard man to kill."

"You are right," retorted Fandor, without an instant's hesitation. "Prisoner though I am, I think my head is more firmly set on my shoulders than yours, Fantômas!"

Nor were the words spoken at random. Every time he found himself in the presence of the Monster, every time the course of his adventurous life gave him the chance of speech with the Lord of Terror, he took a malicious pleasure in making some al-lusion to the guillotine. Well he knew that the mere thought of the red machine of death sufficed to fill the wretch with terror.

Fantômas clenched his fist in fury as he heard the young

man's taunt.

"Silence!" he thundered. "No man may speak aboard my ship!"

"So Fantômas apes the part of a sea captain?"

"Jerome Fandor, I have ordered you to hold your tongue."

"Be it so! But first I would congratulate Lady Beltham."

Tightly bound, arms tied behind his back, ankles firmly secured, he was incapable of the slightest movement. Fandor had to rest content with turning his eyes towards the unhappy lady, who stood a little apart, her face as pale as death, in a state of manifest prostration.

"Yes, madam," he addressed her, "I must surely offer you my very sincere congratulations. The farce was marvelously well played… You enticed me into a trap with ridiculous ease… I am ashamed at letting myself be cozened—cozened I say—by a woman I had deemed innocent but a few hours ago."

He was endeavoring by dint of mocking, biting sarcasm to express all the scorn he now felt for Lady Beltham. For had she not in truth been playing the most odious of comedies, pretending not to notice that he was "shadowing" her—the same vile comedy she had staged from the first moment of her arrival at Juve's lodging?

A tragicomedy, verily, that visit paid to the detective under pretense of warning him against the danger run by Helene. Had Lady Beltham in truth had any other object in view but to entice Juve to follow on her track, albeit it so happened that Fandor had undertaken the task?

But the young man's gibes came to a sudden stop. At the mere sound of his voice Lady Beltham seemed to rouse herself from an overmastering torpor, to wake from a horrid nightmare.

"Jerome Fandor," she panted, "will you believe me if I tell you on my oath that I am innocent?"

"Be silent, madam!" interrupted Fantômas.

"No!" protested Lady Beltham. "I, at any rate, will say my say, and you cannot hinder me," and she resumed:

"I swear to you, Monsieur Fandor, that I never knew you were on my track… I swear that my visit was inspired by no other wish but to dissuade you from a pursuit that fills me with terror… Again, I swear I was in ignorance that Fantômas was at Le Havre."

"So you are trying to justify yourself?" mocked Fantômas, who had moved away, going aft and taking the helm again, steering the boat in a fashion that at once proved his dexterity as a seaman.

Lady Beltham seemed oblivious of his gibe.

"Fandor," she went on, "I will gladly give my life to save yours… Do you believe me?… I knew nothing of Fantômas being at Le Havre. It was only on landing from the steamer that I caught sight of the boat. Discovering him to be there, what was I to think but that he had come to pray me not to leave him? That was why I went to the harbor, that was why I consented to go with him when I recognized who it was… You feel I am telling the truth, don't you?"

"Yes, madam, that is so. I feel you are not guilty. There is only one coward here—and that is Fantômas."

But the journalist was mistaken if he thought to rouse one feeling of shame in the hardened ruffian's breast. Fantômas only shrugged his shoulders at the taunt.

"Enough!" he ordered. "I act as I think good, and when I so please I put an end to such as are my bitter enemies… Fandor is to die… Juve is to die… I am weary, too, of Lady Beltham's everlasting jeremiads. Let her say one more word, and I will pitch her overboard."

The wretch was grinning odiously, heedless of the scalding tears that stood in the eyes of the woman who had loved him— nay, who loved him still!

Fandor for his part bit his lips and buried his nails in the flesh of his palms. How atrocious the suffering to see himself thus in the hands of the Monster, and to be absolutely unable to throw himself upon him and punish the blackguard for the hideous cruelty of his sarcasms!

"Juve! Juve!" thought the unhappy man, "why are you not here? Why cannot I call to you for help? What vengeance you would wreak on the villain!"

But he must needs keep silent; he must perforce resign himself to endure anything, to submit to any atrocity.

"Now begins my death agony," thought the journalist; "a little sooner or a little later, more or less slowly, with more or less ingenious cruelty, I shall be tortured to death. So much is certain. I am doomed. What need to think of anything else?" And he shut his eyes and tried to sleep.

Was not sleep in fact the only alleviation the unfortunate young man could hope for? How else could he hope to find forgetfulness? He forced himself to lie motionless. He was shivering with cold; he was exhausted, tired out; his limbs ached painfully. No matter! Such was his courage, so perfect his resignation to the inevitable, that soon he was breathing gently and regularly, wrapped in slumber, while unconsciously his lips repeated two names that called up dreams of affection and love: "Juve... Helene..."

*   *   *   *   *

Meanwhile, at the same time, Juve was very far from being asleep, by no means sharing Fandor's calmness, though involved in no such tragic plight. The fact is, the police officer was in a towering rage because once again he was confronted with what filled him with utmost loathing, with what was above all things most fitted to infuriate him, to enrage the official mind.

Scarcely was Lady Beltham gone and Simon installed in one of the two rooms composing the little flat, before he fell into one of those profound fits of abstraction and earnest thought that were specially characteristic of the man.

"Devil take me if I understand Fandor's behavior one scrap," growled the detective presently. "He has insulted Lady Beltham, knowing all the while that she is completely innocent. He has treated her with violence into the bargain by putting her in handcuffs. And he did the like to me... By the Lord! unless the fellow has gone mad, I must suppose he has some motive for acting in this fashion... But what motive?"

Question himself as he might, however, cudgel his brains as he would, Juve could discover no plausible explanation of his friend's conduct.

"Then hardly had he clapped them on before he was off… Where the devil can he have gone? It's against common sense to be so headstrong and impatient."

Not that Juve himself was guiltless of the same fault, for as he spoke he was stamping impatiently about the room.

"But there! what call have I to bother my head about the confounded fellow? Still, I want something to occupy my mind. By-the-by, what's the meaning of the visit Lady Beltham paid me just now?"

Juve left the question unanswered for a moment. The truth was that, if he was in a rage, this was less because he was puzzled by Fandor's attitude than because of the strange impression made on him by the interview with Fantômas' wife.

"Coming to inform me that the wretch no longer loves her… To warn us he intends to murder Fandor and me… Hmm! I can only conclude it was just a bad excuse. Why, there's nothing new about it at all. For many a long day, unless I'm much mistaken, the Lord of Terror has cherished such feelings… There much have been something rendered the visit necessary… Now what was it?"

For a moment Juve thought of Helene… It was true Lady Beltham had declared she longed to see the police investigations stopped because she feared that Fantômas, in his excessive fury, would attempt some act of violence against his daughter.

"But that," Juve assured himself, "I do not believe. Fantômas loves his daughter. Fandor and I, we have both had many proofs of the fact… No, no, on this point Lady Beltham is deceiving herself… or else she wishes to deceive us… There's something else behind it."

As he thought thus, Juve was marching up and down the little room where the others had left him. It was now five o'clock in the morning, the hour when Fandor, shadowing Lady Beltham, was just arriving at the London terminus. Presently Juve crossed the floor and, going to the window, laid his burning brow against the glass, looking out at the grayness of the breaking day.

"And still no sign of Fandor," he muttered again. "It's enough to drive a man mad."

A moment later he had resumed his pacing up and down, still soliloquizing:

"For after all," he repeated, "she had some reason for coming, that's self-evident… And I'm bound to find out what it was, unless I'm to deem myself a positive fool, as stupid as an owl."

But Juve need not have passed so severe a judgment on himself. As for the twentieth time, perhaps, he was making the passage from a shabby sofa to the window, he stopped dead, his brow furrowed, lost in deep, absorbing thought.

"Oh, oh!" he growled. "Suppose it was…" And there he stopped, for now the police officer's face was clearing under stress of a new thought that filled him to all appearance with intense satisfaction.

"Well," he muttered again, "unless I'm much mistaken, it's a grand, a very grand discovery—an amazing, a wonderful discovery," and for a moment he stood stock-still, his breath coming in gasps, his eyes staring, like one in a trance. The he resumed:

"And I am not mistaken. I cannot be mistaken… Yes, it's that, and nothing else… I know now why Lady Beltham came to see me… I know now," and rubbing his hands in triumphant delight, he concluded:

"And upon my word, this proves Fandor an idiot—a downright idiot! Oh, but I'll give him a fine dressing-down when he deigns to come back… By God! the thing is obvious. How the devil came I not to think of it sooner?"

Juve said no more, but with the very utmost pains fell to a task—a very odd one for a man who never paid much heed to the elegance of his appearance. Fetching his round felt, he proceeded to brush it up with the most loving care.

11. The Tempter

Juve had never been a dandy, but this morning he was evidently bent on making the most of himself. After a painstaking toilet, he went out and, visiting a barber's, had himself shaved, then into a haberdasher's where he selected a pair of gloves with all the careful deliberation of a young blood.

"There!" he ejaculated as he left the shop, hat brushed, a clean chin, a pair of gloves, "I think I can present myself with everything in my favor… But will he know me, I wonder. He must have aged a tidy bit—and naturally I've followed his example."

At the moment Juve was in the Strand. He noticed a tea shop, went in and ordered a cup of coffee, and then he buried himself in the perusal of the books of reference he had asked the waitress to bring. Reading English imperfectly, he found it difficult to make out the information contained in the different directories and wasted a good deal of time. He was in no hurry, however, that was plain, for after paying for his coffee and copying an address in his notebook, he strolled off at a leisurely pace, a cigarette between his lips, like a man who is killing time so as not to arrive at an inconvenient hour at his destination. As he went the police officer was talking to himself again.

"In France," he muttered, "the thing would offer no difficulty at all… Of course, it is entirely illegal, liable to all sorts of pains and penalties, capable of bringing down on your head the worst troubles, but it is fascinating to the last degree. A couple of words would be enough to attract our man… Here, on the contrary, I'm bound to admit I run but a small chance of overpersuading my friend. The English character is more serious, more calculating, colder—in a word, saner—and they're not very sane the proposals I'm going to make."

Indeed, Juve seemed by no means convinced he was not

running great risk of a failure.

"Yes," he went on, "that's all quite true. But it is no less true that for a man of his sort the affair will be extremely tempting. The great thing is for me to put it to him in a good light, that I prove myself a tempter there is no resisting. Bah! if only I put my heart and soul into the job!"

Reaching this point in his reflections, the police officer looked at his watch and nodded his head with an air of satisfaction.

"Half-past ten," he observed. "Well, that's all right; I can call now without seeming a 'bounder'... If only he's at home, by-the-by"; and five minutes later he was ringing a peal at the door of a little house of cozy but unpretentious appearance standing in a quiet suburban street. His hand was trembling as he pulled the bell, and a sigh of relief escaped him the moment a servant appeared at the door.

"You wish, sir?" asked the man.

"To see your master."

"Excuse me, sir, but my master is away."

"Evidently!" growled the detective. "But tell him—"

"You don't understand, sir," returned the domestic. "I told you he was away—traveling."

"Yes, yes! But that ought not to prevent my seeing him."

"You're fond of your little joke, sir, I see. Good day, sir!" And the man was on the point of shutting the door in the visitor's face, had not Juve, anticipating the action, thrust the toe of his boot between the two folds of the door.

"You're over quick!" he protested. "At least let me tell you my name."

"It's no good. My master is not here."

"I am Juve... Juve, do you hear?... Detective Juve! It's out of the question Detective Shepard isn't in for me."

Juve's persistence, in fact, was quite justified. He was well aware—for had he not many a time give the like orders to his own old servant Jean?—how police officers always have the same answer given to casual callers—to wit, that they are abroad traveling. It is a mere matter of prudence, the only means they possess to avoid finding themselves face to face with undesirable visitors.

But was his name going to break down the barrier? It seemed so, for now he caught a gleam of intelligence flash in the fellow's eyes, and his confidence revived.

"Well," he said, "is your master come back from his travels now?"

"I… I… I don't know. I'll go and see."

"That's right… And come back quickly… Tell Mr. Shepard it's a matter of grave importance—and that I wish to recall myself to his memory."

While the domestic, impressed by the name of Juve—a name as famous, or almost as famous, in England as in France—was making up his mind to go and inform his master—who, of course, was at home all the time—it was a host of old a exciting memories that filled the police officer's mind.

This man Shepard he had known some years previously, and that in the course of one of the most terrible investigation he had ever undertaken against Fantômas. At the time Shepard was one of the famous Council of Ten, which constitutes, as is well known, a sort of committee of the ten ablest detectives in England.

In those days the two had been in cordial sympathy one with the other. Juve had qualities he owed to his French birth; Shepard had others due to his English origin. The two were complementary and mutually helpful rivals in skill and courage.

Was it to no purpose, then, he proposed to appeal to this old-time friendship? Shepard, in fact, was living in retirement. A happy accident had enabled him to render an important service to a big bank in the Strand, and he was now a rich man. Would he, under these circumstances, be willing to enter upon a fresh adventure as the result of which there was little or nothing to hope for save the formidable risk of incurring Fantômas vengeance?

"Nay!" thought Juve. "Once a man has tasted the excitements of police work, he loves the profession for its own sake. Old soldiers are agog for battle when they hear the guns. No,

Shepard cannot but be stirred by what I am going to say." And so it was; the servant was coming back again at a run.

"Mr. Shepard begs you to come upstairs, sir. He says he would have been very vexed to have missed seeing you… I will ask you to follow me."

"I desire nothing better, my man," and in another two minutes Juve, his face beaming with satisfaction, entered a study of imposing dimensions.

Then he stopped dead in utter amazement. At the far end of the room, behind a great writing desk, his legs wrapped in a rug, a black skullcap on his head, spectacles on nose, sat a man who, bending feebly forward and extending a trembling hand, greeted his visitor in a shaking voice:

"Good day, Juve! Good day! Do come in!… You find me greatly changed, eh?"

And in fact Juve's face had paled with sympathetic emotion. Could Shepard, whom he had last seen a few years before a sturdy and robust figure of a man, vigorous and muscular, have changed into this little old man who seemed hardly able to speak above a whisper?

"Oh no!" he stammered. "Not at all! not at all!"

"You're very kind, Juve. But your face speaks for you… Yes, I'm an old man now… Take the armchair there… Your hand, my dear fellow… And to what, tell me, do I owe the pleasure of your visit? Business, you said?"

"Yes, serious business, my old colleague!… But I don't know…"

"If I could be of use to you? Well, do you see, I'm not one of the men to whom they make bones about telling the truth."

"No doubt! no doubt!… Well, I was going to ask you to accompany me on a perilous enterprise."

"I'm sorry for you."

"I was going to do this because I don't know where Fandor is… and because you are the only man except him I can trust…"

"It's a question of Fantômas, then?"

"Of Fantômas, yes! In two words, it's a question of tracking him down at his own house… Oh, well, you're not in a condition to go with me… But you may be able to put me in touch with one of the present members of the Ten. You can facilitate matters… I'm going to tell you my story."

"Very good, my dear sir."

Without further hesitation, in a few plain but precise sentences, with the clearness of statement that was characteristic of the man, he put Shepard is possession of the late series of events that had occurred since his arrival in London.

"Not to trouble about details," he concluded rapidly, "there remain two important facts: firstly, I have discovered one of Fantômas' haunts and have made my way into it; secondly, I have had a visit from Lady Beltham, who, probably in perfect good faith, advised me to go back to France… Well, I put the two facts together, and I draw this conclusion—"

"Stop a moment," interrupted Shepard. "I quite understand. You draw this conclusion, that Fantômas finds it needful to return to the house in question, and that, dreading to encounter you there, he has decided to try to induce you to go away."

"Precisely so. It seems obvious enough," declared Juve. "Further—"

"Further," Shepard completed the other's sentence, "further, you have decided you ought to do exactly the opposite of what they would fain suggest your doing: you purpose to go back to the house and keep your eye on the villain there."

"You read my thoughts, Shepard."

"Yes. But at the same time your intentions frighten me."

"Because?"

"Because you have no right to act so."

But these very words of the English detective Juve had been expecting from the first opening of the conversation.

"Oh, I know that," he admitted. "I hold no warrant. I am not here on any official duty. In a word, if I found myself in Fantômas' presence, even if I arrested him, I should have all the trouble in the world to put the matter on a regular footing."

"That's quite certain."

"My dear Shepard, that is the very reason why I wanted to ask you to come with me."

"But, Juve, no more than you can I—"

"Yes, yes," interrupted Juve; "no more than I would you be entitled to act… But you are an Englishman; you bear a name famous in the annals of Scotland Yard… But first and foremost it is a question of ending the career of a wretch who is the scourge of all mankind… Surely that is worth the risk of doing something illegal. The law is a fine thing, but duty is more imperative than the law… If only I had found you in sound health, I should have overpersuaded you, I swear I should."

"What a tempter you are, Juve!"

"Yes, indeed, I should have tempted you."

"Still, suppose we did get into the house; suppose even we found Fantômas there… We could not arrest him!…"

"We could… hmm! We might have fetched in the policeman at the next corner; on the authority of your name he would have given every help, believe me! You realize how after that, Fantômas once in custody, matters could have been managed."

"No doubt!… But…"

"But what, Shepard?"

"When would one have to go there?"

"Why, at once I suppose; the sooner the better! If you can suggest one of your friends…"

"Oh, Monsieur Juve, it's not a business on which one sends a friend!"

"Still—"

"No, sir! Either one leaves it alone, or one goes oneself."

"But, Shepard, in the state I find you in…"

"Ah, Juve, when an old warhorse hears the trumpets blow, he gets back his strength," and Shepard sprang to his feet.

A shout of triumph rose to Juve's lips. A weak old man, this erstwhile detective? Not a bit of it! With a laugh he tore off his spectacles, his skullcap, his wig, sent his rug flying… and stood revealed, tall and slim and active, still hale and hearty, not having changed a hair!

"You'll understand," he proceeded to explain, "when my men gave me the name 'Juve,' I was suspicious; it might have been a trap… Now, my boy, I see I was mistaken, so I go back to my customary appearance… Now I shan't be having to leap at a moment's notice at the throat of some ruffian thinking himself face to face with a graybeard"—and he broke into great shouts of laughter.

"Ho, ho!" he finished, "a fine feather in my cap! I have out-witted Juve!"

"Completely! No, I never suspected the truth… Never mind, I'll give you as good back."

"Don't be so sure! I have a sharp eye of my own. But we've long been rivals, Juve, you and I… Well, you're after making me do a foolish thing. No matter! I do it with a good heart, if only to convince you we're as daring fellows in England as in France."

"My good sir, I am fully convinced of that!"

*   *   *   *   *

Two hours later, after an ample and substantial meal—it was as well to take proper precautions as the ambush might well mean a long period of waiting—Juve and the English detective stood before the house haunted by Fantômas, to which the former proposed to repeat his visit. Fortunately there was a dense fog, and the streets seemed as deserted as could be desired.

"For getting in?" questioned Shepard.

"Mere child's play… I've studied the lock already. Just an electric alarm bell to avoid, that's all"—and in a few seconds Juve had picked the lock.

On the threshold of the vestibule, however, he halted his companion. "Be careful; there are threads, silk threads, that may give us trouble—and tell us into the bargain whether Fantômas has come back again."

He advanced cautiously. Then in less than a second he checked a cry of satisfaction.

"Come back!" he announced in two words, for again the thread was stretched as before across the stairs. Only Fantômas had changed its place, now fixing it on a level with the arched openings of the balustrade, where only Juve's perspicacity would have guessed its all but invisible presence.

At his side Shepard was gesticulating in great excitement: "Oh, but that means a lot… The audacity of the fellow to dare to come back here again!"

"Bah! to come or not to come—a mere question of temperament. The odds were so heavy against his coming back that actually he was running little risk."

The two men were conversing in whispers. Both carried revolvers and were provided with handcuffs and ropes, ready for all emergencies.

"Do you hear anything?" asked Shepard.

"Not a sound!"

"Your plan of operations, Juve?… To search the house, no doubt. Give your orders! I'm all obedience."

"And I am asking your advice… No, I'm not wishing to search the house… We may, unawares, set off an alarm and betray ourselves. To my notion the best thing is for us to hide, each on a different floor. If Fantômas comes, he must pass one or the other of us… All success to that one!"

"You are right, Juve. Your prudence is a match for your courage. Where do you wish to conceal yourself? Here, at the entrance?"

"On the contrary, I prefer to leave *you* here. I shall go up to the library. I was bested there, and there I should like to enjoy my revenge—if that is agreeable to you."

"Perfectly! So do as you say. Now to fix up one thing—how are we going to hail each other in case of danger?"

"You, Shepard, hoot like an owl… I… hmm… I… I'll cry 'Peewit!'"

"Agreed! Good luck, Juve."

"Good luck, Shepard."

And the two men instinctively wrung each other's hands before separating. It might very well be that all their trouble would come to nothing; but were it not also possible for it to lead to a life-and-death struggle?

Slowly Juve mounted the stairs, listening hard, every sense strained to the utmost tension. The impressive silence that reigned in the house added to his ever-growing suspense. Was he really come to the tragic moment looked forward to for so many years—the moment when at last he could arrest the villain? Juve observed nothing suspicious on the stairs, which he mounted with a wise deliberation. The first-floor landing appeared equally peaceful. In the library, however, he noticed a faint smell of cigar that startled him.

"He has come back," he thought. "He is here! He is close at hand!"

Then he gasped as his eyes fell on the bookcase; the books had been put back in place—yet another proof that Fantômas had dared to reappear on the spot.

"Well, well!" growled the police officer, "that settles it. Let's have a look at the hiding hole."

He pulled out the heavy volumes, and barely checked a cry of horror. There, carefully laid out and neatly folded, lay the ill-omened garments—black silk tights, black hood, black gloves and shoes.

"The cast-off raiment of crime!" shuddered the police officer. "What audacity to leave it all in a hiding place Fantômas knows I am acquainted with!"

The police officer in fact felt more and more perturbed. Such manifest tokens of his return had the scoundrel left behind that this very effrontery gave cause for alarm. Had he indeed re-turned, but returned for the last time? Or even supposing the villain again risked his life on the premises, how long would it be before he reappeared?

"There's a thousand chances to one against our venture suc-ceeding," Juve confessed. "Nonetheless I did well to try. After all, I risk nothing but Shepard's making fun of me, who has already had a good laugh at my expense."

Downstairs, on the ground floor, Shepard was arguing much to the same effect.

"Juve is a first-rate detective," he was thinking. "But he is overimaginative… Fantômas has been living here. Granted! He has come back here—granted again! But it is foolishness to suppose he will ever come here again… Ah, well, I couldn't well refuse; besides, it'll be diverting to see Juve's face when we take our departure, badly baffled as ever."

The English detective had reached this point in his lucubrations, still engaged in concealing himself as well as he could behind a curtain, when suddenly he stood stock-still, his heart thumping wildly…

Immediately over his head, on the first floor, the noise of a mêlée had suddenly broken out.

"Eh, what?" he ejaculated, and felt himself turn cold with apprehension.

Piercing, terrifying, on a note of anguished horror, a cry had rung out—the call agreed upon:

"Pee… wit!… Pee… wit!"

Juve was appealing for instant help!

12. The Fate of Juve

Shepard was gallantry personified, as he had proved again and again. But so terrible, so tragic, above all so unexpected was the grievous cry, that he stood for a moment horrified, nailed to the floor, incapable of a single movement, while his heart actually stopped beating.

"God Almighty!" he groaned. "God Almighty help us!"

But this inactivity, only too natural in such a case, this paralysis of the faculties, lasted, could only last, a few seconds.

Juve's voice was still trembling on the air—subsequent inquiry was destined to verify the fact—when the erstwhile member of the famous Council of Ten was again in possession of all his presence of mind, all his accustomed energy.

Not another instant did Shepard waste. "Courage, Juve!" he shouted. "I am coming!"—and at a bound he was halfway up the stairs.

He could not tell what awaited him on the first landing, but he was surely convinced he was about to see some abominable sight there. Yet little could he foresee the appalling shock he was to experience, so incapable was his imagination of picturing the full horror of the thing.

Not a sound was to be heard. No voice was audible in the house, now restored to absolute peace and quietness. Not a soul seemed to be stirring but himself.

Shepard, however, saw instantly what direction to take. No sooner, in fact, had he reached the landing than he caught sight of a pocket torch, Juve's electric torch, lying on the floor. It was burning and its light revealed a neighboring room. Into this room he dashed, revolver in hand, shouting:

"Juve, Juve! I am here! Where are you?"

No one answered, and at the first glance he received the impression that the library was empty and unoccupied. But at that moment, as he stood hesitating on the threshold, ready to turn back and go elsewhere, a hoarse whisper, a faint sound of breathing, panting and half stifled, met his ear.

Then he saw clearly. In one corner of the room, a dark corner to which the light of the torch barely penetrated, a man lay huddled on the ground, both hands pressing on the boards, whose head swayed slowly from side to side with an unceasing continuous movement, as though he were struck with madness.

A man? Nay, rather a nightmare creature, a fantastic, incredible figure inspiring a horror beyond belief, an ineffable terror. This strange being was clad in black from head to foot. It wore a hood whose flying folds showed only through holes in the stuff the flash of two fierce, haggard eyes. A suit of black silk tights was drawn closely over the stalwart frame; gloves and shoes of black enhanced the grimness of the horrid costume.

"Fantômas! Fantômas!" yelled Shepard, and hurled himself at the man…

Alone as he was in this house where accomplices of the Lord of Terror might at any moment appear, Shepard gave proof of unparalleled bravery. Nor was his courage without its reward. The brigand offered no resistance; as his assailant fell on him, he rolled over on the ground.

"Captured! Captured!" cried Shepard again. "Juve, he is taken!"

But no answer came; the silence was unbroken. Yet a prisoner he was, no doubt of that! Quick and adroit, as all English police officers are, Shepard had already drawn a pair of handcuffs from his pocket and, clapping them on the man's wrists, had secured his arms behind his back.

"Juve! Juve!" he shouted again, and persisting in his task, he lashed the villain's ankles together and wound a stout rope round his body.

Yes, this time it was victory indeed—a sure and certain victory. Fantômas was caught, vanquished, brought to bay at last!

Then Shepard rose to his feet again. He was one of those men who think quickly and are coolheaded in the worst emergencies. He remembered his colleague.

"Juve! Juve!" he called again, for a frantic dread was again growing upon him. Juve gave no sign of life; he never answered his shouts. Could he have fallen at Fantômas' hands? In two steps he ran back for the electric torch, which was still burning. Picking it up, he threw its faint beams all round the room. This done, he saw that the library was in perfect order. Only a chair had been overturned; no other token of a struggle was visible. But Juve, dead or alive, was not there!

"It's like to drive one mad!" groaned Shepard. "Yet he can't have vanished!"

He looked to make sure his prisoner was quite helpless, though really this precaution was unnecessary. Bound as he was, his wrists handcuffed, he could not possibly escape, even if he had not been in the lamentable state he was.

"So much the worse for him!" Shepard observed. "I've tied him up; now I'm off to find Juve. He cried for my help and he must need it."

Shepard stepped up to the window and made sure the bars were firm. Then he went to the door, shut it and tested the lock.

"Right!" he growled again. "This time he's tied up good and tight"—and he left the room, double locking the door and putting the key in his pocket.

Be sure his heart was beating joyously in his bosom. Yet at the same time the satisfaction he experienced at his triumph over the greatest criminal of all time was marred by the disquieting, agonized thought: "Where was Juve?" How came it that, after uttering that cry for help that still rang in his ears, he had disappeared?

"I am the more at a loss to understand," Shepard confessed, "as Fantômas is evidently wounded. It follows Juve was the victor, yet there are next to no traces of a fight."

As he spoke he was searching the other rooms, which Juve on his first visit had also examined, but they were in the same undisturbed state, nor was there a vestige of Juve to be discovered.

"Enough to make one bang one's head against a wall!"

groaned Shepard, coming to a halt in the middle of the garret. And a sudden thought occurred to him that struck his heart with a spasm of despair.

"There were several of them, perhaps? An accomplice has made off dragging Juve with him!… But, if so, how was it he abandoned Fantômas to his fate?"

And the alarming idea took on substance in his mind:

"The library must comprise a trap… The confederate intended to return. He did not know I was there… Good God! Perhaps he has come back while I've been up here!"

This sudden fear was, in fact, very natural. If Juve had been spirited away from the room—and it seemed certain he had been—it followed that the library communicated with a secret passage. How fail to surmise that by this secret passage they had returned for Fantômas, who had been left in the hands of the police?

"I shall find nobody there now," faltered Shepard, and he felt a cold sweat break out on his forehead. If Juve had disappeared, if Fantômas after his capture had likewise been carried away, this meant utter, heartbreaking failure, a defeat that would cost Juve his life without winning any result.

Thereupon the detective abandoned his search. The mere notion that possibly his prisoner had disappeared as mysteriously as Juve set him trembling with terror. In two bounds he was down the stairs again. Then, as he opened the locked door, behind which Fantômas ought to be lying, he thought:

"He is gone! I'll take my oath he's gone! I ought never to have left him. It's my fault he's no longer there—and he *is* no longer there!"

He kicked the door violently open—and checked a wild cry. Fantômas had not moved, stretched on the carpet, lying perfectly still, he appeared to be unconscious or lifeless.

"So now?" Shepard gasped in amazement. Finding Fantômas on the same spot, positively his prisoner still, he deemed even more incomprehensible than Juve's disappearance. Time was passing and every minute made the situation more critical.

"What to do?" gasped Shepard. "Yet Juve *must* be found! He

cried to me for help… Perhaps they have killed him whilst I stood hesitating."

The detective came to a quick decision, the only one that was in fact feasible. He left the room again, taking care to shut the door afresh and pocket the key.

"I will hurry to the nearest police station," he made up his mind. "I will bring ten men with me; we'll pull down the house if needs be, but I am determined to find out if there is a secret passage… And then we'll remove Fantômas…" and he dashed away, running like one demented, after banging the house door behind him.

Now it was not ten seconds after Shepard had left the house before one of the mirrors in the library turned on itself, just as a door pivots on its hinges. Through the opening thus made a man issued, a man of gigantic stature, who seemed anything but easy in his mind. The newcomer cast a look about the room, then with a start of amazement caught sight of Fantômas where he lay unconscious.

"My God!" he faltered. "The chief collared! Great heavens! I'm only just in time"—and springing lightly down with an agility hardly to be expected of a man of his heavy build, he landed on the ground.

"It's Juve, I wager, has done the trick," he muttered. "Oh! the cursed villain! If only I knew where he's got to!"

Then, bending over the prisoner, he called in a low voice:

"Fantômas! Fantômas, I say! Speak, master!"

But the wounded man never moved.

"Dead, eh? That *would* be a pretty go!"—and he put out a hand to feel the face under the hood.

Then an amazing thing happened—an attack so sudden, so swift and unexpected, the fellow had not a chance to defend himself.

Fantômas had sprung to his feet. While his manacles fell about him, while his handcuffs rattled to the floor, unlocked as if by magic, he had gripped the miscreant who was coming to his rescue, had hurled him to the ground, and in less than three seconds had gagged and secured him with another pair of handcuffs he had taken from his pocket.

"Now!" threatened the victor. "Now I give you fair warning… Try to say one word, and I will break your skull… You understand?"

The manacled wretch was green with fear.

"Yes, I understand, Fantômas," he whimpered.

"Call me Juve, you idiot," ordered his chief—and tearing off his hood, removing his mask, he revealed his features—and there stood Juve, grinning.

"So there!" he went on; "it is I wear your master's costume. That surprises you? Well, it only proves you to be as simple a fellow as Shepard… Ha, ha! but it makes me laugh to think of the face he will pull when he comes back… Ho, ho! he'll take you to prison, eh?… Anyway, he tricked me; I may very well pay him back in kind."

Juve was laughing gaily, as calm and unperturbed as though he were not in a house full of peril, in the middle of an adventure that promised to be fantastic in every sense of the word. The fact is the police officer never lost his head and was genuinely amused when he thought of the comedy he had just played with such rare adroitness.

No sooner inside the library than he had an intuition that somebody was lurking hidden nearby.

"I mean to have myself arrested by Shepard," he had decided instantly. "After that, when I'm tied up and seemingly incapable of making a movement, Shepard must leave me. I still remain quite still… Upon my word, if some accomplice of Fantômas is on the premises, he'll never resist the temptation of coming to kill me—if he knows I am Juve; or else to set me free—if he takes me for his master!"

Thereupon Juve had at once set to work to disguise himself with the help of Fantômas' clothes which he had discovered a few moments before. To call to Shepard had been the work of an instant. To take advantage of the short struggle with the police officer to filch his handcuffs and slip another pair into his pocket, a pair the locks of which had been faked, had offered little difficulty. Only he had found some trouble in freeing himself from the cord with which the detective had bound him. He had not foreseen this additional precaution, but had nevertheless succeeded in undoing the knot Shepard had made, this luckily being underneath him, behind his back.

"There!" resumed Juve, delighted by his exploit and stretching his stiffened limbs, "that's a fine success accomplished. That accomplice fellow will be able to gas to some purpose. So there's a passage by way of the mirror; but no, a mere hiding hole… A pity, for I should have loved to explore a bit of a subterranean passage…" Then he broke off to exclaim:

"Ah, here's Shepard coming back! Now for some fun!"

Laughing to himself, Juve moved to the door. A big voice now made itself heard, speaking in a tone of great respect.

"Certainly, Mr. Shepard, I will take five men to remove the prisoner. Oh! never fear, he's not going to slip through my fingers… You'll keep the other ten here to search the house and hunt for poor Mr. Juve…"

"The Chief Inspector!" thought Juve. "Oh God! ten men to hunt for me! Capital! They think a lot of me!"

The key turned in the lock. Shepard was evidently in a hurry; his high state of agitation was manifest.

"I'll take post before the door," thought Juve, "and greet him affably… Ho, ho! if Fandor was here he'd be highly diverted…"

Then the door opened—opened briskly.

"Oh!" was all Juve found to say. It was not Shepard! The man who walked in, his face masked by a black hood, identical with the one Juve had just snatched off, wore black silk tights, black gloves, black shoes.

Oh—that grim figure, the same he had copied himself a few moments previously—Juve had no need to look twice to recognize it.

"Fantômas!" he cried.

"Fantômas, who has no love for such as try to play his part," retorted the spectral figure, and the brief words had a ring of blood-curdling tragedy—one of those tragedies that last one second to be remembered with horror for a lifetime. Juve sprang forward—and his arms closed on empty air. With marvelous agility Fantômas had dodged to one side. He mocked:

"Juve, have a care! You can't ever hope to capture me; now come!" and in two steps he was across the room. He held a knife in his hand, while Juve leveled his revolver.

"Hands up!" the police officer challenged.

"Never!"

"Am I to fire?"

"Fire away, Juve!"

But the detective pressed the trigger in vain; the charge had been withdrawn.

"My good man," explained Fantômas, "you may be sure I didn't let you enter my house without taking precautions…"

He stopped, for Juve had sprung at him again—only to stumble over a chair Fantômas had pitched between his feet.

"Have done!" ordered the brigand. "First to settle accounts. My idiot of a lieutenant has let himself be taken. I have no use for clumsy fellows!"

Hurled with unerring aim that showed an astonishing dexterity Fantômas' dagger whistled through the air, and buried itself to the hilt in the heart of Juve's prisoner.

"Murderer!" screamed Juve. "But you shall pay the forfeit of your crime!"

"I don't believe it."

"But I do. I have you in my power."

"No!"

Juve had darted to the door. He shut it and turned the key. He thought for certain he was sure in this way of hindering his enemy's escape.

"Juve, you are a fool," scoffed the brigand.

"Fantômas, surrender!"

"Never! I have said so already."

The two men stood facing one another, each at one extremity of the room, keenly on the alert, watching every movement of his adversary.

"You will know me again, Juve?" scoffed Fantômas.

"Coward! You keep your face hidden."

"You're not clapping your handcuffs on me, Juve?"

Scorning to reply, for the third time the police officer sprang forward.

But positively it seemed as though Fantômas had foreseen the attack. At the very instant Juve was upon him, Fantômas leapt, both feet together, on to the great writing desk that stood in a corner of the library.

Juve could not check an involuntary cry of rage and disappointment.

Lo! the top of the desk had pivoted on itself, suddenly swinging round, and, disappearing as if through a trapdoor, Fantômas had vanished before the detective's very eyes.

"Goodbye!" he shouted in tones of ironical courtesy.

But this cry of triumph was nevertheless premature.

Fantômas had been quick-footed, but Juve had been quicker still. Barely had the trapdoor closed before the police officer, copying the other's maneuver, had likewise leapt into the yawning cavity.

*   *   *   *   *

It was one of those dreadful, appalling moments when a man gives his life to the task he has chosen, when nothing else is of any account, when self-sacrifice is absolute, and one thought, high and clear, alone survives, the thought of the end to be attained. All heroes, all such as are the glory of the human race, have known these times of great-hearted courage. Juve had known many such. Plunging into this abyss in pursuit of his flying foe, he was surely sacrificing his life of his own free will.

Into what new peril was this leap in the dark to lead him? Into what fresh snare was he to fall headlong? Starting on a road that was doubtless familiar to the Lord of Terror, while he knew none of its intricacies, he was surely at the villain's mercy.

But Juve never counted the cost. Steadfast in pursuit as the hound that tracks down the game the sportsman drives from covert, he ever went straight to the mark, braving all obstacles, ready to confront every danger.

Hardly had he dropped through the trapdoor ere he experienced a startling surprise. The writing desk artfully contrived to conceal this hidden exit opened on a sort of toboggan slide that appeared to plunge deep into the earth, not unlike those contrivances one sees in big fashion shops serving to convey parcels and packages rapidly to the delivery counters in the basement. The slope was no less rapid, all but vertical in fact, and Juve had no time to examine it in detail for the good reason that he was instantly entrapped on the slippery surface and shot downwards at top speed.

"The devil!" was all he had time to ejaculate before next instant a cry of satisfaction escaped him. The slide had made a bend, revealing a further length beyond. In full view, five yards perhaps ahead of him, he beheld Fantômas, aslide like himself, flat on his back, his whole body rigid, carried down passively in the same giddy descent.

"Halloa! so we're bound for the infernal regions, are we?" thought the police officer.

But at the very same moment he was chuckling at his own joke, a fine token of his perfect coolness, he suddenly gave a yell of rage. Yes, truly Fantômas was a genius among criminals. Even in his most audacious enterprises he never forgot a carefully calculated prudence that left nothing to mere chance. True, when he had contrived this sort of toboggan slide he must have felt certain of eluding all pursuit, sure of being the only one to dare the risk of this extraordinary way of escape. Yet nonetheless he had remembered that possibly some other daring individual might be tempted to dash after him down the perilous slope, and had actually so arranged things as to assure a sure and certain triumph over any who should be rash enough to pursue him to this last extremity.

Pursuer and pursued were plunging downward at the same giddy pace, when suddenly, unexpectedly, Fantômas threw up his arms with outstretched hands. In an instant, before Juve could gather what the movement signified, the chase was at end and the villain saved…

Part way down, at a point Fantômas knew, but which Juve of course could not guess, the former had fixed a strong iron bar, a sort of trapeze in fact, spanning the passage from one wall to the other of the toboggan slide.

Result, the one stopped dead in mid-career, the other, not foreseeing this simple acrobatic feat, came hurtling like a bombshell up to where Fantômas hung suspended by his hands, and shot past, sliding by under his lifted body, and continued his giddy descent with ever-increasing speed.

"Goodbye, Juve!" mocked Fantômas—and only a smothered cry, a scream of rage and despair, answered him.

Alas! it was easy for him to conjecture that on a level with the bar there must be in the wall a concealed door through which Fantômas would be free to escape and in all probability to reach the cellar of some adjacent house.

But into what abyss was *he* to fall. Into what depths was he being carried by this slide whose slope was so precipitate he could do nothing to check his fall or stop his giddy descent?

"Done for!" thought the unhappy man. "Overmastered! Beaten, shamefully beaten!"

Then the ground seemed to fail beneath him altogether, and he was conscious of falling—falling into a void, a bottomless pit. His last thought was for his beloved comrade.

"Fandor! Fandor! Ah, I shall never see you more! Avenge me! Avenge me!"

Another second that seemed an eternity at once brief and infinitely long, and Juve dashed to earth with a shock to bruise his whole frame, to break every bone in his body.

Yet, strange to say, such was his energy, such the lucidity of his mind, that he was fully conscious of the seriousness of his fall.

"No luck!" he thought. "No. I am not killed!"

And again he considered, yielding to a growing torpor of the senses.

"Yes, it is surely an *oubliette*… I am to die of slow hunger… and cold… and exhaustion…"—and he lost consciousness altogether.

As a matter of fact, he had been picked up, carried off and tended. His wounds had been bandaged and two dislocations set that threatened to rob him of the use of a limb... But he knew nothing of this.

What length of time actually elapsed between the moment of his fall and that of his regaining consciousness? Was it a day, a week, a month—or only an hour, perhaps?

At first he sought no answer to the question. Life dawned again in a mist of vague uncertainty. He realized he was not dead, but the knowledge remained at first indefinite, and he felt a sort of fear to make it more precise by any mental effort. He was no longer in pain. He lay stretched on a cushioned couch, and was telling himself:

"If I move, I shall wake up altogether and find myself back again in an atrocious plight. No, not worth the trouble! Better stay asleep!"

It was, in a word, the vague, restful feeling of a man still half asleep when he is still dreaming, partly aware it is a dream he finds pleasant and fears to interrupt.

But now Juve was muttering:

"Strange—why, someone seems to be speaking to me?"

He caught a distant murmur, a muffled, indistinct sound of words whispered rather than clearly articulated—something in his dream no doubt! The voice he half heard was faltering:

"Juve? Juve? Are you still asleep? Juve, my good Juve, my dear Juve, don't you hear me!"

"Why, yes!" the police officer said at last. "It's Fandor speaking to me... Fandor is at my bedside..."

But he knew very well it was only a dream, and that Fandor was not there, and could not be there. Very curious this state of semi-consciousness—these hallucinations that fevered brains experience and which come to an end only too soon to give place to reality, always so disappointing in comparison with the visions of dreamland!

Suddenly memory came back to the detective.

"The slide! My fall!" he stammered. "Fantômas!"

But he had hardly said the words, or tried to say them, when he was startled by a fresh surprise.

But no, he was not asleep! It was no dream, this voice, half stifled by emotion, that addressed him. No, there was no doubt of it—someone *was* speaking to him… asking if he were in pain… It was Fandor; no possibility of mistaking the tones of the young man's voice.

Then, awake at last, with a violent effort of will, Juve opened his eyes. But it was at the very moment he was coming to after a lengthy period of coma, which soporifics had further prolonged, and even now he thought himself in a dream.

"I am going mad!" he faltered in a feeble voice, and he looked about him on all sides.

Yes, he saw, but what he saw so far exceeded the limits of possibility that he doubted the testimony of his own eyes. He was in the middle of a structure, as extraordinary as it was terrifying; bars of iron, strong, thick, solidly bolted together, formed underneath him, underneath the mattress on which he lay, a sort of gridiron. This rose vertically before him and behind him, to right of him and to left. There was but one word to describe such a thing; yes, it had a name—it was a cage and nothing else.

"I… am… in a cage!" groaned Juve, and he broke into a discordant laugh—a laugh that had a ring of insanity in it.

"Caged!" he groaned again. "I am caged! Fantômas has clapped me in a cage!"

It was a wailing cry, at once ridiculous and heartrending, at once tragic and grotesque. Then suddenly the wretched man gave an anguished exclamation:

"Fandor! Fandor! He is caged too!…"

Impossible as the thing seemed, it was literally true, and Juve made no more delay in examining the details. The cage in which Juve was confined—similar to the iron cages wherein of old King Louis XI was wont to imprison such of his courtiers as had lost his favor—stood in a chamber of some size, feebly illuminated by a single electric lamp of a red color.

By the beam of the dull ruddy light thrown by this lamp Juve could quite well make out that another cage, in every respect like his own, was placed a short distance away; and in this cage was Fandor, standing upright, his hand gripping the bars, his eyes fixed on his friend.

For a moment, just recovered from such a state of prostration, Juve was still so heavy-witted that he realized nothing else. But only a few seconds elapsed before he caught sounds to which his condition of terror had at first made him deaf. Yes, it was really Fandor in the cage yonder, and his comrade was speaking to him, beseeching him to answer.

"Juve," the young man was appealing to him, "for pity's sake, give me some sign that you hear me, that you understand what I say! Juve! Juve! I am frightened. You are not ill, Juve? You are not…"

The police officer had to call up all his determination and energy to find strength to answer his friend. He did reply, however, completing the sentence Fandor had not dared to finish.

"No," he said slowly and painfully. "No, you need have no fear. I am not mad!"

"Juve, you are only now awaking!… Where have you come from? What has happened to you? You have been here since this morning… It is four days Fantômas has held *me* prisoner."

"Fantômas?"

"Why, yes! Fantômas, Juve! We are caged by Fantômas' orders. Ah, my dear old friend, pull yourself together. You're never going to afford the scoundrel the pleasure of seeing you so dejected?"

Instinctively, at a venture, Fandor had hit on the argument of all others best fitted to bring back Juve to the full possession of his faculties.

"You say well, Fandor," began the police officer. "You are right…"

He got to his feet, took three or four deep breaths to free his lungs of a deadly feeling of oppression, then in a moment thoroughly awakened:

"By God! Yes, Fandor, you are right. We are caged, eh? But is that any reason for behaving like imbeciles?"—and this time the laugh that rose to the detective's lips was a natural one—a laugh that rang out like a defiance.

"Still, it's mighty queer," he confessed. "I could not awake…
Yes, just that; I simply could not rouse myself."

"But now, Juve?"

"Oh, now I am my own man again."

"How did Fantômas capture you?"

"I ask your pardon, Fandor, but don't ask about me; my adventures can wait… Rather tell me how you, too, come to be a prisoner. Tell me what you know as to our probable fate. We are condemned to die of hunger and thirst, no doubt! We are abandoned to perish here!"

"Why, no! Nothing of the sort! Jailers come regularly to bring me food to eat."

"And water to drink?"

"Yes, to be sure!"

"And you have seen Fantômas?"

"Yes, yesterday… He informed me you were doing better… I did not know you were in his hands… Imagine my feelings when I saw you—I who was waiting for you to come and rescue me!"

"Hmm, better wait for someone else to do that, Fandor! I fear I might not be quite in a condition today to undertake the job."

"Oh, Juve, my dear old Juve! How happy it makes me to see you."

"Indeed? For my part, I should be happier not to see you, Fandor."

"Capital! You know very well what I meant."

"Doubtless. But I don't know how *you* come to be here."

"No matter for that, Juve. It's simply yet another proof that I'm a noodle."

"Lord, how you miscall yourself!… Anyhow, speak out and tell me, noodle that you are!"

Juve had in truth recovered all his accustomed powers of mind, as he showed conclusively by the close attention with which he now listened to Fandor's account of his adventures at Le Havre and how he had fallen into Fantômas' hands.

"You see," concluded the journalist, "Fantômas' boat was

only a fishing boat to look at. In reality it was a well-found, swift pleasure craft, fitted with a superb motor. In her Fantômas found no sort of difficulty in crossing the Channel and landing us, Lady Beltham and myself, in England."

"And then?"

"Upon my word, Juve, that's about all there is to it. At the landing place three cars were waiting. Lady Beltham went off in a limousine, Fantômas leapt into a racing car, I had the privilege of riding in a lorry into which they pitched me underneath a great heap of vegetables—"

"And they drove you here?"

"Here, yes!… Or at least into some sort of cellar into which I was shoved through a low door without a notion what was on the other side of it… As you can guess, Juve, it was the cage all ready for me. The door shut to behind me, and there I was a prisoner…"

"And after that?"

"After that?… Well, I'm here still."

"And Fantômas tortured you?"

"No, he hasn't yet…"

"Yes, you're right, my lad; we shan't go far wrong in waiting for such a thing."

"I quite think so, Juve… Perhaps he was spying on you, eh?"

"Yes, very likely."

For the moment the police officer was thinking things over, his eyes fixed on the ground.

The episode in Fantômas' house which had ended with his slide and fall had taken place on the evening of the day after Lady Beltham's visit. It was therefore evident Fantômas had arrived there directly after landing from the vessel that brought him to England. Now was this not proof positive that he had actually made use of that lady to suggest to the detective the idea of going back to the house?

"I guessed as much," thought Juve. "Murderer as he is, Fantômas is a devilish clever fellow too."

Then he looked up and called, "Fandor!"

"Yes, Juve?"

"You're not armed, of course?"

"Haven't so much as a pin on me."

"A pity, that! We might have made an end of it…"

"Yes, Juve, I'd thought of that… But there, after all, we've been in worse holes before now."

"Oh, no!" protested Juve, "never! This time we are at the end of our tether…"

But he left his sentence unfinished.

A sudden gleam had shone out from great lamps hitherto unlighted, while at the same moment the sound of approaching footsteps made itself heard.

"Gentlemen, my respects to you!" came a grave voice.

The police officer looked round with a groan.

"Fantômas! It is Fantômas!"

The Genius of Crime had just entered the cellar.

13. An Appalling Alternative

Instantly the detective had recognized the Lord of Terror, the Arch-Criminal, the Monster who no more deserved to be counted among men, so far had his notorious cruelties set him apart from the rest of mankind.

Yet for the moment Fantômas bore no resemblance to himself. Gone was the ill-omened uniform he chose to wear as if to make himself akin to black night each time he was bent on committing a crime; gone the black hood, the tight-fitting black silk suit, the black gloves and black shoes, that rendered him impossible to recognize. Instead he bore all the aspect of a perfect man of the world. In frock coat well cut and worn with ease—that garment that makes so many poor devils of the inferior classes ridiculous—with a well-fitting white waistcoat making a bright contrast with the broadcloth, Fantômas might have been taken for the most elegant of club men, a personage not out of place in any drawing room, had he not still worn over his face the indispensable addition to his costume that always hid his features whenever he chose to disguise himself—to wit, a mask of black velvet.

Another step or two across the cellar, now brilliantly illumi-nated, and he repeated his greeting:

"Gentlemen, all my best wishes to you! I trust my coming does not annoy you."

But Juve interrupted brutally:

"Have done, Fantômas! Doubtless you have come to kill us. Kill us then, and make an end of it. Try to behave like a gentle-man—and not like a foul brigand, as you usually do!"

"My dear Juve, I cannot say you are polite."

"If you think, Fantômas, to divert yourself at our expense, I warn you you are making a mistake. Neither Fandor nor I will answer you; no, not even listen to you."

"Oh, indeed? On the contrary, I am convinced that Fandor will hear me. I have to speak to him of someone he holds dear."

The words put Juve beside himself. For all the resolve he had adopted to affect complete indifference to whatsoever the Torturer might say, he wheeled about on his heels and, turning to Fandor:

"My dear lad," he besought him, "shut your ears. This scoundrel wants to talk to you about Helene—"

"Nay, Juve, you are entirely wrong!" broke in Fantômas. "There is no question here of my daughter…" And he laughed a while, then proceeded to explain:

"It is *you* are in question. Has not Fandor informed you of what is afoot?"

Juve's eyes questioned his friend, or rather sought in vain to question him, for the young man had seated himself on his mattress and buried his face in his hands, avoiding the other's eyes.

"No," replied Juve quietly. "Fandor has not told me."

"Well, well! I should have thought he would. He is such a talker—"

"Bah! He must have deemed the matter of no importance."

"You are first-rate, Juve, at a gibe. Upon my word, you show astonishing coolness. Oh, what an admirable lieutenant you would have been in my band!"

"Really, Fantômas? Indeed, I have often told myself as much—what a capital headsman's mate you would have made. You have all the qualifications."

"Thanks, Juve. One for you! You have hurt my feelings…" And the wretch gave a short laugh, then continued:

"But a truce to nonsense!… I had told Fandor I would kill *you* first… before his eyes… very slowly…"

"Coward!" snarled the police officer.

"Not at all! An act of good nature, rather, on my part. A man of your age would have taught your young friend to die becomingly…"

"You are the stronger, Fantômas; do as you will with us. I can answer for Fandor as for myself. He will not show the white feather."

"Yes, quite likely. You are both of you exceptional beings. There, you see I compliment you—the condemned man's last cigarette! I recognize your merits for the last time—"

"No need for that, Fantômas. You are mad; one does not heed what a madman says."

"You repeat yourself, Juve. And you are listening to me all the time… However, to go on. Well, that is what I meant to do; but I have changed my mind. I have decided to do the opposite—to kill Fandor before your eyes."

"One day, Fantômas, you will suffer—on the scaffold. Remember that!"

"Not I! I never think of any such thing. I am not of the sort they execute. My name is neither Juve nor Fandor!"

The Monster laughed again, then resumed, calmer and more sarcastic than ever:

"We were saying how I meant to kill Fandor first… Hmm! Just fancy now, I have changed my mind again after mature reflection. Yes, I have changed my mind because I have thought of something better still, you may be sure of that…"

"Better or worse, Fantômas?"

"That depends on the point of view. Worse for you! Better for me! But it will come to the same thing… Anyway, I have had a grand idea. You're not curious to hear it, Juve?"

"I am above any threats of yours."

"Things like that are said; they are not really thought. And you, Fandor?"

"I am ready, Fantômas; I know you are capable of anything."

"My dear Fandor, that's the first pleasant word you've spoken to me!"

"I meant, Fantômas, to insult you… I meant—"

"Enough! I forgive you, Fandor. Doesn't one always forgive the dying?… Well, I was telling you I had found a better way than to have you killed. You understand?—killed by someone I hate now as heartily as you love that same person… Ho, ho! you are curious to hear? Come, now, I am going to help you guess the riddle."

The wretch took a silver case from his pocket, chose a cigar at his leisure, cut the end and lit it; he puffed at it two or three times, then in the same deep, expressionless tone continued:

"I was bound, you understand, to avenge myself on you and on the one you love and I now hate. Upon my word, to condemn that person to kill you was a mighty pretty plan. But how force a decision... So I have made a sacrifice. You can't guess what it is?"

Fantômas appeared to wait a minute or two for an answer, which neither Juve nor Fandor vouchsafed. Well he knew, the cruel villain, how to torment the victims he had resolved to execute. Well he knew how to prolong the horrid pangs of anguish and suspense.

"Strange," resumed the Lord of Terror, "how dull you both are at guessing. Here are two childish problems neither of you can solve. Well, no matter! No doubt you are afraid, and fear impedes your powers of mind."

"You coward! You coward!" ejaculated Fandor.

"Not I! I am generosity itself... Judge of it yourselves. I was telling you I had made a sacrifice, in order to induce the person you will see directly to murder you... This is the sacrifice: I shall ask the person in question to kill only one of you. Why, yes, only one of you is to perish—and I shall send the murderer away with the other, the one she has spared... You quite understand me? Only one of you two is to die—but to die by her hand... The other will depart with her, a free man. What say you to that?"

With one voice, both together, Juve and Fandor besought their tormentor:

"I! I! It is I who must be killed, Fantômas!"

But the brigand forced a laugh.

"Oh, but I beg you," he protested with sudden emphasis. "I must ask *you* to do *me* a favor... The matter is now no concern of mine; it is to the person I refer to you must address your prayers. She has entire freedom of choice. She will spare whichever of you two she loves best... Nay, even if she chose to kill both of you... But no! I am convinced she will not... I cannot tell if the one she lets live will still continue to love her. You see, she will have killed his friend… But there, again, that is no concern of mine. I am going to have her brought into your presence. She will be at perfect liberty to act. I shall have nothing to do with the matter; I shall not be here, in fact… But mark that I shall take measures to compel her to choose. Look you, from the moment she comes, she will be a prisoner here. Neither you two nor she will be given anything to eat or drink. If then she refused to make a choice it would mean suicide for her and murder into the bargain, for all three of you would have to die… Now is not my little scheme a diverting one? You will not answer? Well, no matter. Goodbye! You force me to cut short a highly interesting conversation… Goodbye, gentlemen—or rather goodbye to one of you—but I cannot say which."

Fantômas gave a little patronizing wave of the hand and turned to go. But suddenly coming back:

"By-the-by," he added, "there is one thing I have not told you—a fact you ought to know. I would warn you of this: the person who is to kill you is Helene—Helene, whom Fandor will never marry, whether because she will have killed him to save Juve's life, or because she will have become hateful in his eyes by preserving his life at the cost of slaying Juve. Goodbye, gentlemen—goodbye to the one, 'till we meet again' to the other!" And the wretch went off with an odious laugh.

Yes, this time in very truth Fantômas had reason to be proud of his vile scheme. Far worse than physical pain, which a brave man may endure and defy, mental agony is terrible. It rends the heart and maddens the mind; it opens abysmal depths of misery that border close on sheer insanity.

Could a more atrocious torture have been contrived to punish Juve, Fandor and Helene for having dared to defy the Arch-Criminal? Could Juve consent to live at the price of Fandor's death? Could Fandor agree to go free if his freedom were purchased by Juve's blood? Could Helene, an innocent, gentle girl, hope to escape madness when it came to choosing between these two men, one of whom she loved like an honored father while the other was dear to her as a lover?

Which was she to kill?... Fandor? But Fandor was the man she had chosen from among all other human beings to be her husband... Juve? But if she slew Juve, Fandor would hate her.

Oh, but the snare was artfully laid! The pass to which Fantômas had brought his victims was veritably an appalling one. Whichever way the unhappy creatures turned, horror faced them—fatal, inevitable—the horror of a decision before which the spirit recoils affrighted.

Hardly, indeed, had Fantômas turned his back before a grim struggle, a dreadful rivalry, began between Juve and Fandor. Both, conscious of the pressing danger, knowing how the seconds were flying with alarming rapidity, had been quick, each to out-argue the other.

"Fandor!" panted Juve. "I have something to say to you."

"I, too, Juve!" interrupted the young man. "I must speak to you—"

"No, no! I know, Fandor, what you are going to ask of me. But it is imperative I speak first. I have a right to... I am your elder... Listen to me! It is of Helene we must think—"

"Helene! Helene!" groaned Fandor. "Oh, the unhappy girl!"

"I see, of course, we must take pity on her—"

"Yes, Juve, yes! But how?"

"How deliver the poor child from this horror?... Well, that is simple enough—by dictating her choice, by convincing her she is to do what we have decided on... Both of us must be of one mind... You understand me, Fandor? She must not be left to choose. That would be too dreadful; it would drive her mad—"

"Juve, I was going to say the word. It is I she must kill!"

"No, Fandor, no!... It is *I!* It is *I!*"

"Juve, you have no right to say that—"

"Fandor, you talk beside the mark... Listen now! I will explain."

"No, no, Juve! I will not hear a word... Let me be! I am sure I am right."

"Fandor, I beg you hush... We have not a second to lose. It must, it shall be I—"

"Juve, again I tell you you have no right—"

"But you are all wrong, my lad! I am the older man, look you. You are a boy compared to me. My life is over—a little sooner or a little later—"

"But, Juve, Juve! You are the only one can carry on the struggle and one day overmaster Fantômas!"

"Fandor, I beseech you to be reasonable—I beseech you in Helene's name—"

"And *I* beseech you, Juve, in the name of all humanity, of all mankind!"

"Fandor, you are an imbecile. If I die, that only concerns myself. It is only I am struck down; but if you die, Helene is as much hurt as I… Oh, you could never wish to give Fantômas this victory into the bargain! You would never wish Helene to bewail you all her life long! You have every right to happiness. It is only right for you to live for her."

"It is senseless, Juve, infamous, what you are saying… Happiness indeed! To marry Helene… But if she had killed you, I should hate her. She would be my enemy. I should see blood upon her hands."

"No, no! The executioner is not responsible for the sentence he carries out. You will forget; love will make you forget."

"Juve, you must not say such things. You know they are not true."

"Nay, Fandor! I, it is bound to be I who die!"

"It is cowardly of you, Juve, to speak so. You have a duty to fulfill. You are Fantômas' adversary. You dead, his reign of terror will continue undisputed. *I* am not capable by myself of carrying on the battle. To choose to die is to play the part of a deserter."

"When you talk, Fandor, of sacrificing yourself, you are betraying Helene."

Then both fell silent, breathless with agitation, both realizing they would never convince one another.

"My poor Fandor!" groaned Juve.

"My dear, kind Juve!" sighed Fandor.

Standing each in his hideous cage, they extended their hand in a last greeting, an eternal farewell.

"It is all my fault," cried the journalist. "I ought never to have been so obstinate in following up Lady Beltham."

"Not at all, Fandor. It was *my* fault. I was in the wrong in choosing to make a search in Fantômas' house without calling on the English police for succor… My pride was my undoing."

"Juve! Juve! I forbid you to speak so. Neither of us was to blame. No man is ever to be blamed when he is doing his duty."

"Fandor, Helene will soon be here."

"That is true, Juve. We must have come to a decision by then."

"I beseech you, Fandor, to consent."

"Never, Juve! Never! You know it is impossible."

"Shall we draw lots, Fandor?"

"No, Juve! I refuse to accept the decision of mere chance."

Again there was a moment's silence, while a thousand thoughts coursed through their minds, a thousand phrases hovered on their lips. But they had not the heart to dispute further.

Time was passing. Before long a choice must be made between two alternatives of the most hideous sort. This they knew, and fully they realized the inflexible determination of the Monster who held them at his mercy. Priding himself on being a great-hearted bandit and observing the laws of honor—the very name of which in truth he had no right to utter—Fantômas would surely keep his word.

One of the two would leave the cellar alive; one of the two would escape a free man from the cages where they were now languishing. For Fantômas it would be one of the audacities he was proud of, when the tale was told by the survivor of the dreadful adventure. Yes, one or the other, either Juve or Fandor, would go forth from that torture chamber… But which?

"Fandor!" Juve began again, "weigh my words well. You must agree to my death, for—"

But Juve never finished his sentence. This last effort to induce Fandor to agree to a plan which in truth the young man would under no circumstances have adopted remained abortive.

A door creaked, and the two men knew that someone was

coming in; and next instant they were aware that the time was almost up and the fatal moment close at hand that would force them to a decision that must leave one of them alive and the other a corpse. Into the place where the dread choice was to be made two men had entered—doubtless a pair of Fantômas' accomplices. Both wore tied over their faces a handkerchief pierced with two eyeholes; like all the Monster's satellites, their features were unrecognizable.

They were talking together.

"Have a care!" one of the villains warned his mate, "the chair ain't heavy, but seemingly it's summat special; the Master told us not to knock it against nothin.'"

"Righto! Then don't do it. Got to be planked down between the two cages, eh?"

"Yes, and the little table too. The revolver to be dumped on the table—them's the orders."

"Nothing else to be done?"

"No, nothing! Seems it's for the girl; *she's* got to sit there… Anyways, we're to be there too. The Master's going to play off his little game before us… A fine bit o' fun by what he says."

With one accord Juve and Fandor stopped their ears in horror, refusing to hear more.

Yes, these low fellows, these confederates of Fantômas', would be ready enough to applaud when they learned their master's shocking ultimatum. As they put it, these henchmen of the Arch-Criminal, it would be "a fine bit o' fun" for folks of their kidney.

Then a worse shudder shook the two condemned men. This armchair they were bringing in, this table on which they placed a revolver well in view, it was for Helene they were arranging all this! And they stood transfixed, their eyes riveted on chair and table and revolver, and felt their reason must desert them.

Fantômas' two myrmidons, their task finished, fell back a little way, and again there was a brief pause.

Then another step was heard approaching, a faltering, stumbling footstep, the footstep of one racked with anguish, half demented with grief.

Fantômas' daughter stood before them. Helene had entered the dreadful place.

14. Juve Makes His Choice

Such, however, was the horror involved in the dreadful predicament that confronted the three actors in this cruel scene that at first neither Juve nor Fandor dared look at the unhappy girl, while she herself averted her eyes from their faces.

What agony of mind was that of the gallant young man as he felt growing within him a feeling of hatred and abhorrence! Yet in now way was the girl responsible. How could she be held answerable for the monstrous wickedness her father had decreed?

Fandor told himself so, enraged at what he knew to be an injustice. Above all, he decided to anticipate Juve, to induce Helene to make her choice before he could influence her decision. Accordingly he was the first to address her.

"Oh, Helene, Helene! What joy to see you—even at this terrible moment!… I am convinced you will understand my wish, that your heart will approve the decision I have come to… You know everything, Helene, do you not?"

She whispered a reply:

"Yes, I know all; I know the abominable dilemma Fantômas sets us to resolve."

"Well, then, Helene, I beseech you listen to me… There is no dilemma; it is resolved already… It is Juve who must leave this place a free man."

"Juve? Juve? And you?…"

"Me you will kill, Helene. Yes, you will kill me. Nay, keep calm! You must listen to my advice… Helene, come here beside me. I wish to say something in your ear."

But the girl shook her head, signifying how it was physically impossible for her to approach Fandor's cage. About her waist a thin steel band, almost invisible, but nonetheless strong, was coiled. One end was attached firmly to the wall and limited the girl's freedom of movement; she could sink back exhausted into the chair, but could not advance a step further.

But at the same moment Juve broke in. Trembling, and now choking with indescribable emotion, he seemed to have recovered if not all his self-possession, at least his presence of mind.

"Hush, Fandor!" he cried. "We are not going to begin again; argument is useless. It would only mean prolonging Helene's suffering; it would be cruel to the child… And then, we must make an end of it… Let me speak!"

The police officer turned to Helene and declared:

"I do not mean, Helene, to make appeal to your heart. I know your heart holds less empire over you than your conscience. So it is to your conscience I appeal… You love Fandor. To save Fandor alive will free you both. I ask you in all sincerity to kill me."

"Kill you, Juve? What! Kill you?"

"Nay, Helene," groaned Fandor, "never listen to him. I swear by the love I bear you that if you chose him for victim I should hate you to the end of my life. It is I who should die… Juve is indispensable! Juve is a hero! His life may mean the salvation of hundreds of other lives… It is I you must slay!"

"Fandor! Fandor! I cannot do it; I cannot!"

In his cage Juve was stamping with rage.

"Great God! Hold your tongue, Fandor! It is disgraceful to torture the child like this!"

"Juve! Juve! I cannot understand you. Come, sacrifice your scruples! Consent to live!"

"Never! Never!"

Their faces pressed hard against the bars, the unhappy men were straining towards each other, crying out their fixed determination to die.

Suddenly Helene gave a great cry: "I cannot choose! I must not choose! It is I—I myself who should die!" And with a frantic gesture she seized the revolver and put it to her temple.

But instantly, with one accord, Juve and Fandor besought her to stay her hand.

"You have no right to kill yourself, Helene!" expostulated Fandor. "Suicide is a sin. God keep you from this wickedness!"

"Stop! Stop!" vociferated Juve. "The idea is idiotic! Once you were dead, Helene, Fantômas would kill us both. It means sentencing us to death to take your life. He will avenge himself on us."

And for sure the police officer had hit on the decisive argument that was bound to carry conviction to Helene. Otherwise with what eagerness would the generous girl have vowed herself to annihilation if only her death could have saved those she loved, if thus she could have evaded the dreadful dilemma, the impossible and cruel choice!

Yes, Juve was right. Furious at the failure of his plan and the death of his daughter, whom he loved perhaps as passionately as he hated her, Fantômas would surely wreak his vengeance on the two heroes, putting both to death after atrocious tortures.

Helene put down the weapon again. The wretched girl was now so deathly pale, so trembling and distraught, she seemed barely conscious of her surroundings.

"Helene! My beloved!" besought Fandor. "I conjure you hear me!"

But the words had not left his lips ere a sudden cry of exultation answered his appeal.

"Why, I was mad! I was forgetting! Oh, now I know I can save you, Fandor. This time, protest as you will, I can force you to submit… And you will have no cause to blame Helene… And you will be happy—happy in spite of yourself!"

At this moment Juve appeared to be the prey of some sort of feverish exaltation, speaking with all the excitability to be noted in those experiencing the most crushing grief or the most intense joy.

"Above all," continued the police officer, "understand this, my children: let us have no false sentimentality, no useless silliness… Life is life; we must take it as it comes, and we have a duty no less than a right to be happy. I command you to be happy. That will be my revenge. Juve's revenge. It will be my day of triumph, the day of your marriage."

"But, Juve, what is it you mean? What is it, Juve?" But the young man's voice failed in the excess of his emotion, and he could say no more.

"Nay," resumed the police officer, "it is all settled, provided for, concluded. There is no going back upon it. Yes, you will marry, my children. And sometimes you will think of me—of me who loved you fondly... Well, farewell, Fandor; farewell, Helene... Fandor, you were my son; I loved you like a son. Goodbye! You will honor my memory. Again, goodbye!"

But neither Fandor nor Helene realized the truth at first. Juve, for all his eagerness and emphasis, was so self-possessed, so self-controlled in speech and gesture, he could hardly be suspected of meditating anything momentous. Only the two young folks were now assailed by a new dread. Had Juve lost his reason? Had he suddenly gone mad?

But it was another matter altogether. Juve had suddenly recollected a precaution he had taken in former days in view of the dangers he was constantly exposed to.

Rapidly, with a furtive movement, he had wrenched off one of the buttons of his jacket, had put it between his lips and was breaking it up between his teeth.

"Oh!" groaned Fandor in an accent of agonized grief. "Poison!"

"Poison, yes! A deadly poison! Yes, with my death Fantômas will be satisfied... And I shall feel no pain, none whatever... Say no more... I... I... I am cold, deadly cold... And, Helene... Fan... Fandor..."

Juve beat the air with his arms. Then he collapsed, falling headlong to the ground. He was a tall man, and looked even taller lying thus stark and stiff at full length on his mattress.

For long years he had been the very incarnation of the most valiant courage, the very spirit of unselfish self-sacrifice. His end was worthy of his life—sublime.

Rending sobs echoed through the dreadful place. Fandor had fallen to his knees. Helene, fainting, half dead, was crying bitterly. Minutes passed. Then a step was heard approaching.

"Juve has cheated me of my vengeance." Fantômas spoke in chilling tones. "He has killed himself... I ought not to let you two go free... No matter! You shall live to remember. You shall live to hate one another… For you *will* loathe one another. You will ever have betwixt you a corpse, a dead man who died for your accursed love! Ho, ho!…" And the Monster broke into a peal of fiendish laughter.

Yet what meantime were his real thoughts? Did he truly believe that Fandor would never forgive Helene for being the involuntary cause of Juve's death? Or was he perchance thinking he had gone far enough in villainy and horror and could not endure to deal yet more vilely with his unhappy daughter? Or was not his chief motive to have witnesses to prove the indubitable fact of Juve's death?

He gave a savage gesture of scorn and hate.

"You shall be free in a few moments… Never, either of you, cross my path again—neither you, Fandor, nor you, Helene!" And Fantômas took a step towards the door.

But Fandor could contain himself no longer.

"No, no!" he protested. "Kill me, kill me now, murderer! Kill me if you value your life! For, by God I swear it, I shall never enjoy one second of repose till I have punished you, till I have avenged Juve's death!"

"I scorn threats," was all Fantômas vouchsafed in reply. "I am above all reprisals… You shall live. If you trouble me, I shall make you prisoner again at my own time and pleasure, whenever I think good… and I will kill you, as I have brought Juve to kill himself."

This was the Torturer's last word. But hardly had he gone before masked men entered the cellar, threw themselves upon Helene, gagged, bound, and blindfolded her.

"The car is come?" asked one of them.

"Surely!" replied one in command. "The orders are to drive her fifty miles away from here, and drop her in the open country."

"Same as Fandor, then?"

"Yes. But they will not be taken to the same spot… Anyway, the chauffeurs have their instructions."

But just then Fandor was not even listening. His eyes were riveted on Juve's body, and he was a prey to an agony of suspense that was near akin to madness. He thought he saw the dead man's chest still rising and falling slightly, still inhaling the air that is the breath of life. Had death, then, not done its fatal work?… Or perhaps…

He dared not complete the thought. Some hopes are so wild, some dreams so preposterous, that the mind refuses to accept them, at the same time it finds itself led to conceive them.

Nor did the young man attempt the least resistance when Fantômas' men pushed their way into his cage, bound him with strong cords and gagged him tightly. Nothing mattered now. Juve was dead. Life had lost all savor; he was utterly indifferent to everything. For was not the victory definitely and for always decided in Fantômas' favor, and what was left for him but to continue a hopeless struggle, to seek vengeance he could never hope to wreak unaided? Still, if he was actually to live, if from one motive or another the Monster should let him go free, he would have no hesitation in devoting his life to the punishment of the murderer. He had taken his oath; he had publicly proclaimed his purpose. He would keep his word; he would faithfully perform the duty his conscience laid upon him.

"Come, let's be quick about it," said a voice, and Fandor cast a last look at the corpse of the man who had redeemed his life by the sacrifice of his own.

But lo! Again the journalist had to bite his lips to check a cry.

Yes, Juve's heart *was* beating. Slow, wavering, interrupted, the breath still stirred in his bosom. There was no doubt of that. As fire smolders beneath the ashes, life still smoldered under the rigidity of death.

But alas, he dared say nothing! How could he proclaim the fact when Fantômas' fellows would have been only too happy to extinguish this feeble spark of life?

Then, again, was he not perhaps mistaken? Was it not insane, ridiculous, grotesquely childish to imagine possible a miracle such as this!

Jerome Fandor said no word. He let them bear him away, while great tears poured from his eyes—tears he was in no wise ashamed to shed for Juve, his lifelong friend.

Nevertheless, the journalist had made no mistake. Juve was not dead, albeit he displayed very nearly all the tokens of death. His body was cold; his limbs were rigid; a mirror put to his lips would have remained undimmed, so slight was the breath his lungs exhaled, so feeble the respiration. The heart, too, was beating so weakly that even a doctor's ear would surely have been deceived, and the throbbing of that muscle that drives the blood through the arteries and veins and forms the chief organ of life were imperceptible.

Yet, low as was the ebb of life within him, Juve was perfectly conscious. Like the opium smokers whom that evil drug so stupefies they become incapable of movement while the over-stimulated brain gives birth to extravagant dreams, Juve would at this moment have found it an impossibility to stir a finger, though this in no wise prevented his preserving an entire and complete lucidity of mind.

"Extraordinary stuff," he was thinking, "this Indian drug they call curare. Never will science discover precisely all the effects it is capable of producing when given in carefully regulated doses. I am in a state of apparent death. My life is in a way suspended. Upon my word, if Fantômas is deceived by it, it may yet be possible for me to come out of the business all right."

And at the same time Juve was tormenting himself with the thought of the terrible grief in which his pretended suicide must have plunged Fandor and Helene.

"Yet how could I warn them?" the police officer continued his reflections. "I had to appear to be acting at the last moment, when there was no possibility of drawing back... We may be sure Fantômas was not far off, and was no doubt listening furtively to our farewells, Fandor's and mine... If I had failed to convince Fandor and Helene I should have had still less chance of cajoling Fantômas."

Juve was quite right in his suppositions. After the Torturer had quitted the cellar where stood the two cages in which his victims were imprisoned, and after his two minions had brought in Helene to carry out the odious task he had imposed on her, he had taken good care not to retire to any distance.

Atrociously cruel as he was, Fantômas was too delighted to listen to the last agonized speeches of his victims willingly to forgo a scene so attractive in his eyes.

A witness, therefore, of the terrible scene between Juve and Fandor, and their prayers and expostulations, watching through a peephole artfully contrived in the wall the expressions of the two men's faces, Fantômas had perforce been deceived by the amazing comedy Juve was in reality playing off on him. It had, indeed, been part of the police officer's ingenuity to feign so profound a despair as to seem convinced that no possible vestige of hope was left him. To see him, a man of such energy and determination and ingenuity, giving way so utterly was a spectacle so uncommon that underlying the tragicomedy Fantômas had suspected no trick, any more than Fandor and Helene had felt any doubts.

Yet no sooner had Juve heard Fantômas announce the punishment he had decided on than his thoughts had turned to this supposed button that warranted him in looking for a possible way of escape.

But, as a matter of fact, had he any real assurance of success? Thinking it over with the clearheaded acumen that was characteristic of him, he found himself bound to admit that failure was much more likely. He was not dead, yet showed all the signs of death, so much was certain. Well, it was worth trying; but it was very far from certain what the end would be. True, this drug curare, does possess valuable properties if, by slowing down to the last degree the pulsations of the heart and the action of the lungs, it provokes in persons entirely alive all the symptoms of dissolution, but it is no less a fact that this is the limit of the powers of this marvelous Indian poison.

Completely master of himself, Juve was reckoning up his chances.

"Now the situation is perfectly simple… I pass for dead, and I may be expected to be treated as a dead man… On the other hand, I am incapable of moving, unable to utter a single word; unable to show that I am alive. Consequently my whole fate depends on one thing—what they are going to do with my supposed corpse."

Who but Juve could have had the coolness and courage under the circumstances to argue with so clean a realization of the facts of the case?

What, indeed, was Fantômas going to do with Juve's body? According to all probability, fearing police inquiries and the information Fandor and Helene would not fail to give, the cowardly Lord of Terror would make all haste to get rid of the mortal remains of the man he believed his victim.

"If he buries me," reflected Juve, "I am done for. I shall die in my grave without having been able even to attempt to make a way out. If they throw me into the river it will be just as bad—I shall be drowned… Now it seems to me one or the other of these two alternatives is bound to be my fate…"

But the police officer's reflections came to an abrupt conclusion. Close by his side—yet he could not so much as turn his eyes in the direction of the speaker—a voice had spoken, the voice of Fantômas.

15. A Tragicomedy

Very calm, entirely indifferent now to the triumph he evidently believed himself to have definitely achieved, Fantômas was giving his orders to one of his confederates—and Juve missed no word of the infamous conversation.

"See here, doctor," the brigand was saying, "I did not save you from the hulks for the mere pleasure of sparing you a punishment you had well deserved. I was sure that one day or another I should stand in need of your services."

"They are entirely yours, Master."

"I presume they are. Anyway, I am not going to ask you to do anything very complicated."

"Complicated or not, the thing shall be done."

"You came from Marseilles, doctor; your talkativeness is proof enough of that. Remember, I don't like people answering me when no answer is required. To say you will do as I wish is just talking for talking's sake. My orders are always obeyed."

"No doubt, Fantômas, but…"

"Enough! Enough said!"

The tone in which this rebuke was couched was indeed enough to convince the Arch-Criminal's confederate that it was best to say no more, and he held his tongue accordingly.

After a pause Fantômas resumed:

"I have brought you here, doctor, because I wish you to certify a death."

"A death?"

"Yes. Nothing to be surprised about in that. One of my enemies, the most dangerous of my opponents has just died."

"A natural death?"

"Naturally, the death of an enemy is always to be desired, doctor. But this man's death was more or less forced upon him."

"Let's call things by their right names, Master. You mean you dispatched him to the next world?"

"Not at all! You make a mistake. He dispatched himself."

"Suicide, then?"

"Next door to it! Say an execution. Juve executed himself..."

"Juve? Juve?"

"Yes. Does that surprise you?"

"Say rather I am delighted. Juve dead! By God, there's nothing could give me more pleasure."

"Why, pray?"

"Why, because the man was a standing danger to you, Master."

"Doctor, you're no better than an ass. No man is a danger to Fantômas... Those who take their orders from me must be convinced of that. I am afraid of no one."

"I know that, Master, of course. You fear nobody; but we who love you fear for you."

"You are a bigger ass than I thought, doctor. However, what matter? I am full of indulgence today. So I am asking you to certify Juve's death."

"You want a formal death certificate?"

"You are joking, doctor, I take it? I only want you to assure yourself that Juve is really dead."

Still lying motionless athwart his cage, a deathlike chill circulating in his veins, Juve could hardly fail to realize that his fate was now definitely decided. If this foolish confederate of Fantômas' was really a doctor, was he not certain to diagnose his condition of lethargy? Was he not sure to inform his master of the fact and thereby condemn him to die in very truth?

"Well, then, I am doomed to die," thought the police officer, resigning himself to his fate. "I have saved Fandor and Helene; now I am going to pay the penalty for that supreme satisfaction. I have no reason to complain. To die—after all, is that so dreadful?"

But now he was listening again. If death meant nothing to a brave heart like Juve's, might not the circumstances still be terrible? Finding out that Juve had played him a trick and was actually and veritably alive, what tortures might not the Lord of Terror devise in his devilish ingenuity to punish the audacity of his wily enemy?

"Well?" pursued Fantômas in his calm voice; "you do no answer my question, doctor."

"Oh yes, Master! What you ask me is quite simple."

"Really? Now how will you set about it?"

"Oh, I have only too many ways to choose from."

"Very good. But go on."

"There are many different signs of death, Master."

"I want a sure sign."

"Rigidity of the limbs."

"No, doctor. That can be seen in certain cases of nervous spasm."

"True; but such cases are rare… Well… the extinction of all reflex excitations."

"Somnambulism suspends these."

"True again! But Juve was not a sleepwalker… However, there are other means… The pulsations of the heart are no longer audible."

"You may be mistaken."

"Oh no. But there's something better still. To make quite sure of a patient's death, you can burn the heels. The pain is so intense that even if the man is in a lethargy he will wake up."

"You don't know Juve, doctor. He would have it in him not so much as to give a jump."

"I doubt that, Fantômas… but never mind; there is one certain sign there is no mistaking—decomposition; once the corpse begins to decay, it stands to reason…"

"Enough said! We cannot wait, we might have to remain in doubt for several days. I wish the death to be certified here and now."

"Then, by God, I don't quite see… I—"

"Doctor, I'm not of your profession, but I know a decisive method—one that can leave no room for mistake or trickery."

"What is that, Master?"

Fantômas' eyes flashed fire beneath his hood, which he had put on again, as he declared:

"All that is wanted, doctor, is to kill over again the man who is already dead. Having escaped the first time, he won't escape the second."

"Your words are of gold, Master. It's a sure thing, if you tell me to cut off Juve's head…"

"No, there's no need to go so far as that; I have no ideas of resorting to such violent proceedings. I don't wish his corpse to be an object of horror."

"As you please… So you have a particular notion of your own for killing him over again?"

"Yes. I don't know how you are going to operate…"

"Hmm, but it's I who… Still, after all, I don't care. What is your way?"

"You are simply, doctor, to take this long gold needle and plunge it in his heart. That will leave a hardly perceptible mark. Yes, that is what I wish!"

"Bravo, Fantômas! A capital idea! It shall be done straight away."

"You're not over clever, doctor, but you are pretty quick to act. Now take this needle."

"Willingly, Master. Where is Juve?"

"Turn round. In that cage there."

"God Almighty! You had him shut up in… You take my breath away. I really begin to think you're more than human, Fantômas."

"Operate, doctor… And don't talk!"

"It'll only take a second, Master. Only, how does one get into the cage? I can see the door, but I haven't got the key."

"Here you are, doctor."

"Thank you. Give me a moment to bend over him, and you can set your mind at rest. I haven't dissected bodies for years to boggle over a little matter like this"—and the fellow gave a cheerful laugh.

Now, who and what was the man, a person of education, who held a diploma difficult to obtain, demanding years of study and serious application, yet who had fallen so low as to be ready to perform the basest services Fantômas? Only the man himself and his master could have answered the question. Those whom the Lord of Terror recruited for the needs of his criminal enterprises were invariably unknown to all the world. Escaped convicts, murderers who had cheated the gallows, wretches going in fear of the police, they belonged to the lowest depths of society where evildoers lurk in shame and degradation, earning a precarious living by crime.

The doctor was almost unknown to the rest of the gang. If he was something of a noodle with his inconsequent chatter, he was, to make up, a man who, no vestige of shame, no sort of scruple left, was ready to undertake the vilest and most cowardly tasks. The notion of piercing the heart of a dead man did not trouble him in the very least. Nay, he found it actually amusing, and admired Fantômas for the wisdom he displayed in wishing, as he had just said himself, to kill his enemy twice over.

Yet would he have leapt so promptly into the cage where the unfortunate police officer still lay had he known that Juve, for all his look of death, was really alive and actually aware of the conversation that had just passed?

How terrible the situation of the unhappy man, lying there incapable of movement and looking like a corpse, as he watched the scoundrelly doctor approaching, in his hand the long fine needle with which he was preparing to transfix his heart!

"This time," he thought, "it is all over with me! I can cherish no illusions as to that… Still, one piece of luck—it won't be very painful!"

He would fain have shut his eyes not to see the hand that crept nearer and nearer to his bosom bearing death between its fingers. He would fain have not heard, not even thought.

At a moment when, fully conscious, he knew his death to be certain, inevitable, he would have wished to collect his thoughts to ponder the unknown mystery of another world into which he was so soon to be hurried. But far from this, his mind was in a wild whirl, boiling with thoughts of hate, of fury and impotent rage. So Fantômas, then, was to have the last word? It was the Arch-Criminal who was to table the last card and win the dreadful game?

Then tenderer thoughts filled his mind. Fandor was safe and Helene too. Alas, their sorrow would be deep, their grief intense, yet there is no sorrow but comes at last to be forgotten; no tears but are dried up by time. In these last moments of his life poor Juve clung to thoughts of hope. Fandor would marry Helene and be happy... The two would build a home for themselves... In future days children would learn from their lips the tale of the hero who had saved their parent's lives... No, he was not to perish altogether, if assured of surviving thus in the fond memory of those he had loved and of the children that would be theirs.

But, alas, he could but see and hear, poor wretch.

"Once... twice!" cried the doctor. "Nobody has anything to say? Nobody any objection to make?"

"Get on with it!" from Fantômas.

"Well, I have my orders!" laughed the doctor, and he laid his hand on Juve's chest, and he felt under the shirt the contours of bosom and ribs, explaining as he did so:

"You know, it's a very curious thing, Master, but in a living man the heart does not lie in precisely the same place as in a dead body. Of course, the displacement so far is only a matter of a fraction of an inch. However..."

"Get on with it, do!" Fantômas ordered again.

"There! I'm just going to begin. I've located the exact position by the strictest rules of anatomy... Don't be impatient, Fantômas. I'm on the job... Now I stick it in!..." declared the wretch, calmer than ever.

Meantime Juve, lying there stark and stiff, was tasting the pangs of death second by second. Unable to see the doctor's hand, as he could not so much as move his eyeballs, he had no means of telling the exact moment at which the needle would penetrate his heart... Would he in fact, he wondered feel the pain of the death-dealing thrust; or had the Indian drug that kept him thus at one and the same time alive and dead abolish all sensibility?

"I do not feel him touching me," he thought to himself. "No, I don't think I shall suffer any pain at all.. But there, what matter? It will be very soon over."

But, on the contrary, the seconds seemed eternities, to drag on as though they would never end. What was the rascally doctor waiting for? Why did he not drive his needle in?

Suddenly Fantômas appeared to lose patience.

"Well?" he demanded.

"Well… the job's done."

"You've driven the needle home?"

"Till it came out the other side."

"Then he is dead for certain?"

"By God! I don't quite see how he *could* still be in this world."

Nevertheless, Juve heard perfectly well what the man was saying. He was alive, and he knew he was alive. Nay, he even felt less distressed than he had a while before.

"Is it witchcraft?" he asked himself. "Can the thing be possible? Has the fellow not stabbed my heart after all?"

He longed to cry out, to move, to show he was alive. He never thought of the danger the least imprudence would have brought about for him. Curiosity to understand what had happened overcame every other feeling.

"No, no!" he assured himself. "I do not believe in miracles. I have no faith in wizardry. It is not true this doctor has killed me!"—and his own words stuck in his throat—words at once amazing and absurd. How was it possible a man could ever be asking himself such a question—asking *if he had been killed?*

But Juve was not one who could endure such uncertainty. His mind, accurate, precise, well-versed in difficult police investigations, demanded clear-cut facts, definite and exact explanations. Why should this accomplice of Fantômas' have spared him? Why should this man he did not know, who actually proclaimed the instinctive hatred he bore him—why should he have hesitated to put an end to his life? Was he not running the risk of being unmasked by his master? Was he not playing with his own life by not obediently executing the orders given him?

"I am certainly mistaken," Juve finally decided. "No doubt the doctor did drive home the needle that was to kill me. But the needle did me no hurt. Now, why was that?"

And in an instant, with the rapidity with which luminous discoveries flash across the mind, the truth stood plain before him—simple enough in fact and evident after a little reflection.

Why had the needle not wounded him mortally by piercing the heart? For the simple reason that it had *not* transfixed the heart. But why had it not reached that vital organ? For the reason very lucidly explained beforehand by his executioner in the presence of his victim. Had not Fantômas' accomplice expounded to his master in his own garrulous fashion how the heart did not lie exactly in the same position in a living man and in a corpse?

Now, as he bent over Juve, the doctor had believed himself bending over a dead man. He had driven his needle where, logically, the police officer's heart should have been supposing he were really dead; but, seeing his patient was alive, the surgeon's scientific knowledge itself occasioned his mistake. The deadly instrument had grazed the organ without actually touching it.

"A piece of luck!" thought Juve—"luck for which I owe thanks to nobody... By-the-by, I wonder how it comes about I feel no pain, and suffer from no internal hemorrhage, for after all, if the needle did not pierce my heart, it did go through me from one side to the other—a treatment of a sort not much to be recommended."

Juve conjectured—and this was the truth, though he could not be sure, not having any very profound medical knowledge—that the curare had most likely played a part in the phenomenon.

"In a word," he reckoned things up, "my circulation is greatly slowed down; my blood is almost stagnant. That I suppose is why I do not bleed. It even seems probable this will allow the tiny wound to heal up quickly. Four-and-twenty hours' rest and it won't be visible at all."

But as he formulated the thought, for all his energy and courage, his spirits sank. Twenty-four hours' rest! Why, he was by no means sure yet he would not have all eternity to rest in. They had not killed him; he was still alive by a miracle, and in a few hours more the soporific—for curare is a stupefying drug that acts like a soporific—would no longer condemn him to immobility. But his fate was not decided for all that… He passed for dead; indeed, in the eyes of all he seemed more dead than ever. After what fashion was Fantômas going to give him burial?

"How will they dispose of my body?" Juve asked himself. "Will they pitch me in the river or dump me in the ground? Devil take it if I'm not recovering my taste for living, and I don't feel any great wish for either of these alternatives."

Again the unhappy man knew the anguish of being incapable of movement and of doing anything whatsoever to defend himself, and of knowing that even at that very moment his fate was being decided.

Fantômas had withdrawn a little to one side and was talking under his breath to the doctor. What was he saying to him?

Oh, to know what was to happen to this body of his which no longer obeyed the behests of his will, and was yet full of life!

16. Bouzille Redeems His Character

Juve remained yet another full hour in absolute uncertainty of what was to become of him. There was undoubtedly talk going on beside him, but it was in whispers, and he could not hear what was said. He was not even sure if Fantômas was still there or if he had gone, doubtless with the purpose of contriving fresh wickedness, sure now of impunity, seeing Juve was no more, or so he thought.

Meantime the curare was beginning to act in odd ways on Juve's bodily system. This drug, the toxic qualities of which are still imperfectly known to the medical profession and which in different doses produces effects sometimes of an entirely contradictory nature—temporary paralysis or feverish stimulation—had been given to Juve many years before by an old colonial, who had explained its properties to the police officer in a very summary fashion. Consequently the latter was in the dark as to the sensations he was now experiencing—a fact which did not fail to cause him no little anxiety. For some time he had felt a violent burning in the stomach, a tightening in the region of the heart and a distressing buzzing in the ears that half deafened him.

"Well, it's one thing or another," thought the police officer with his usual imperturbability. "Either I am poisoned, and this is the beginning of my death-agony—or, on the contrary, the effect of the curare is diminishing, and little by little I am going to find myself in perfectly good condition again."

But neither one nor the other of these possibilities was without its terrors. If poisoned, he was doomed to a speedy death, for no one would dream of succoring him, in as much as all thought him a dead man already. If, on the other hand, he woke up, it was certain he would lose his look of being a corpse and Fantômas' men who stood about him would not fail to notice the fact.

"To the last degree disconcerting!" he reflected. "I really cannot see any way out of it… In any case Fantômas is waiting to get rid of my supposed dead body. I wager that at any moment they are going to nail me down in a coffin… Well, I suppose when that happens I've only to give up my life once again."

Yet Juve had no real notion what was actually to be his fate, so true is it that the most clear-sighted intelligences, the most ingenious minds, are liable to make the worst mistakes.

He had been a long while, a very long while, alone, entirely left to himself, it seemed, when suddenly he saw two men approaching his cage, talking together as they came.

"D'you think it's dark enough yet?" one of the men asked.

"Surely!" replied his mate. "Anyway, the place is quite deserted."

"Oh, so without that the job would be a dangerous one?"

"Why, no, not a bit of it. They'll only suppose we're with a tipsy man. In this damned country they're just as plentiful as in France. Only difference is here drunkards are more melancholy like, and are always crying instead of singing."

As they talked, the two fellows had opened the door of the cage and Juve could now see them bending over him. He did not recognize them, never having seen them before, but he did his best to fix their features in his memory.

"Just to think," remarked one of the pair, "to think it's Juve, the great Juve, that terrible fellow Juve! Don't that strike you as a funny go, eh?"

"Say rather it seemed to *me* a mighty fine thing. Why, a chap like Juve is all on his own more pestilent than the whole Criminal Department lumped together."

"Surely! That's just what I think myself… But this here go off…"

"Oh, this go off he won't worry folks never no more! His number's up… Lift, man—it's a bit lumpy."

For the moment, for all the tragic aspect of the situation, Juve felt somewhat heartened up.

"There's nothing very cheering about being dead," he told himself. "Still, it has its consoling side. It comforts me a lot for my decease to know what a worry I was in my lifetime to these fine fellows."

But this thought was short-lived. Little though he suspected it, believing it was mere curiosity which prompted these two henchmen of Fantômas' to come to have a look at him, they were in reality the gravediggers appointed to remove his dead body.

"To remove me to where?" wondered the police officer, and he listened with all his ears to what the two were saying, but just at first he found no great interest in their remarks.

"You'll take him by the heels, eh?" asked one of them.

"Yes… You catch him under the arms."

"Oh, don't you trouble your head about me. If I find him too heavy, I'll drop him. No fear of his breaking, eh?"

"Delightful talk!" thought Juve. "These fellows have a way of showing respect to a dead enemy that is truly exquisite. But what are they going to do with me?"

To that question he invariably came back, for it was the only thing that really concerned him. But it seemed to all appearance likely to receive an answer. Picking him up, as they had settled, by the legs and arms, the two men proceeded to carry him away. To begin with, Juve was not at all distressed by the transit. He had been thrown a trifle roughly onto a plank of sorts, and he was still asking himself where exactly he was when, by the shaking and rattling that supervened, he guessed he was lying on the floorboards of a truck.

"So then," concluded the police officer, "I am to have another half hour or thereabouts to live. If they use a motor vehicle to remove me, that means in all likelihood that they propose to drive to suburban parts. But that proves nothing. They can dig a hole in a remote district in the first plot of waste land they come to; but it's every bit as easy to make their way to the Thames and pitch me into the river."

Juve had reached this point in his reflections when he felt the truck slow down, and then after a sharp turn come to a sudden stop.

"What!" he guessed; "so we're there already?"

A few seconds more and his guess became a certainty, for, jumping down from their seat, the two men exchanged sundry remarks in a low voice the import of which was unmistakable.

"You don't see nobody anywheres about?"

"Not a soul!"

"No cops especially?"

"No, never a one… What a funk you are?"

"Why, lordy, a pretty game it would be to get ourselves nabbed with this here piece of goods on our hands!"

"O' course!… But we shan't be nabbed… Now, right away… All change here!… Now, Monsieur Juve, for the honor of shifting you down… Nothing broke? No… you won't forget the tip for the remover's men, will you?"

At that moment Juve was assuring himself that he was less and less able to understand what could have been decided as to the disposal of his body. Not only was he not beyond the confines of London proper, not only was he on no plot of waste ground or on the banks of the Thames, but, more than that, he perceived that he was in a street. Still incapable of any attempt to shift his position or even move his eyes, Juve was obviously unable to identify the street. But he was sufficiently well acquainted with the English usage to know that police patrols traverse at stated intervals day and night every street of the town.

"Thus," he concluded, "from one minute to the next they are liable to be seen… How, then, can they have the effrontery to dismount here from the conveyance in which I lay concealed? Whatever are they going to do with me in a street?"

"Heave ho!" cried one of the pair forming Juve's bodyguard at that moment. "Come, let's have him down. There we are!… But I say, he won't be too warm on his bench, eh?"

"Oh, well, if so be he catches cold, he can complain to Fantômas when he comes to pay his respects to the defunct… You ain't forgot the placard?"

"No, no! Not I. But let's carry him there first, and we'll stick on the placard after… But what and all's the use of it? The

Master does complicate the job so with his whimsies."

"Never you mind! It pleases him, anyways."

But just then Juve found it difficult to hear more. Gripped under the arms and legs, he was again being transported by his escort; but, as ill-luck would have it, his face was turned to the ground, so that all he could see was the paving stones.

"Where am I?" the unfortunate detective was again asking himself; "and what can this bench be they spoke about?… So they're not going to bury me yet?"

The next minute one of the men said:

"Are you ready? Shall we turn him over?"

"If you like."

"Say now, what about sitting him up?"

"Shall we be able to? He's all stiff."

"Not a bit! He ain't all stiff. What a chap you be for making difficulties!"

"No, I ain't. But the job's not much to my taste."

"The gentleman's looking cross, is he? The gentleman may get us into trouble with the boss, eh?… Anyway, go and fetch the placard."

This time Juve only wished he could have cried out to relieve his feelings, so surprised and overjoyed was he. In one second all his anxieties had vanished and once more he knew the joy of being alive, the delights of being delivered from his worst apprehensions.

Where was he? Why, in the very street in which was the furnished lodging he and Fandor had hired on their arrival in London. The stone bench whereon the Arch-Criminal's two accomplices had just installed him was not two hundred yards from the door of the house!

Now everything was plain at last, easy and simple to understand. Anxious to prove to all the world what was the might and grandeur of the victory he had won by Juve's assassination, Fantômas had pushed his effrontery to the pitch of dispatching his enemy's supposed dead body to a point within a few yards of his abode.

He was having him deposited on a bench. There he was

leaving him all alone in the street, after first taking the precaution of having a placard pinned on his chest to indicate his identity beyond any chance of doubt, so as to avoid any possible blunder on the part of the police, or even any delay in his identification.

"Then," thought Juve, "why, then, I am saved—saved for good and all! Directly they find me they will carry me to my own lodging... So I shan't be buried right off, but shall have time to awake from my lethargy."

No sooner, in fact, had he conceived this hope than further reflection actually increased his satisfaction. He noted how the men who had just seated him on the bench had found no difficulty in bending his body and knees. From this he argued that his rigidity was diminishing; in other words, that the curare was little by little losing its paralyzing effect.

"Who know," pondered the police officer, "if I'm not going perhaps to come to completely in a few minutes?... I feel quite able to get home all by myself... Great heavens! Suppose I should find Helene, suppose I should find Fandor there!"

The roar of the motor which the ruffians were cranking up preparatory to getting underway now gave him a feeling of indescribable pleasure. It betokened his final and definite deliverance from danger. It was, after such cruel defeats, a sign of an assured victory won by dint of his genius. It was he who had thought of the Indian drug whose extraordinary effect had saved him by deceiving Fantômas and his satellites. It was he who had had the courage to resort to a ruse the results of which might have been terrible, but which had actually rescued him from the most perilous of situations. Free, safe, assured that Fandor and Helene had likewise escaped the toils of the Lord of Terror, had he not every right to feel a well-justified pride in his achievement?

But he checked his self-glorification as he thought:

"Still, this is only a momentary victory. I have escaped Fantômas, but Fantômas is still at large, still able to renew his criminal exploits... Here and now I swear that I will disarm him and make him my prisoner. I shall have no rest nor respite till I have vanquished him, as he thought he had vanquished me."

The truck had driven off. Juve could hear the noise of the engine getting fainter and fainter in the distance. Then he remembered another thing:

"There, I never thought of taking the number! How clumsy of me! This might someday be a useful, even an indispensable piece of information. Wherever were my wits gone to!"

Yet surely it was very excusable to have been a trifle absent-minded under the circumstances. At the same time, such was his regret for having neglected this detail of police duty, that he now made a desperate, a supreme effort to move and turn his head. There followed an agonizing spasm that seemed to tear and rend every muscle, as if it would break the very sinews and bones. By sheer force of will Juve was shaking off the paralysis induced by the poison he had had the hardihood to swallow. He had won the day against pain and utter exhaustion.

He turned his head, and his eyes followed the motor now almost disappearing in the far distance. But it was too late; he could not make out the number.

But he had gone beyond his strength, done more than was humanely possible. Nature never suffers her laws to be broken with impunity, and she was taking her revenge.

Juve staggered to his feet, "I have moved," he said. "I am sav…"—and then he fell, measuring his length on the ground in a dead faint.

He did not come to again at once, but lay there for a while motionless, lifeless, entirely unconscious.

Meantime what momentous events were happening! What joy if only he could have taken cognizance of them! Scarcely had the detective collapsed on the pavement before chance, in combination with the strict and admirable organization of the London police, brought on the scene the constable whose duty it was to keep an eye on the block of houses before which Juve lay. Seeing a man stretched helpless on the sidewalk, the policeman began by making a not unnatural mistake.

"So ho!" he exclaimed, "another drunk and incapable? Devil

take the fellow! I shall have to get him to the station"—and with the toe of his boot he gave Juve a shove in hopes of extracting some token of intelligence from the unknown, or at any rate inducing him to get up.

Though the latter never stirred, the constable nevertheless made an important discovery, now catching sight of the placard Fantômas had had pinned on the detective's chest:

"This man is the French police officer Juve, Inspector in the French Criminal Department. He has been executed by order of Fantômas, to which the journalist Fandor will bear witness."

As he read the words the constable at first asked himself if he was not dreaming, if it was not all a nightmare. Then he felt panic-stricken. The names of Juve, Fandor, Fantômas, were, of course, familiar to him. Was he to believe he saw before his own eyes one of these champions?

The worthy man swore all the oaths in his vocabulary. Then, leaving the body lying there, he rushed to the police officer's house, the address of which was given on the placard, and rang a peal on the bell to summon witnesses to his aid.

But he had not said a word, or even roused the attention of the inmates, before a young man, his face pale, his looks distraught, his eyes red with weeping, dashed out, hurrying to the spot where Juve's body had just been discovered. It was Fandor!

How describe the sorrow of Helene's unfortunate fiancé at what he saw! He had only just returned—and it was to find the corpse of the dearest of his friends!

"My poor Juve! My poor Juve!" he sobbed, falling to his knees beside the body.

Never for one second had it crossed his mind that Juve was only in a swoon and that his grief should by rights have given place to extravagant delight.

*   *   *   *   *

Jerome Fandor was not in any case to be blamed if he failed to divine the state in which he had found Juve, and that the only thing that hindered him from showing he was not dead was a fainting fit of no serious importance.

Only partially recovered from the toxic effects of the curare, he still retained a certain deathlike rigidity proceeding from what doctors call tetanus of the muscles, and which perfectly simulated the "rigor mortis." Again, his circulation was not yet completely restored. Thus his hands were icy cold, while his face was so pale and his nostrils so pinched that Fandor, aware of what had gone before, could entertain no doubt as to the unfortunate man being dead.

Moreover, such was the young man's grief at this terrible moment when he believed himself to have come upon his friend's mortal remains, that he was in no condition to reason things out. Energetic and courageous as he was, inured to the worst perils and accustomed to face the worst storms of life, Fandor's spirit was for once vanquished and reduced to despair. One desire, and one only, was his—to be alone, to be able to weep his fill—above all, to be free from all importunate curiosity. By good fortune, whereas in France he would infallibly have been assailed by a host of inquisitive folks lavishing useless consolations upon him, or tormenting him with ridiculous questions, here in England all were well content to leave him alone with his sorrow.

The constable had given the alarm, telephoned to the nearest police station; a detective of a superior grade arrived almost immediately, and the necessary investigations, or, to speak more precisely, the preliminaries to a more thorough investigation, had been rapidly carried out with all the sympathetic discretion Fandor could desire. In less than three-quarters of an hour after Juve had been discovered lying in the street Jerome Fandor found himself alone with the body of his friend in the modest lodging, which compassionate neighbors had already beautified with flowers.

For a time Fandor was in a state of prostration that bordered closely on total incapacity of the faculties. But already he was struggling to throw off this paralysis of the will.

Presently, when the last interruptions had ceased: "And now," the young man cried, "I must avenge Juve."

It was the sole clear and definite thought left in the journalist's mind. Yet how could he even now begin preparations for this vengeance which in his secret soul he so ardently thirsted for? But, like the good man he was, he did not hesitate one second.

"Juve is dead," he decided, "because the official police have never backed up his efforts as they should have done. Fantômas has triumphed because the sacrifices have never been made that were necessary to capture and punish him."

The young man's heart was boiling with ever-increasing fury. In his eyes, as with all men who knew his crimes, Fantômas was a public danger, a monster that terrified all the earth and was a menace to whole nations. Men had perforce witnessed his evil deeds in almost every country of the world; he had marked his passage in all parts of the globe. How came it, then, that all peoples did not unite to hunt him down? How came it that civilized nations did not reach an understanding to declare war to the knife on this villain who was the enemy of all mankind?

"Crying will serve no good purpose," Fandor suddenly observed in a determined tone. "What we must see to is that Juve's death proves useful to humanity. That is the best way to honor the memory of the departed hero."

The journalist seemed buried in thought for a moment; then, turning his gaze away from Juve's pallid countenance, he sat down before a table, drew out his fountain pen, took a sheet of paper and began to write.

Since Juve was dead, Fandor was about to appeal to the whole earth to unite to punish the murderer. As a journalist, did he not possess in his pen a redoubtable weapon, more powerful by itself than all individual efforts combined?

He was about to publish a manifesto, to denounce the cowardice of those who suffered a Fantômas to exist, who allowed a Juve to be assassinated.

"Millions are found," he wrote, "to get up fireworks displays, to undertake useless enterprises, to maintain a host of functionaries who spend their time in reading the illustrated papers; yet the few hundred thousand francs cannot be found that would suffice to organize a league of defense whose special task it would be to hunt down Fantômas! It is scandalous! No matter if we shock accepted conventions and convictions! Public opinion must be roused. The people must demand that the necessary measures be taken."

Jerome Fandor, when he chose, was a first-rate controversialist, well able to find the words that strike the imagination, the phrases that make men think, the expressions that bring conviction.

Never hesitating, he wrote on:

"Juve is dead. La Capitale will publish above another signature than mine the details of his death—his martyr's death. My eyes are full of tears. I think my heart is breaking. Not today must I be asked to follow my trade as a journalist. A man does not sell his grief, he cannot speak of his sorrow, cannot lay it bare to the curiosity of readers.

"Nevertheless I write. I write sitting beside the corpse of my lifelong friend. I write because I do not wish his death to go for nothing, because he must be avenged, because it is to all honorable men I address my words—men for whom Juve fell, and whom I would have understand the imperative duty his death imposes on them.

"Juve is dead, murdered by Fantômas. Fantômas must be brought to the scaffold. This is a point of honor for all mankind. This must be done, or the word justice be expunged from human speech…"

Behind him a voice spoke softly:

"Very good copy that, Fandor!" it said. "First rate!… But there are one or two inaccuracies—"

"Eh?" exclaimed the journalist. "In—"

He had answered instinctively, so deeply preoccupied he felt no surprise at being accosted. But suddenly he awoke to a sense of reality… He was alone with a dead man… Who, then, could have spoken to him?

Fandor sprang up so hastily his chair toppled over behind him. Was he going mad? Was he the victim of a hallucination?

Juve was there, standing on his feet; he had got down from the bed, where the depression left by his body could still be seen! It was Juve, who had just read what he had been writing over his shoulder! It was Juve who with a smile was stretching out his arms to embrace him! Oh, he was dreaming, dreaming!

"Juve! Juve!" stammered the young man.

"Why, yes, it is Juve! It is I! So come here and embrace me."

"Juve!… Alive!"

"Very much alive, Fandor, my lad… Fresh as a daisy!"

"Juve! Juve!"

"Come, come! You said that before… I tell you I am not dead… Obvious, isn't it?… Why, you're never going to faint like a silly woman? No?… Well then, smoke a cigarette—sit down! It's monstrous; so I've got to see to *you* now! Oh God! I've always been told joy never hurt anybody… Does it put you out, then, to see me alive?"

But joke as Juve might to hide his feelings, half swoon away as might Fandor and grow paler than Juve himself had been, it is nonetheless true that joy, if it frightens, is never, for all that, dangerous.

Oh, the exquisite, the intoxicating hour that then struck in the room but now so sad and now so gay and full of boundless happiness!

"Juve, how come you to be here? Tell me…"

"Oh, leave me alone. My adventures cannot be told in a word. I was dead, and I am no longer dead. You were writing a fine screed for your paper, and your paper will never print it. No matter! It's of no great interest… But you, what of you?"

"Never mind me, Juve. I don't count."

"Come, come! Just look here. You say you don't count—but Helene, does she, too, count for nothing?"

"Oh, if only she knew you were alive!"

"She shall know, never fear! In fact, I have my own little project on that point… Where is she?"

"I don't know, Juve."

"You don't know? You don't know? Why, whatever are you after, then? You ought to know."

"Juve, we were carried off, she and I, in two cars, and deposited in two different places… I came back here in the hope she would have telegraphed—"

"Ta! ta! ta!… Scatterbrain! I can imagine Helene, but just released, coming to join you here after all that has happened!"

"But you, Juve?…"

"Never mind me! I don't count either—in the past, at any rate… For the future, that's another matter. I might still play a minor part."

"Oh, Juve!"

"You're past bearing! Come, calm yourself! Juve is alive. Tell yourself so once for all, and let's change the subject. At what o'clock are they to bury me?"

"But—"

"Answer my question, do!"

"But, Juve, again I don't know."

"Why, good Lord, you don't know anything! Look here! I don't want to scold you; but you *are* negligent. Next time you must try to manage a bit better. I wish for a fine funeral, and you don't so much as give a thought to the matter."

"You're mad, Juve, upon my word!"

"I beg you, Fandor, to treat me with proper respect. Yes, that's how young people are! If I was dead you'd write articles ten pages long in honor of my memory. Because I'm alive, you call me cracked."

"But, Juve, you go talking of your burial. Hang your burial, say I."

"That's a pretty way to talk, Fandor."

"Listen here, Juve! *I* want to be cheerful; I've had enough of melancholy… If you come to life again only to talk to me about coffins and hearses—"

"You advise me to die over again, do you? Charming!… I beseech you, Fandor, to be logical—"

"I am, Juve."

"Not at all! You want cheerfulness, and you won't let me speak of my funeral. By God! Can't you see there's nothing more diverting than a funeral where everybody's there—barring the corpse?"

"Juve, I do assure you you're talking nonsense."

"There you are! Go on! Insult me, do!… Fandor, you make me regret I'm still in this world… But to return to my funeral. Here, in England, things go fast. The death is verified by the police. The newspapers will report it with much luxury of detail. In short, I opine they may be ready to put me in my coffin about five in the afternoon, and carry me to the cemetery the next morning. You don't believe it?"

"What I do believe, Juve, is that the ceremony won't take place. I am afraid the chief actor in it will fail to be at the organizers' disposal—"

"Excuse me! The chief actor at this funeral is myself, so it seems to me."

"It really strikes you in that light, Juve?"

"Then, why should I balk the organizers? What do you know about my intentions? I shall be punctual, never fear!"

"Juve, I begin to think you're past understanding…"

"Because you don't think… Listen to me, my boy! I intend to have myself interred. Certainly I do. To begin with, one don't have a chance every day of attending such a fête, and I should be foolish to miss it… Indeed, the same thing happened to me once before in France, the same thing, or near about, when they set up the commemorative tablet on the walls of the Prefecture of Police; but I wasn't pleased with the speeches. Here I feel convinced things will be better."

"Juve, these sorry jokes…"

"I'm not joking, Fandor. Let me finish… Well, then, I want them to bury me—yes! And give me a very fine funeral. I want many people to attend—a regular crowd, in fact."

"The devil! Then what about the invitations, then? Why, we don't know a soul in London."

"Never worry about that! There won't be many invitations to send out. You know very well that the funeral of a celebrity is always a draw; there'll be hundreds of idle spectators… And, by-the-by, I particularly wish for certain persons to be able to attend with impunity by mixing with the crowd—with *apparent* impunity, because I'm quite expecting—"

"So, Juve, you're thinking…"

"There, you've caught on at last! That's a good thing! Emotion doesn't sharpen your wits, Fandor. Obviously I'm thinking of arresting Fantômas. By God! He killed me, and there would surely be some spice to it if I should arrest him—I, the dead man…"

"But will he come?"

"If he doesn't I should be surprised. Surely he owes me that much… In any case, Lady Beltham… Bouzille… Helene…"

"Oh, Helene!"

"Why, certainly! Being free to come, she will, you may be sure of that. No, Helene won't be taking tea at the hour I'm being borne to my grave. I feel certain she will be there… Ah, you've no more protests to make against my plan now?"

"I'm lost in admiration of you, Juve."

"I'm pleased to hear it, but I don't see why."

"You think of everything. Hardly out of a fearful adventure and you're scheming how to renew the struggle!"

"I am a police officer, and I have no desire to resign my post. Accordingly I practice my profession. It's all quite simple."

"It's just that simplicity, Juve, I find so admirable."

"Then, my lad, admire yourself too! Just now you were in great grief; well, for all that, I found you following your trade. You were writing an article, remembering you were a journalist—"

"It was to avenge you, Juve."

"Exactly! And if I wish to be buried, it is…"

"Is for what, Juve? Tell me."

"No, I refuse to speak. Since I have been dead officially, I have learned to be discreet… Now tell me where Simon is."

"I don't know for certain. The man told me he had gone to join Shepard."

"Ah! Poor old Shepard!"

"Say, rather, admirable old Shepard. Ever since your disappearance, night and day, without a moment's rest, he has been in search of you. Simon seconds him. They are hunting for you everywhere."

"Very good! Shepard and Simon will read of my death in the

papers and will come to the little ceremony you know of. I am keeping a special place of honor for them… It's all working out excellently… Now another question…"

"Say on, Juve!"

"Have you a big sack handy?"

"No… whatever for?"

"To go and fetch some sand in."

"You require sand, Juve?"

"My good Fandor, you never think of anything. Why, of course I want sand—a hundred and fifty pounds or so."

"For what purpose? I can't see—"

"Of course you can't! Listen to me, Fandor! I wish to be buried, certainly, but I prefer to have it done in effigy rather than in fact. So you will have to do a clever bit of playacting. When the time comes to put me in my coffin, you must ask to be left by yourself to do the job. So you'll remain alone with me. But never fear! I'll give you a helping hand. We shall put a hundred and fifty pounds of sand in the coffin—and I shall slip away quietly. I shall take a cab—"

"You're going to follow in a cab?"

"Certainly! I shall follow the funeral in my carriage. Surely I may afford that expense for myself; I owe myself that trifle, don't I?"

Really, it was as good as a play to see Juve making his arrangements for his own funeral. Self-possessed as ever, he was, as usual, speaking in jest without a word to betoken the real gravity of the affair.

"Now," he proceeded, "I wonder if you've got anything else to supplement the sand. I don't make it an essential point to be represented simply by pebbles and soil."

"There's a cupboard, Juve, full of old illustrateds."

"Capital! That will do first-rate—indeed, it will be more of a compliment to me. You see, my boy, everything is working out beautifully. Oh, I think I can see the faces that will bend over my grave and bid me an eternal farewell! How furious they would all be could they guess they were simply gazing down at a bundle of old illustrated papers!"

"I don't feel any pity for them."

"You show a want of heart, Fandor… But meantime we want a bit of fresh air here. The neighbors have brought all these flowers and the smell is overpowering. Don't you find it so? Well, take them away, my boy!"

"But if the neighbors notice?…"

"You'll invent some excuse. You can say you have found a will in which I ask for no flowers or wreaths at my funeral. It's the fashion now."

"You have an answer for every objection."

"Why, bless my soul, if I *am* dead is that any reason I should risk getting a sick headache? That would be going altogether too far… Now look here! We've nothing more of immediate importance to discuss, have we? And I'm dead sleepy."

"Same with me, Juve! And yet, when I see you here alive, when I look at you, I cannot make up my mind to leave you. I seem to be in a dream…"

"Say right out, in a nightmare!"

"Juve, you know very well that, for nightmares of this sort, I am only too delighted to have them."

A swift wave of emotion passed over the police officer's powerful face. Yes, it was indeed true; Fandor loved him and he loved the journalist. This deep feeling of sincere, ardent affection that united the two men and made them inseparables, was it not sufficient recompense for many sufferings, was it not consolation enough for many hours of anguish?

We often speak of the brotherhood of arms that unites men who have fought under the same flag for the same good cause. Were they not more than brothers in arms, these two comrades who for long years, without ever losing heart, had together waged the most ruthless of wars?

But Juve shook off the emotion that was mastering him.

"Come, my lad," he said, "let's get to sleep. Tomorrow will be a hard day. You will have to receive the idiotic condolences of a heap of silly people… And besides, who knows, besides all that you will perhaps have to bear the brunt of other emotions."

And as he said the words, Juve was smiling, a sly smile that bore the look of foreseeing events he did not choose to specify.

*   *   *   *   *

Juve had not been mistaken in his surmise that the day preceding the funeral would be tedious and the ceremony itself
would cost fatigues and emotions without number. Albeit the
journalist was actually lighthearted enough and had all the
difficulty in the world to refrain from whistling a merry tune,
he nevertheless felt bound to feign the deepest sorrow and put
on an air of dejection, to reply with mournful mien to all the
numerous expressions of condolence he received.

In very truth the police officer might well be proud of the
universal sympathy and the worldwide grief aroused by his
"death."

To begin with, a flood of telegrams had poured in, coming
from all parts of the country as well as from foreign lands. Following this flood of written condolences, a crowd of intimate
friends and mere acquaintances, not to mention relations and
connections and others simply moved by curiosity, had arrived
on the scene.

Dupont de l'Eure at their head—for the kindly editor of *La
Capitale* was greatly attached to Juve—a French deputation had
come, embracing all the heads of the magistracy and all the
chief officers of the police.

"Ah, my poor fellow! How I sympathize with you, Fandor!"
murmured M. Havard.

"An irreparable loss!" declared M. Fuselier the magistrate.

"How true! It was with tears in my eyes I read the news,"
asseverated with touching sincerity a humble inspector of the
Criminal Department, who had come to London at his own
expense and who greeted Fandor with heartfelt cordiality.

"Oh, the noble fellows!" thought the journalist, whose arms
were beginning to ache with continual shaking of hands—"and
to know that in two or three days they will learn the truth!"
And in his own mind he noted sincere condolences on the one
hand and empty phrases on the other, drawing a distinction
between such words of sympathy as were undoubtedly genuine

and others which denoted nothing better than cleverly-veiled hypocrisy.

What to say, for instance, of Shepard's handshake and the words the Englishman had used: "The best way, you know, to mourn him is to avenge him. I mean to devote my life to the task." Could he forget Simon's cry: "Poor Monsieur Juve!—to think that nobody can replace him—not even you, Monsieur Fandor, because *you* are not of the trade!"

Not a doubt of it, throughout the long day that preceded the interment Jerome Fandor had ample opportunity for making a study of the human heart that was not without interest. But the study was too tedious; the evidence that offered was too voluminous.

"It's very shocking," thought the young man; "but these people are really boring me to death. Yet they come here with the best possible intentions"—and from time to time the unfortunate journalist would make his escape and slip away into the next room, where Juve, in great comfort, his feet on the fender, was smoking a comfortable pipe and absorbing a whisky-and-soda.

"Things going all right, master of ceremonies?" he would ask each time.

"Quite all right! You're doing good business… But give me a cigarette, will you?"

"Never in this world, you wretch! Do you want to smell of tobacco? Does a man dream of smoking at a funeral?"

"Juve, you're too hard on a fellow."

"Fandor, you lack the most elementary sense of delicacy… But there, smoke if you will; you can suck a cachou afterwards."

The two, in fact, could not look at each other without grinning.

"It's going like clockwork," laughed Juve. "There'll be three thousand people there tomorrow."

"Yes," agreed Fandor. "But there's one missing I'm surprised not to see here."

"Why, who?"

"Jean—your old servant Jean. I'm astonished he hasn't come.

He is so attached to you."

"No doubt of it! But it doesn't surprise *me* that he hasn't budged."

"Why?"

"Why, because he knows perfectly well this is all make-believe. I have promised him once for all to write to him after my death"—and Juve burst into a great shout of laughter.

Thus, relieved by cheerful interludes when he went off to gossip with Juve, Jerome Fandor passed a strange day—a day which, for all that, he found so tiresome that he gave a heartfelt sigh of satisfaction when next morning the hearse at last moved off, presently breaking into a trot, as the custom is in London.

"There, that's a good job!" he told himself. "Now the only thing left to wish for is that Juve's predictions may prove well founded… If only Helene makes her appearance! If only Fantômas comes!" and in spite of himself, every time the line of carriages following the hearse turned a corner, Jerome Fandor threw a glance in the direction of a certain motor brougham with blinds drawn down, in which, very much alive and in excellent spirits, the "dead man" was taking part in his own funeral procession.

No special incident marked the drive to the cemetery. There, indeed, the crowd was so dense that the carriages had to pull up, and it became to the last degree difficult to force a way to the platform from which the official speeches were to be delivered.

"Oh, no!" thought Fandor. "I'm not going to the seats of honor To have to listen to all these mournful farewells would be beyond me. For a dead certainty I should finish up by exploding—and that would look so bad!"

Taking advantage of a movement of the crowd, Fandor slipped quietly into the ranks of idle spectators and was lost among the general public.

"I have something better to do," he reflected, "than to join in this comedy. They'll think I hadn't the heart to go right up to the grave," and there and then, seized once more by the passion for investigation that was part of his nature, Fandor set to work to examine his neighbors in the crowd, seeking to discover which of them might possibly be Fantômas—supposing Fantômas to be really there.

But Jerome Fandor was quickly to forget the Lord of Terror, so true is it that the wisest of investigators is, all said and done, only a man like another. It was not, in fact, five minutes after the journalist had alighted from his conveyance when he felt a gentle tug at his coat-sleeve, while a timid voice hailed him in muted tones:

"Monsieur Fandor? Monsieur Fandor?"

It was Bouzille. Wearing his glossiest top hat and sporting his finest clothes, the old man nevertheless looked ill at ease. His eyes red, sniffing and coughing, trembling in every limb, Bouzille seemed the victim of the greatest agitation.

"M'sieur Fandor, I want to tell you," he stuttered. "I ain't dared to go and see you; but… but… I be sorry… M'sieur Juve… he was such a teasy man… but there, he means well… means well, he do."

But Fandor had gripped the tramp by the arm, and was hauling him forcibly away from the press. Hidden from the eyes of the curious by a monument, he gave the old vagabond a good shaking.

"Ho, ho! So there you are!" he cried. "Delighted, I'm sure! You're not going to take me off today, are you, to get me pitched into a tank with a pack of rats?"

But Bouzille was on his knees. "Stop, M'sieur Fandor!" he whimpered. "Believe me or not as you like… but I didn't know—I take my davy I didn't!… And look'ee, if I be here, if I stopped you as you went by, it was to tell you so… And mind you, I didn't need to have come if so be I didn't want to… But there, I says to myself, anyways, you did ought to go; you owes it to M'sieur Juve, you do… If you see M'sieur Fandor, you'll explain…"

"Well then, explain, Bouzille. You didn't know you were leading me into a trap when you took me to the rat pit? You weren't carrying out an order of Fantômas'?"

"No, M'sieur Fandor!… They'd given me half a quid, they had, to let the Americans have a peep at you. I was to get you

to sign postcards for 'em. I'd been told this, that and t'other…
But there, it was all lies, so it was… But I didn't know; I didn't
know, M'sieur Fandor!"

The old fellow had started crying again. His clean-shav-
en face looked both comical and piteous… Fandor debated
what it was best to do. No doubt the vagabond had led him
into an abominable trap. But he had been cajoled, perhaps,
by Fantômas' confederates. May it not have been Fantômas in
person who, after disguising himself, had sent Bouzille to meet
Fandor without revealing his identity?"

The journalist was still turning things over in his mind when
Bouzille mopped his eyes and started afresh:

"Then look'ee here, M'sieur Fandor, I'm a-going to prove I
ain't no dirty scamp… You come along o' me, M'sieur Fandor.
I'm a-going to take you to see somebody—somebody you'll be
mighty glad to meet. I caught sight of 'un by chance as I was
a-searching round."

"Who, Bouzille? Who?" gasped Fandor, who already guessed
the name Bouzille was going to pronounce.

The tramp wagged his head, his face suddenly wreathed in
smiles:

"Mam'zelle Helene, then… She's here… and she's crying…
Oh, but you should see her! For sure she loved M'sieur Juve…"

"Quick, quick, Bouzille! Take me to her!"

"Then you'll forgive me?"

"Oh, I don't care one fig for you and your betrayals. Get on!
Get on, do!"

But a few seconds later Fandor was feeling the bitterest disappointment. Bouzille had come to a dead stop before a mortuary chapel with a look of regret and astonishment.

"God bless my soul!" ejaculated the tramp.

"Well?" demanded Fandor breathlessly.

"She must have seen me… Now she's gone!"

"Gone?"

At that moment Fandor felt so keen a pang as left him
almost dazed with despair. Helene had gone without seeing
him, gone without ever suspecting that Juve's burial was only

a farce. Should he ever see her again? Should he ever recover a trace of her?

The young man was still prostrate with grief when Bouzille set about consoling him.

"Nay, never be so downhearted, M'sieur Fandor! She mayn't be so far off… Guess she's gone off only for a bit. We shall come on her, perhaps, at the gate of the cemetery."

"Good God! Bouzille, come on then, come on!" the journalist cried the next moment, and running his hardest, never paying the smallest heed to the bewildered looks that pursued his mad career, he dashed back to the entrance of the burial ground and hurried to Juve's carriage. When still a dozen yards away he saw the blind raised a little and a hand beckoning him.

"Fandor! M'sieur Fandor!" a cheerful voice hailed him.

It was Simon. For the moment he had been puzzled to see this carriage with the lowered blinds, and, peering in, had beheld with utter amazement Juve's face inside. But the man was thinking of something else now.

"Come here!" he called softly. "They're hunting for you everywhere. Whatever have you been after not to be at the official stands? What strange behavior! Quick, jump in! The other gentleman is with you? Well, let him come in too; where there's room for four, there's room for five… Come on! Come on!… and don't get excited!"—and the door was opened.

Fandor never knew how he scrambled in, or how the carriage got into motion, or who had given the driver his orders. One thing and one thing only the young man knew, for that was the one and only thing that now counted for aught in his eyes.

Helene was there, pale but smiling, a soft greeting on her lips and tears of joy dropping from her eyes.

"Oh," sighed the girl, "when you called to me, Juve, as you went by, I thought I was going mad…"

"I think you have gone crazy," interrupted Juve; "you don't so much as say good day to Fandor…"

But the two young people had exchanged a look—and it said so many things, so many soft words of love, that all other words were superfluous.

"My children! My dear children!" murmured Juve, "what a bright and happy day!"

"Oh, yes," put in Bouzille, "a burial like this here, why, it's as good as a christening!"

But no one took any notice of the whimsicality of the old fellow's phrase. Fandor had suddenly turned pale.

"Juve," he faltered, "we are not doing right. We ought you know as well as I do, we ought to stay yonder…"

He dared not speak out what was in his mind before Helene. But she was clear-sighted enough to fathom it. Should not duty have kept within the cemetery those who had laid on themselves the obligation to pursue Fantômas without truce or respite? To go elsewhere, was this not to lose, perhaps, a unique opportunity of encountering the villain?

Juve's only answer was to burst out laughing:

"You are mistaken, Fandor… Fantômas has given us a holiday… Why, certainly! Look, a paper has been flung into the carriage. Read there!"—and he handed over a visiting card, on which was engraved a name—a name of horror. Underneath, two or three lines of writing completed the missive:

> *Fantômas offers Juve his best congratulations on his resurrection. He would hate to trouble a victory which he is the first to admire. But he would remind Juve that in every game revenge is always possible.*

"The sting's in the tail," observed Juve, who had been reading the card over Fandor's shoulder. "In any case we are free… Now to get out, and let's go up again to the mortuary chamber. Bouzille, my lad, I've got a word or two to say to you."

But Juve was smiling so pleasantly that Bouzille was not at all intimidated.

"Here you are, M'sieur Juve," he declared. "You are teasy whiles, but all the same I likes you better alive and dead; it's more cheerful like… And now then, if you was to send me along to buy some champagne it wouldn't do you no hurt. The doctor don't forbid it, does he?"

On the stairs two minutes later Juve—without Bouzille—re-joined Helene and Fandor, a silent pair.

"Ho, ho!" he greeted them, "here's a couple of young lovers who dare not dream their dreams out loud! My presence doesn't put you out, I suppose?"

Finally, when the door stood open, he broke into a laugh at sight of the flowers heaped up in his room as funeral offerings.

"Tell me this, Helene," he grinned, "you're not superstitious, are you? I may offer them to you?"

He saw the girl smile sadly.

"Flowers, Juve?" she said. "I love them so… But I'm so little assured of happiness."

"Why so?"

"You know why very well."

"I know nothing, Helene, and I don't wish to know. See here! You are not responsible for the acts of another. Neither Fandor nor I will ever ask anything of you, neither information nor assistance such as might hurt your conscience… Then let's be merry! I want to see you smile. Fandor's fiancée has no right to be sad…"

"Fiancée—and never anything else," sighed Helene.

"Nonsense! It's a long lane that has no turning. Life is made up of surprises… A burial… a marriage… one succeeds the other."

"You know very well, Juve, that Fantômas has sworn to commit an atrocious crime if a marriage…"

"If a marriage took place? Yes, and I know another thing, too—and that is that even if this marriage has *not* taken place, Fantômas will have no scruples about attacking us—Fandor and me… My poor child, do I wound you by speaking so? But what would you have? I must force you to see things clearly. After that we will never mention these matters again. Come, be reasonable, Helene! Has your father respected the agreement you and he had made? You know he has not. He has attacked Fandor; he has attacked me… In a word you are entirely wrong not to send your scruples packing. Happiness is within your reach. The wise thing to do is to put out your hand and grasp it."

Juve had spoken with grave emphasis. Now in a softer tone he asked:

"Tell me, my child, am I not right?"

"I cannot say yet; I cannot see my way clear before me yet. I require to think it over, to consider…"

"My dear little girl," replied Juve, "I am very ready to give you five minutes for reflection—not a second more!"—and turning his back to Helene, the police officer, whose madcap spirits were certainly overpowering, proceeded:

"Fandor, my boy, it's still Italy where you're going to spend your honeymoon?"

"Oh, Juve, a truce to joking!"

"But, good Lord! I'm not joking! I think you might take ship at once and begin with Naples… I have charming recollections of Naples—and *I* was not on my wedding trip!"

Juve went off in another peal of laughter, then asked another question:

"And pray, what are you looking about for now?"

"For Bouzille, poor old Bouzille. Where has he got to?"

"Don't worry. He has gone for a little walk; he'll be back directly."

"If you only knew, Juve, how the poor fellow wept for you!"

"I don't doubt it. At bottom, he adores me, that chap. I frighten him, do you see? He's one of the sort who love to cry at the play. The more afraid he is of me, the more he loves me. Ah! here he comes, I think."

Steps, in fact, could be heard in the vestibule just outside and Bouzille's voice saying authoritatively:

"This way! Right before you! There's the door… What a blessed bit o' luck I met you!"

"Who is Bouzille with?" demanded Fandor.

The door opened, and with one and the same impulse Fandor and Helene sprang to their feet, both faces paling, while Juve's wore a gentle smile… Bouzille was accompanied by a clergyman!

"Sir," the police officer addressed him, "I am infinitely obliged to you and sorry to have disturbed you. I am not very well acquainted with the English customs on such occasions, but I felt sure you would be so very kind as to oblige us… There, reverend sir, are two young people to be married. Of course I have all the necessary papers here."

Neither Fandor nor Helene ventured to say a word. Juve's peremptory way of settling their marriage left them so dazed with joy they could not speak.

Meantime the clergyman, an old man of a grave and gentle mien, turned to the young couple pointed out to him.

"The young people are consenting parties I need not ask?" he questioned with a benevolent smile.

The answer he could read in the lovelorn glance that passed between Jerome Fandor and Helene.

Turning to the rest of the company, the clergyman put another question:

"I presume the necessary witnesses are here?"

"Certainly!" replied Fandor eagerly. "There stands Monsieur Juve, reverend sir, the celebrated police officer, ready to act as my witness."

"Juve? The great Juve? But… I thought… I had read… I had been told…"

"You had been told, sir, that Juve was dead?" observed Juve quietly. "It's only a silly rumor put about by evil-minded persons."

"I am delighted to hear it… The young lady has also chosen her witness?"

"Certainly!… You are agreeable, Bouzille?"

"You choose me, Mam'zelle Helene, you choose *me?* Ah! That's something grand, that be! That's a fine feather in my cap! My character's redeemed," and he turned red with pleasure, poor fellow.

"My children," resumed the clergyman, "bethink you heedfully! I call down the blessings of Heaven on your union…"

And in truth, simple as was this marriage service, it was not lacking in a certain impressive solemnity.

When, the sacramental prayers duly pronounced, the ritual phrases uttered, the marriage of Fandor and Helene was veritably an accomplished fact—in accordance with the law of England—Juve could be seen wiping his eyes with unwonted vigor, while for his part Fandor found *his* dimmed... and Helene, without an attempt to hid her emotion, let the tears flow unchecked down her blushing cheeks.

"True," remarked Bouzille at this point, throwing himself into Simon's arms, finding in him a highly sympathetic friend, "it be a grand treat to be a witness—only it's all too soon over."

Meantime the clergyman had discreetly taken his leave, after receiving a handsome gratuity for the poor of his parish.

"So that's that!" cried Juve, struggling against his emotion and forcing himself to put on a jocular tone; "and just as easy as easy!... You'll be passing through Paris on your way back from Italy, and you can have your marriage registered... Come now, don't let us give way to our feelings... This is the end of a story, the final wind-up of a romance... Well, we've no reason to complain; the last act finishes up happily."

Juve smiled benignly, and setting his two hands to his mouth in the guise of a speaking trumpet, sang out:

"All aboard! All aboard for Italy! All aboard for the Land of Happiness!"

"The car's waiting at the door!" announced Bouzille gravely—the old fellow seldom failed to say the decisive word—"and they'll soon be at their journey's end."

17. Epilogue

Two hours later Juve was returning alone to the modest lodging which henceforth was to seem to spacious for him. He was happy, and sad at the same time. Joy, even the purest joy, is never unmixed. A tear is ever mingled with our laughter, fears with our hopes.

"All very quaint!" he muttered to himself. "It's Fandor is married… and it was I brought off the abduction. I didn't give them time to say 'knife'! Very good! It had to be so. If I hadn't taken advantage of the youngsters' emotion, they would never have agreed to leave me. Yet Fandor and Helene have surely a right to enjoy a truce"—and the police officer repeated the word, so fraught with unspoken thoughts—the word that spoke of the future—a Truce.

Juve was on his way back from the railway station. As he said, he had carried out a sort of abduction by hurrying on Fandor's marriage, then escorting the young couple to the station and packing them off to a seaport, whence a few hours afterwards a steamship would bear them away towards the wide horizons of the open sea and eventually to the sunny shores of Italy.

"Yes, my mind is quite at rest," he soliloquized. "I am going to receive sundry telegrams and postcards… Yes, the postman will soon know my address." And he concluded: "That will soothe my nerves, and help to distract my thoughts."

The fact is he suddenly felt himself very old and very tired. Fandor was no longer at his side, and yet the ruthless struggle was not ended. Fantômas was at large. Somewhere in the wide world, just as his grim and cruel caprice prompted, he would surely reveal his presence by one of those fearful crimes, one of those horrid deeds of darkness that always marked his course. Juve must renew the battle, investigate fresh mysteries, face new and appalling dangers.

"There is nothing ended," he told himself; "a new home set up, and that's all." And he set forth again on his way back at a leisurely pace, lost in the London crowds, thinking still:

"Moreover, I have certainly many big difficulties ahead of me. From the legal point of view I am actually dead. My death certificate is lodged with the authorities… Besides that, as an official, I must not expect congratulations. Hmm! the fact is I have made mock of the powers that be. Serious, very! I cannot tell if they will ever forgive me."

But even as he spoke Juve was shrugging his shoulders carelessly like a man whom suchlike petty details left entirely indifferent.

"A fig for all that!" he exclaimed next second. "I am bound to do what I deem my duty. That is all that counts. The rest is of no importance."

Presently he reached the house, where he climbed the stairs, holding by the banister, for he was tired out, no doubt of it, and not yet fully recovered from the violent shock occasioned by the drug he had swallowed.

"I can barely keep my feet," he confessed. "I think I will go straight to bed."

Opening the door of the rooms, "Why, what!" he exclaimed. "Did we leave a light burning in the parlor? Or perhaps it is Simon and Bouzille come back already? I quite thought they were gone to make a night of it." And, suspecting nothing, Juve made for the lighted room.

Suddenly he stopped dead. A man had appeared on the threshold, who bowed to him, and whom Juve had no need to look at twice.

"Fantômas!" he cried.

The man was in everyday attire, and he carried over his arm a light topcoat with an air of careless ease. But across his eyes a black velvet mask was fixed.

But he, too, seemed weary; he, too, appeared fatigued, worn out.

"Yes," he said simply, "it is I, Juve. I was waiting for you. I want to speak to you."

"What! You dare—"

"I dare anything and everything, Juve. You know that. Nay, never feel for your revolver, and never think to arrest me! I have taken my precautions. You have been robbed of your weapons and I have thirty confederates in ambush, all ready to fly to my rescue in case of need."

"This means yet another fight, Fantômas?"

"By no means, Juve. I am not even armed; I give you my word I am not. I have come to see you to conclude a pact with you."

"A pact between you and me!"

"That astounds you? Nevertheless it has to be."

"*Has* to be?"

"Assuredly! Oh, I know quite well the word strikes you as a piece of effrontery. Still, listen to me. Whatever you decide afterwards, it is important you should hear me first."

"Speak, then, Fantômas!"

"Juve, you have married Fandor and Helene. You think you have united them indissolubly and won a triumph over me."

"Can you deny it, Fantômas?"

"Juve, I prefer not to answer you. One day you will understand why I do not speak. But no matter. You profess to have married Fandor and Helene—so be it! But do you know that aboard the same boat they are going to embark in one of my lieutenants has booked a passage? Do you know that if I chose to send him by wireless a message in cipher, tomorrow morning Fandor, who has no suspicions, and Helene, who is all wrapped up in her happiness, would have ceased to live?"

"Fantômas! Fantômas! Such a crime would surpass in horror—"

"All those I have committed. Yes, I know that. But also it would avenge—"

"Avenge you on whom? It is I who am your enemy."

"Very true, Juve! But by annihilating Fandor or Helene I should wound *you* to the heart... Can you deny it?"

"I do not deny it, Fantômas."

"Well, Juve, it depends on you whether this atrocity is perpetrated or no. *You* are going to decide the point."

"I?"

"You! By refusing or accepting the pact I am about to propose to you."

"Fantômas, I think I am dreaming."

"No. You are perfectly in possession of your senses. You even realize that the offer I make is a serious one. Juve, you love Fandor, and I love my daughter."

"You love her! No, no! It is not true! If you loved her, you would not have tortured her in the cellar…"

"The revolver I had given her to kill you or Fandor with was not loaded!"

"A lie!"

"Juve, remember this: I have set Fandor and Helene free! Why should I have done so had I not felt pity for my daughter?"

"If Helene's revolver was not loaded, Fantômas, if you did not wish to kill us, why did you have a needle plunged in my heart?"

"Juve, have I said I did not desire *your* death? It is Helene, and Fandor whom Helene loved, I have spared…"

"So be it! But I do not believe you…"

"Well, as you please; I care not… This, Juve, is the pact I am going to propose to you… I am rich, enormously rich… And I am afraid, I am horribly, hideously afraid of the guillotine… You see, Juve, I am speaking to you with perfect frankness?"

"Proceed, Fantômas!"

"Juve, I am ready to swear to you never to commit another crime. Juve, I am prepared to pledge my honor—"

"*Your* honor!"

"My honor as a brigand to live henceforth as an honest man. But you will swear to me never to pursue me more. It is only you I fear. The rest of your detectives, one and all of them, I care nothing for. Juve, send in your resignation, abandon your profession, and I will give up mine."

"I do not believe you, Fantômas! No man credits the oath of a wretch like you."

"Juve!"

"Let me speak... I say it is only just that retribution should overtake you. You are to be captured, condemned, and executed."

"You are pitiless, Juve. You forget that my retribution is already begun?"

"Since when?... In what way?"

"Juve, I have let you... let you marry Fandor and Helene... I have given... I have given... you have given my daughter to your ally."

"Fantômas, what is it you hint at? What is the hidden meaning of this reticence with which you intersperse your speeches?"

"That you will know later, Juve—perhaps. You will know it if you do not agree to the pact I now propose."

"Never, Fantômas!"

"Juve, consider well! The first act of the new war you declare on me will be the death of Helene and Fandor."

"Fantômas, I cannot play traitor to my duty."

"That is your last word?"

"You cannot doubt it."

"Then it means nothing to you, Juve, my undertaking to lay down my arms forever?"

"It would mean everything, Fantômas, if I could put faith in you."

"You insult me, Juve!"

"Do you not deserve it?"

"Yet are you certain you are not making a mistake? Think! Oh, think!"

Then came for Juve a minute of agonizing doubt, a terrible minute of which he was destined to keep an imperishable memory. What was he to do? Was he not making a mistake in binding himself to continue the battle?

But even as he hesitated he thought of all the miseries this villain was answerable for, all the rascalities he had committed, all the lies he had uttered. To curse him did not a thousand specters hold forth their skeleton arms, a thousand phantoms of those he had tortured and done to death, without one pang of pity lurking underneath his black hood, and who cried for vengeance?

No! No pact was possible with Fantômas! No peace could be made with the enemy! He was one of those monsters who must at any cost be punished, chastised, annihilated, because they have lost the very right to draw the breath of life.

"Hear me!" resumed Fantômas. "I do not ask you to answer. What matter, after all? I trust you. So long as you hear no further word of me you will refrain from your pursuit of me. Farewell!"

"No, no! Be done with lies and falsehoods! Be done with artful subterfuges! You think against my will to bind me by an oath I refuse to take! Defend yourself, Fantômas! Defend yourself! So long as Juve shall live he will never spare you!"

"I do not believe one word of it. Farewell, farewell!"

"No, no! I tell you. I see through your game too well… You are planning some fresh villainy. You simply wish to gain a few weeks' respite in order to carry it out in peace."

But was not Juve deceiving himself? He seemed now to see a sudden pallor spread over Fantômas' face under the mask he wore. Did the wretch feel his scheming was in vain?

"Farewell!" he said again, and, quicker than lightning, he sprang to the door and escaped.

"Safe! He is safe!" gasped Juve.

Then he, too, turned pale. In his valise lying in the next room the police officer possessed a box filled with a high explosive. To throw it was to blow up the house—to kill himself, and to kill Fantômas before he had left the building.

"Great God! Ought I to provoke such a catastrophe?" thought Juve.

He knew the house was empty; there would be but two victims—Fantômas and himself.

To annihilate this ill-omened monster of iniquity, this criminal of criminals, who held all humanity under the yoke of his power, was it not become his duty to sacrifice his own life?

So, there would be neither victorious police officer nor vanquished malefactor. Death would be the final end of the grim and tragic history of Fantômas. Was any other possible?

"Oh, I cannot, I must not hesitate!" decided the heroic Juve, and he started to run into the adjacent room, resolved to seize the bomb, throw it, and realize the sublime sacrifice.

But Providence refused to sanction so sublime but cruel an act that punished the innocent no less than the guilty.

Juve took one step—one step and no more. The giddiness that a little before had made him stumble on the stairs seized him again, disabled him.

He staggered and had to lay hold of a chair to save himself from falling. A second passed… Another… It was too late to act.

"Ah!" exclaimed Juve. "So Fate was against my purpose. Was Fantômas perhaps sincere? Is he about to disappear? Shall we hear no more of him?"

But the question, he reflected, could only receive its answer from the supreme Arbiter of the Future—Time!

THE END

THE FANTÔMAS SERIES #1–7
NOW AVAILABLE FROM ANTIPODES PRESS

#1 **Fantômas**
Originally published as *Fantômas* in 1911.
Paperback: 310 pages. ISBN 978-0-9882026-1-0.

#2 **The Exploits of Juve**
Originally published as *Juve contre Fantômas* in 1911.
Paperback: 196 pages. ISBN 978-0-9882026-2-7.

#3 **Messengers of Evil**
Originally published as *Le Mort qui Tue* in 1911.
Paperback: 298 pages. ISBN 978-0-9882026-3-4.

#4 **A Nest of Spies**
Originally published as *L'Agent Secret* in 1911.
Paperback: 336 pages. ISBN 978-0-9882026-4-1.

#5 **A Royal Prisoner**
Originally published as *Un Roi Prisonnier de Fantômas* in 1911.
Paperback: 184 pages. ISBN 978-0-9882026-5-8.

#6 **The Long Arm of Fantômas**
Originally published as *Le Policier Apache* in 1911.
Paperback: 336 pages. ISBN 978-0-9966599-1-8.

#7 **Slippery As Sin**
Originally published as *Le Pendu de Londres* in 1911.
Paperback: 238 pages. ISBN 978-0-9966599-2-5.